Indiana Horror Review 2014

Edited by
James Ward Kirk

Cover Art by John Stanton

Book © 2014 James Ward Kirk Publishing

Internet: jwkfiction.com

Twitter: @jameswardkirk

Facebook: James-Ward-Kirk-Fiction

Cover Art and Design by John D. Stanton © 2014
Illustrations by John D. Stanton © 2014

ISBN-13: 978-0692343104 (James Ward Kirk publishing)

ISBN-10: 0692343105

Contents

Photograph by John Stanton

Dona Fox

The Serial Magician

The fragile cargo shifted as the van passed through the early spring landscape. A crisp wind blew dead winter leaves, greed and The Magician into the small Indiana town.

In the passenger seat of the van, a young man studied The Magician's face as bars of light and shadow played across his features.

The Magician's mass of hair, a bit too long, rolled back from his brow in glossy waves. The skin of his face stretched tight from cheek to jawbone. How often the young man, Phillip, had traced the lines of those bones from beneath his sleepy lashes, and wished for The Magician's face that he saw when he looked into the mirror. Phillip was about to nod off from the quiet ride and the warm, closed air when Maynard, The Magician, pulled the van off the paved road and into a large clearing.

Shaking off his drowsiness, Phillip reached for the door handle. "No, Phillip." Maynard touched his arm gently. "You will never learn the importance of the drama, will you?" He settled back into his seat, so Phillip did the same.

The huge van crouched in the clearing by the woods at the edge of the town. Waiting for the curious people they knew would come. There was no single color to the van but rather a mesmerizing rainbow of colors. The exterior of the van was a complete circus in itself. Every flat surface was decorated with pictures—pictures of clowns, lions, bears, tigers, dancing ladies, strong men, bearded women, flying trapeze artists, and scantily clad dancers performing on the broad backs of elephants.

The largest pictures, centered on the long sides of the van, and were of Maynard, with flowing mustache, top hat, purple velvet coat and his gorgeous ivory smile. Words wreathed in and out of the pictures:

MAYNARD THE MAGNIFICENT.
THE MAGICIAN'S AMAZING PORTALS.
GUESS WHICH DOOR WILL RELEASE THE CHILD

The reading of that final phrase naturally led the reader's eyes to the picture of a young boy with a beatific face walking out one of the four doors of a glass box as a group of people, surrounded by massive piles of sparkling gold, smiled and clapped their hands.

**WIN MONEY FOR YOUR TOWN! MILLIONS OF $$$
WHO WILL BE THE LUCKY CHILD?
BRING GOOD FORTUNE TO YOUR TOWN!**

Oh, yes, at its simplest, the game is "Choose a Child." In each town, the people even came to The Magician with bribes.

The children arrived at the clearing first. They stood apart, little statues, studying the van —waiting for it to entertain them— like the television, the movies, and the teachers at school.

Then the teens started to arrive, which could be a dangerous time for Phillip and The Magician. The teens often got closer to the van, excited by the semi-erotic pictures of the circus performers, and often tried the door handles. However, this was a simple town with well-behaved teenagers, and the parents weren't far behind. The school day was over. The workday was done. Everyone was on the way home. Dinner was not yet in the oven.

The people from the town stood solidly around the van like the monoliths of Stonehenge, lips moving almost in unison as they read the words painted on the van. Their eyes rotated in spirals as they took in the colorful paintings. Body coiled, Maynard let them read as he watched the sky, and then said, "Now."

Maynard leapt out of the van as the sun broke through the clouds.

The crowd gasped.

"Good day to you my fine folks. This will be the finest day of your lives, the day that you will remember forever. I am Maynard, the last real magician you will ever have the good fortune to lay your eyes upon. I bring wealth and good fortune, virtual barrels of gold—and all you have to do is solve one simple puzzle."

"I see that your town is in desperate need of funds. I see the potholes in your roads. The playground is in disrepair—the basketball hoops with no nets, the football field with no bleachers, no electronic scoreboard at all. No library filled with books, and no local newspaper to commemorate your deeds."

"You can have all of those things. You should have all those things. I can give your town mounds of money."

"You've read the tale on my van. All you have to do is choose which door will open. There are four actual doors—I will stay for three days. If you agree to play this little game, I will choose the lucky child or young person, and reveal my choice in the morning."

All the children wanted to be that child—the lucky child in the box.

Maynard laughed. Smiled. "The child has to be someone entertaining. Show us how dramatic, how pleasing, how inventive, you can be. This, my friends, is the circus!"

The children began to dance like monkeys. The young girls smiled and primped, ready for a beauty pageant.

"We will put the child in this box."

Phillip had lowered a box from the back of the van while the stayed focused on Maynard.

"What is it made of?"

"This box is made of visually transparent, military-grade bulletproof glass."

"Who gets to choose the door?"

"The town will, as one, have one choice each day to pick which door opens to let him out."

"What if we pick the wrong door?"

"Every day you pick the wrong door, the money your town receives will be reduced by half."

"Can we call my cousin in Bloomington to drive down and help?"

"If you call for outside help, for any reason, we will take everything and leave."

"How many guesses do we get?"

"You get one guess, from the whole town, at exactly 5 p.m. every day. If you are wrong, we will cover the box until 4 p.m. the next day when you can begin to formulate your next guess."

"If you are correct we will make arrangements to have the money sent to your bank. As I'm sure you can understand, for our security, we do not carry the money with us."

"However, we do have a bank letter we will gladly show to a chosen representative of the town guaranteeing our authenticity. You understand we can't have everyone handling it."

"Soon you could all be holding gold in your hands simply by picking a door!"

The town cheered. Agreement soon followed, as always.

That afternoon a red-faced man in a tight suit jacket approached the young man. "I'm Big Al, of Big Al's Furniture." He slurred his words around the butt of a cigar. "Are you Phillip?"

Big Al had been drinking with Maynard all afternoon, and now flushed and very drunk. "The Magician said to give you this money to ensure everything goes as I wish." He handed Phillip a thick packet. "You need to drive me home and bring back my boy, Little Tater; he's going in the box."

When they got to Al's house, Phillip had to help him find his keys. As they were unlocking the door, Al's young wife opened it from inside.

"Where've you been, Marianne? This here's Phil. Little Tater's the lucky one, he's goin' in the box. Help Phil get me upstairs then give him Tate. You hear me?"

Marianne and Phillip managed to haul Al up the stairs to a bedroom where they let him fall onto the bed. He began snoring almost immediately.

"I'm supposed to take your son back with me," Phillip said.

Tenderly, Marianne wrapped the sleeping boy in a blanket and handed him to Phillip. Dark curls fell onto his face as he slept.

That night Phillip heard screams of pain as he had heard on many nights in many different towns. Sometimes they were the screams of children. Usually it ended with a body wrapped in a blanket, a quick trip to swampy ground, and hours with a shovel, for Phillip—while Maynard began to set up The Box.

Phillip was the only person Maynard would not harm because Phillip was his patient.

Maynard was a surgeon.

He told the story to Phillip, the night he found Phillip in the street, crushed and unconscious. He rushed him to the closest refuge, Maynard's own home, and repaired Phillip's shattered legs. Maynard never returned to the hospital.

Maynard did not tell Phillip of his suspension from the hospital earlier that drunken day—nor that it was his car that ran over Phillip. Maynard promised Phillip that, if, for a short time, Phillip did everything Maynard asked him to do, then someday he would take him home and help him find his family. That short time had stretched into years.

Once again, screams from Maynard' tent—and, unexpectedly, they were cut short. The thunder and the pounding of the rain on the taut fabric of the tent calmed Phillip and he slept.

Hours later Maynard called to him. "Make sure she is okay and get her out of here."

Phillip was surprised to see that Maynard's guest was still alive. He was even more surprised to see that the woman was Marianne. Her eyes were glowing.

"Everything will be alright now. Al suspects that Tate isn't his son, and he thinks the box is evil. That's why he wants to put Tate in the box," she said.

"Marianne, Al's right about the box. It isn't safe. But I've hidden your son," Phillip replied.

"Maynard wasn't ever going to put my son in there. My son and I are leaving with you; Maynard is rescuing us." She was beautiful in that moment of childlike innocence. Phillip stared in wonder at the freshness of her wild eyes and storm-tossed hair.

"It's alright, Phillip. I'm Maynard's sister." At that moment, Phillip knew it was true but he saw no resemblance between the siblings for disparate personalities had shaped their features.

Al arrived before Phillip could take Marianne home. He had slept the drunk off, but the mean stench of alcohol sweat and cigars still clung to him.

"Put her in," Al ordered Maynard.

They argued at the edge of the woods until Maynard relented.

Marianne struggled as Maynard grabbed her arm. He whispered something to her and, meek as a kitten, she agreed to go in.

At exactly 4 p.m., Phillip and Maynard pulled the fabric from the cube.

The crowd was silent, mouths agape. You could have heard the scraping as two adjacent blades of grass adjusted to the turning of the earth.

The box stood transformed.

No longer a simple four-sided box sitting perpendicular to the ground; each flat side of the square had divided, swelled and bent. The clearing had become the inside of a giant kaleidoscope, pirating colors from the painted scenes on the van. The square had multiplied hundreds of times by the clever use of massive curved mirrors artfully placed.

Now there were hundreds of doors, hundreds of symmetrical geometric shapes, each housing a Marianne. No one even thought to complain that Marianne wasn't a child.

Thick ropes surrounded the puzzle so no one could step too close.

"The Golden Rhombus! Archimedes' Rhombic Puzzle! It's a simple matter of tetrahedral symmetry. In other words, for the children, that means stand at the correct point, find the symmetry, and solve the puzzle!"

Maynard moved from side to side, as if solving the puzzle of which box housed the real Marianne would simply be a matter of standing in the right spot in the clearing.

"What is real? What is illusion? Find the quiet place within you that knows." Maynard's majestic voice echoed through the clearing.

Marianne smiled. She jumped up and down, waved and pointed at herself as if to say, "Here, here, this is me, I am the real Marianne." However, all of the hundreds of images were doing the same.

Later Marianne sat on the floor, a tiny smile on her face. It was likely all she could muster at that point as only a small amount of air was able to seep into the box.

The noise of the crowd was deafening as they argued about which door to choose. They walked from side to side and wobbled their heads back and forth, as they looked for the correct point to appear. A number of people became dizzy enough that they had to go home to lie down.

"Oh, bloody hell. It's my wife. Close your eyes, throw a rock, and choose that door. One is as sure as the next."

They had to make a group decision at precisely 5 p.m., and somehow they did.

Maynard reached out for that door, but it wasn't a real door, the crowd sighed in disappointment and Phillip replaced the cover until the next day.

The sun rose on another day. The money was dwindling; the people were frantic, and arguments broke out.

No one noticed that Marianne was listless, or if they did, they rationalized it away:

"The Magician must let her out at night."

"He must feed her at night."

"I'm sure there's air in there."

Finally, someone cried out, "What's more important than the money is if she's really okay or not."

Someone else said, "Surely it's just a stunt."

But, as in every town, they were all greedy and blinded by the possibility of the money, and concern about Marianne faded into oblivion.

At the edge of the crowd, a few souls here and there understood Marianne was dying. They fed on it, as Maynard did. They could not take their gaze from her struggling breath. Their eyes were glowing. Their lips were ripe with lust. They were the ones that understood. They were in it purely for the kill. They were waiting in every town.

Many felt the excitement they told themselves was about the money but in their hearts, they knew it was about more. Some were jealous of her youth, her innocence, or her beauty. Many would be moving up, now they would be the brightest, the prettiest, or the smartest. Maybe Marianne knew one of their secrets, and now no one would know. A death always came as a relief to someone.

So some admitted she was dying, and they were there to enjoy it. Some knew she was dying but denied it to themselves and yet still felt a tingle of guilty pleasure. Everyone pretended all was fine and that the excitement they felt was all about the money.

Phillip admitted to himself that at first, he abhorred Maynard's productions, but then he took his pleasure in Maynard's delight, then in the crowd's excitement. Now, after so many years, he had begun to feel a need of his own, but just for the spectacle, not for the death. He thought there must be some way to accomplish the act without the death, without the slow suffocation.

When the people come out tomorrow, ready for the last day of the puzzle, of the game, their final chance to win any money for their town, Phillip and Maynard will be gone. The crowd will find a box, just one square, and Marianne lying in it dead.

Phillip checked intermittently; he wanted to rescue Marianne, but Maynard stayed with her and watched her suffer through the night.

As Maynard and Phillip packed up the van, the storm arrived. Huge raindrops splattered on the ground.

"Why do you do it? Phillip asked the same question every time; as Maynard expected it of him. Maynard liked to hear himself talk. He craved an audience. For now, that was Phillip.

Maynard chuckled.

The rain intensified as small veins of lightning laced the sky.

"You know she would have died at my hands quite soon if she had come with us. I want everything that's fresh and innocent; I want to crush the innocence, watch as it autumns and dies to winter in my fists."

"I used to take the ones that followed me to my home and finish their little lives in my basement. An onanistic pursuit, it felt so tawdry, so self-centered of me, so selfish, no theatre there."

"But this, this is so grand, this is performance art—I'm giving back. This town was among the smallest, the pettiest of any we have encountered. They spent barely any time wondering if Marianne was in distress. She died beautifully and with such grace. It was a joy to watch. And her son—we should have put them in the box together. Why have I never thought of that before? Mothers and babies. Madonna and child. Whatever became of that gorgeous son of hers?"

A giant lightning bolt ripped through the dark sky, as

simultaneously thunder shook the ground. Phillip's stomach clenched with fright for Marianne's sweet son and for all the innocents that lay sleeping, or yet unborn, in Maynard's path.

They rushed to finish, tearing down the tents as the violence of that first spring thunderstorm increased. Another flash of lightning lit the spectacle of Maynard, bent and straining, as he dragged two crossed poles through the mud.

"No, no," Phillip mumbled beneath the thunder. "You are not the Christ. For so long I have believed you were my salvation. Now I know you were not. Possibly, I was yours. But I can't sever our bond; it is too strong. I'm not a magician. I'm just a young man who would be alone in the world without you. Even so, if I could, I would save the innocent from you and go on with my life alone. I just don't know how." The rain mixed with the tears running unbidden down Phillip's cheeks.

Then the storm itself supplied Phillip with the answer. Lashed by the wind the ropes from the tent wrapped around Maynard's neck. Maynard fought the ropes with storm-reddened fingers, and Phillip knew what he must do.

The events of the next few moments were stored in slow motion memory for Phillip to play whenever insomnia left his mind empty. Maynard looked into Phillip's eyes from across the muddy clearing, Maynard's mouth opened wide as he called out to Phillip for help. Phillip's boots left deep prints in the mud as he crossed the clearing—strange the prints his footsteps left in the mud. He didn't wait to see if they filled up, just went on and made another as he made his way to Maynard. Slow motion. Elongated raindrops fell into the puddles. Maynard called his name again. Phillip looked up; almost there. He couldn't stop to think. He had to get to Maynard. Finish it.

"Phillip!"

Wet hair hid Phillip's eyes, his resolve, as he ran to Maynard— as if to help, one more time. He put his hand on Maynard's sodden shoulder and, instead of muscle, felt bone. Then he realized he was taller than Maynard. He looked down at Maynard, at his wet hair, and saw more scalp than hair. A wave of pity shook Phillip. His resolve wavered. Was this a Magician's trick? For an instant, he wanted to help Maynard.

Instead, he circled the ropes around Maynard's neck again. Then grasping them by both ends, he bound the ropes around his hands and tightened them against Maynard's flesh with all of his youthful strength.

Gasping for air, Maynard reached out and pushed back Phillip's hair. He looked into Phillip's eyes. "Phillip." His arms flailed, but he did not fight back. He could not harm Phillip, even as Phillip killed him.

Phillip dropped his arms and fell to the mud beside Maynard. It was done—that easily. Phillip had not realized how strong his hands had become. Or his resolve.

His tears were lost in the downpour. He could not believe Maynard was dead. He could not believe he had killed him.

Phillip's hands on the steering wheel of the van looked larger now. They resembled Maynard's hands. Strange, he had not noticed the similarity before. Now was not the time to dwell on who or what he had become. Eddies of water blew upon the road. Branches fell across his path.

Phillip planned one quick stop to leave Maynard's body in Marianne's house for her husband to explain. Marianne's son lay hidden in the back of the van, making sounds as he began to wake.

The passenger seat was empty. Phillip was no longer the passenger.

He was in need of an assistant of his own.

Photography by John D. Stanton

Essel Pratt

My Sweet Haley

Screams are short lived as flesh peels from muscle; shock captures her voice rather quickly as her mind fails to compensate for the nature of the horrific trauma. The sound of skin peeling back from muscle sizzles in her ears, blocking out the incessant bitching of her captor. Although he has reason for skinning her alive, the intense pleasure he receives from causing pain is not comforting.

Tanner struggles to pull the last of the flesh free of her twitching toes. With a slight jerk, the skin costume breaks free from the young lady. Her failing lungs exhale a sudden gust of moist breath as her brain still blocks the pain from consuming her. Tanner does not care for the girl; her pain, as well as that of her family, is an unfortunate result of his plan. The hide of skin will be his souvenir from which he will make a custom leather jacket to expand his leather collection.

He waits until nightfall to drive the skinless corpse to the hidden pond behind the old school. Forgotten for years, its murky waters will surely caress the muscle wrapped corpse within the silt-laden bottom. If ever found, only dental records will identify her. Tanner had contemplated removing the teeth and grinding them to a fine powder, sprinkling them in the water. However, he felt she deserved proof of identity if ever discovered.

The waterlogged dock has seen better times; each footstep sinks into the sodden planks. He is careful not to step too hard, fearing he might fall through. Gently placing her lifeless body upon the mirrored pond, he almost sheds a tear as it floats weightlessly upon the ripples it has conjured. A little shove sends her sailing towards the center where the cloudless sky allows the bright moon to shine down upon her muscle-wrapped body, reflecting the most beautiful red glow upon the ripples around her.

Although her body shows no natural movement, her heart has yet to fail her. She stares up towards the starry sky hoping the afterlife is kind to her, knowing that she will not arrive in Heaven any time soon. A single tear escapes her left eye, gliding over her exposed cheek and splashing in the water. The undulations, although small, take their time to reach the shore. Stars disappear as water flows over her face; the world becomes darker until she lands on the bottom of the pond; silt and mud erupt around her, cradling her as they settle.

"Good night, my sweet Haley" whispers the man as he stands from his crouched position. He wonders what the news will say about the disappearance of the shy young girl. Will friends that she never knew emerge from the woodwork like termites feeding on the fame? In reality, he doesn't care. Her flesh was, no is, beautiful, and now it is his to do with as he pleases. His mind focuses on the leather biking jacket that he intends to craft from her leathery flesh. Dyed jet black, maybe with a matching pair of gloves, his skin tingles at the anticipation of his newest creation. To feel her skin hugging his flesh as he rides the open road sends his senses into an uproar.

He doesn't leave right away. Instead, he takes some time to stare at the stars, and see their reflections dance upon the gentle waves of the semi-placid lake. He is happy with his decision to choose her. She was not his first choice, might not even be his last, but after much consideration she was the one.

The northern Indiana summer had almost become autumn as green began to turn yellow and orange. Sitting on his porch with a bottle of beer in hand, he watched the neighbor kids soaking up the last the season had to offer before heading back to school in a week's time. The younger kids were always fun to watch; carefree attitudes propelled their inhibitions to the outskirts of their mind, allowing freedom of creativity to overtake them. On that day, he had his eyes on the wild Goth girl down the street. Her blackened eyes and fuck-it-all attitude seemed a perfect fit for the project rattling around within his head. A leather crafter by trade, he had created masterpieces of various leathers and hides. He had fashioned jackets and boots from exotic skins and even an entire leather chair from found squirrel hides. But never before had he experienced the pleasure of working in the medium of human flesh. A riding jacket to wear while cruising on his hog, with a matching pair of gloves, would be the perfect project to show off the pinnacle of his creations. Who better to wear than the evil little bitch from down the street?

As he gazed upon his prey, another young lady grabbed his attention from the corner of his eye. Haley from across the street had descended from her porch, book in hand, and rested herself on a blanket in the yard. She was shy, a junior in high school, never seen with friends, and had amazingly beautiful skin. She appeared untouched and unscarred. His mind immediately forgot the gothic wannabe and imagined Haley's angelic flesh wrapping around his large frame while causing hell on his Harley. He couldn't get the thought of her virgin flesh out of his head; it would be like cruising around with an angel on his shoulder. She promptly became his newest obsession.

He was careful not to act upon the urge to snatch her up from the lawn, drag her to his basement, and strip the flesh from her frame. Instead, he decided to watch her incessantly and plan out his project in intricate detail. If he was to wear the flesh of such perfection, it was only honorable to construct his design with perfection in mind.

Over the next few weeks, he focused on various designs for his jacket and gloves, every detail sketched out, down to the Haley's Comet design upon the right lapel. He decided upon a rich black dye to stain her beautiful flesh, and button covers the same color as her radiant blue eyes to clasp the over the zippered front. When finalized, the design was as beautiful as she, and ready to be transferred to patterns for use at a later time.

All the while, he focused on his design; he took just as much time to observe Haley and her daily routine. If he were to lure her into his home, let alone the basement where his workshop was set up, he would need to ensure that he went unseen by the multitude of neighbors in the close-knit community. He would also need to find a way to earn her trust, without suspicion by the prying neighbors. It wouldn't be easy for such a large scary man as himself.

To the small Mishawaka community he was the known as a teddy bear member of the frightening biker crowd. He ran a respectable tanning business and had a big heart when helping his community, but remained plagued by stereotype. When something went awry in the neighborhood, whispers rode the winds towards his house. He had accepted the hushed talk about him but worried that Haley's disappearance would draw unwanted attention.

His fears came to a halt when he had heard she was going to take a weekend trip alone to a Christian music festival. The fairgrounds for the event were familiar to him; he had visited it many times in the past to cheer on his favorite rock bands. Cellular service would be almost nonexistent, so her lack of communication with home would not raise suspicion. His mind raced with anticipation as he constructed his plan to lure her. Everyone would believe she disappeared at the festival, and he avoids all suspicion.

Prior to the festival, he cleaned out his attached garage and installed a new bed cover on his pickup truck. His plan decisively devised, yet he felt he needed a place he could take her body without notice if things did not go as planned. Anticipation flowed through his pores as he prepared to set his plan in motion

The following day he waited until she had been at the festival for a few hours before beginning his journey. It was a two-hour drive, giving him plenty of time between her departure and his, and, hopefully, reducing suspicion of him.

The drive seemed like an eternity, despite traveling about ten miles over the speed limit the entire way. He could not wait to get his hand s on her flesh and construct his finest creation, but maintained his cool persona.

She was surprisingly easy to locate sitting on the trunk of her car reading a book. He wondered if it was the same book she read the day he decided she was the one. *Lost in her own little world* and unaware of everything outside of her book, she gave him a smile just the same. Haley was surprised to see her biker neighbor, which is the only name she had ever know him by, at a Christian concert.

He beckoned his best sorrowful face and told her something had happened to her mother, and she needed to come home right away. Her smile melted to a frown. Tanner felt horrible for lying, especially when she began to panic. Haley began to ask rapid-fire questions as to her condition, but Tanner stated that he didn't know the severity, only that he was asked to find her and bring her home. He insisted on driving her due to her frantic state. Haley offered no resistance as she locked her car and followed him to his pickup. Without question, she climbed into the passenger seat and nervously played with her MP3 player. She was in no mood to listen to music, but it comforted her a bit to shuffle through the songs. Tanner was quite surprised with the ease in luring her into his truck, and impressed with his lie.

There was little talk on the ride; Tanner made it clear he did not know any details of her mother's condition. The only reprieve from the silence was the quiet sound of the radio playing softly; Dust in the Wind played on the radio as her mind filed with aimless thoughts in constant motion.

Tanner saw her rub her temples and asked if she was okay; she responded that her head was throbbing. He offered her prescription sleeping pills he easily passed off as aspirin. It wasn't long before she laid passed out cold. He waited for her to be unconscious before pulling over on the rarely traveled back road. She was much lighter than expected as he placed her into the truck bed, careful not to bruise her skin, tying up and gagging her. The pills he gave her would keep her asleep for a few hours, there were only about forty-five minutes left in the trip, but he wanted to restrain and hide her just in case.

The remainder of the ride home was quiet. He tried not to think of it too much, fearing he might change his mind. Instead, he turned the radio up a bit louder and sang along to the classic rock to pass the time.

He pulled into the garage and quickly shut the door behind him. Before fetching her from the trunk, he went inside and made sure the path to the basement was free of obstacles. Once he was satisfied, he thrust her limp body upon his shoulder and hurried to his workshop, careful to catch each step on his way downstairs.

Before she woke from her comatose state, he removed her clothing and prepped his work area. Fearful the medicine wouldn't render her body numb, he injected her with horse tranquilizer and wasted no time making his first cut. He surgically sliced through the skin around the inside of her gums, creating a starting point to rip her flesh from the muscle, then cranked some Black Sabbath to hide any unexpected screams.

Still standing upon the dock, a brisk breeze carried a frigid mist. In his haste, he had forgotten a jacket, and his goose bumps demanded warmth. With a final tip of his hat towards the unseen victim, he turned to walk back to his truck. A loose board slippery with the fallen rain thrust him into the water. He hit his head on the side of the dock and his consciousness faded.

Floating upon the same waves that had ushered Haley towards the center, his limp body did not resist the voyage. He came to a stop rather quickly when the water finally calmed, his comatose body floating without sound. The bright moon shined upon him, illuminating him. Haley slept peacefully below, within her death, waiting patiently for her God to welcome her home, unaware her skin is missing, or that the blob above her was the man that had tainted her.

Gentle raindrops fell on Tanner's face, waking him from his trauma-induced sleep. Panic set in as he struggled to stay afloat; never had he learned to swim. Terror only pulls him deep within the pond; he inhales the water, drowning above the girl he just laid to rest. Death came quickly as his flailing exhausted oxygen from his blood and his limp body became entangled in a patch of seaweed, forever laying him to rest next to his beautiful victim.

Murphy Edwards

Coal Black Talons

Believe me when I say this, they are not human. They may at times look like humans; they may act like humans, even walk and talk like humans. In truth, they are anything but. They are the ultimate predator for they hide in plain sight, not just blending into the crowd, but becoming it.

The first time I saw them they were deep within the inner city, where poverty danced about the landscape consuming buildings and businesses with equal abandon. Lord, how I've grown to hate the city of Gary. Not the sounds or the smells, those I have grown quite accustomed to, rather *like* actually. No, for me it is the never ceasing clot of people, and now the need to look constantly over my shoulder.

I had gone for a walk down Bennington Street to catch some fresh air and a cold pint at Muligans Pub. My sleep had been a bit off the mark, and I was sure the brisk evening air mingled with a bit of strong ale would have me eager for bed and a night of fitful sleep. I took my usual stool at the bar and was soon consumed with the revelry of a night among friends.

Having finished a third pint and a go at the darts with an eager fellow named Cullin, I'd stayed a bit longer than first planned. Since the ale was cold, and the darts were hitting their mark in my favor, I had little concern for the time. At midnight, I cashed it in and left by way of the back door. That's when I saw them.

A thick fog had settled in over the alleyway. It hung over the steam grates and rubbish bins like a woolen horse blanket. The ale had me in gentle spirits, and I was whistling a merry tune to carry me along. Ahead of me by no more than twelve paces was a rather large gent who, by the look of his gate, had spent considerable more time in front of the tap at Muligans than I. He was a bouncing waggle of a man, nearly as broad as he was tall. He lilted from side to side as he walked, caught up in the merriment of a night on the tiles. I amused myself by watching as the fellow tittered to himself and weaved his way down the darkened alley, dodging trash bins, ash cans and the occasional sewer rat. Midway down the alley he stopped short, as if someone had thrown up a traffic signal which had gone to red. He spun towards me and swayed to-and-fro on the balls of his feet. As I drew closer, his body continued its gentle sway, but his face went stone gray.

It was thereabouts that the smell hit me. The smell of something long dead. It wormed into my nostrils and assaulted my sinuses, stirring bile in my throat and tears in my eyes. I leaned against an ash can and began to wretch. At that precise moment the far wall quite simply came alive with their form, as if the very mortar had become them, and they the mortar. When I reached eighteen, I stopped counting them and crept as close to the darkened end of the nearest rubbish bin as I dared without stumbling and causing an attraction. Sweet Mother of Mercies how they did stink though.

The creatures were not lycanthropic, no werewolf or vampire, for none of those beasts could hold a candle to these. Neither were they some legend of distant folklore conjured up to scare children and commoners half out of their rightful wits. Upon appearing from the wall they briefly flashed to a human form, then dodged like a flickering torch before turning full-on into their true selves.

They had no eyes to speak of, merely tight menacing slits high at the top of their protruding foreheads. By the look of their ears and their constantly twitching snouts, I soon made the logical assumption that they moved about largely by the sensing of smells and sounds. Both were quite keen. Roundabout their shoulders and outer thighs were thick wedges of razor sharp bone protruding from the flesh like slippery white daggers. The nape of their necks bore heavy wrinkles, taking on the appearance of a stack of cased sausage links, though the smell of their breath was something else entirely.

The circle of creatures stood stark still, clicking their coal black talons about on the pavement as if signaling one to another. Perhaps they were, for soon they thrust themselves upon the man in a violent and bloody rush. I heard the man scream out, then begin pleading, asking to be spared from whatever fate was about to befall him. Whatever mercies he begged for did him no good. Once they set about their work, there was no stopping them.

Damning myself for leaving my only weapon at home on the bed stand, I crouched as low as I could, willing myself to blend in with the darkness of the trash bin as I'd seen them blend with the brick and mortar only moments ago. My presence appeared hidden from the beasts by the stench from the contents of the trash bin. I aimed to keep it that way.

The first strike opened an ugly gash in the man's belly. His insides soon found their way outside, spilling forth in his palms like a waterfall. Blood gushed between his fingers, staining his shirt like an uncorked bottle of burgundy spilling out on freshly laundered table linens. I struggled to keep the ale within the confines of my stomach. The sight of so much blood sickened me, but not yet to the point of wasting good ale by throwing it up in a darkened alley full of crazed beasts. That was soon to change.

Once the creatures had the man sufficiently weakened, they thrust their powerful talons into his ribs and lifted him onto a loading platform. His body had gone limp, his eyes glazed over from the shock of it all. They approached him at chin level and bit into his neck and thighs as though he were a freshly baked teacake. They didn't eat the flesh so much as merely melt it away. In a matter of moments, all traces of the man were completely gone, save for his clothing and a scruffy pair of hand-sewn loafers. Likewise, the creatures, having eaten their fill, twittered briefly to a human form, then blended into the mortar and brick as cleanly as a knife through creamery butter. No sign of them remained.

Salty tears rolled down my cheeks, hitting the concrete in noisy plops. I dabbed my eyes with the sleeve of my shirt, fearful of what might happen if they heard me and returned to finish their feast. I could smell the man's spilled blood, the raw metallic odor mixing with the smells of taverns and trash. The sound of clicking talons remained trapped inside my head. My hands trembled like those of a feeble drunkard, confident the beasts would return, yet still unsure I had seen them at all.

I waited a full hour, crouched like a frightened bunny behind the trash bin, listening for the two o'clock toll of the central city tower, then exited the alleyway in the opposite direction. I made my way home in less than ten minutes, winded by running at full gate down Bennington Street and up the three flights of steps to my flat. Once there I retrieved the revolver from my bed stand and a bottle of bourbon from the kitchen. I took blinding belts from the bottle, certain the beasts would appear through the walls or ceiling at any moment. I came to on the couch some hours later, the bottle empty and the revolver clutched tightly to my chest. Sharp nailed fingers of pain stabbed at the back of my eyes, bullying me for being so careless.

At dawn I went straightway to the closest station house and filed a report with the Constable, but really how seriously could he take me? Me, shambling into his office smelling of strong drink and going on about hideous, eyeless beasts with black talons and dripping snouts, who appeared from nothing and ate an ape-sized man in the back alley of a local pub. What was he to do? I counted myself fortunate that he chose to let me leave the station with a simple promise to sober up and never speak of it further.

After several days of rambling about from room to room, jumping at the slightest hint of a noise, I determined to keep the whole thing mum. The believing of such a story would be difficult at best, and even my closest friends would likely consider the whole matter nothing more than an amazing bit of tripe. It wouldn't be the first time I stood accused of allowing my liquor to do the talking. I didn't want to be considered daft as well.

I eventually returned to work, explaining to my employer, Winston Deaver, that I had taken ill and was bedridden with chills and fever so severe I had been swept into delirium. The sallow look on my face, coupled with swollen, bloodshot eyes made the story convincing enough to pass muster. Deaver was no fool. After missing two weeks work, I counted myself fortunate to still be in his employ. I determined to bury myself in the mounds of paperwork stacked at my desk and put the whole duff behind me.

When I had all but forgotten my encounter with the creatures, resigning it to the consumption of one too many pints and the exhaustion brought on by a demanding job, I again began to venture out in the evenings. Most of my trips were short, brought about by the need to visit the local chemist for scripts or a market to fetch tea and baked goods. My life had returned to normal, save for the occasional nightmare to disrupt my sleep. On the evening I walked to the tobacconist for a fresh fill of pipe tobacco, everything changed.

I had decided to forego the usual meal from a tin and go out for a quick bite at Gaston's Chop House after fetching the tobacco. I had regained my taste for red meat and as far as a well-portioned porterhouse goes, there is none so fine as Gaston's. The evening sky was clear, with only the slightest nip in the air. The walk to Gaston's was a short one, so I elected to save the cab fare and leave on the heel. I grabbed my jacket and left for a night on the town, but not before sliding the revolver in my pocket.

At the corner of Lennox and Calvert, I stepped to the crosswalk and waited for the signal to change. The first scream hit my ears when I was well into the midst of Lennox, and a ten-ton tipper truck was baring down on me at break neck speed. Had I not rolled to the curb, there would have been little more than bits and scraps to load into a funeral coach. The driver held fast to his horn with one hand while extending a finger in my direction through the open window. He rounded the corner at full gate, having one last go at the horn before speeding off into the night.

I fingered the freshly torn hole in my trousers and dusted bits of ash from my jacket. The scream came again, louder this time, and more urgent than the first. Whoever it was, they were close, and from the sound of it, in extreme pain. I dashed toward the scream, unsure what help, if any, I could offer.

A block up Calvert and through a bit of hedge and I was right on top of it. The screaming turned to a mournful wailing so fierce I clapped my palms over my ears to block it out. What I couldn't block out was the sight sprawled out on the cobblestone before me. A young woman, no more than twenty, was thrashing about as though she were possessed. She was bleeding. So much so that I could not distinguish from where, nor could I detect the extent of her wounds.

As I approached her, the hedgerow came alive with a clot of shifting shapes, first human, then creatures. *Those* creatures. I squinted, balling my fists into my eyes in case I was seeing things, yet knowing full well I wasn't. They were back, and they had seen me. There was no hiding among the trash bins, no pretending to be invisible, no wishing it away. I was caught up in it full on, whatever *it* was.

I folded myself into the hedge, pulling the revolver from my jacket on the way in. I had six rounds in the revolver and enough for one reload. I counted fourteen of them. I was two bricks shy a full hod. There was little to do but aim carefully and pray. Always pray.

The woman by this point was putting up an admirable fight with a can of hair lacquer and a nail file, but she was no match for those coal black talons and thick wedges of razor sharp bone. A pair of the beasts went to work on her midsection, having a go at her front bits like she was a shepherd's pie. I watched her thrash about, knowing full well struggling would only prolong the agony of it all.

From my place in the hedge, I opened up on the beasts with the revolver, hitting one at the base of the skull and two others in the upper chest. They dropped like a two hundred stone weight. My fourth shot went low and wide, bouncing off the cobblestone and burrowing harmlessly into the trunk of a nearby oak. I had hopes the gunfire would bring help, but knew it likely wouldn't since Calvert was at the back of a section of abandoned industrial dredge that had yet to be rehabbed.

The creatures scattered, taken aback by the sudden eruption of a .38 caliber handgun. It lasted no more than a moment before they were back at the woman with renewed vigor. The three creatures who'd taken my bullets flickered for an instant, then blended into the cobblestone and disappeared.

One of the creatures, by appearances the leader of the group, turned his attention to the hedge. His ears pricked as he sniffed his way to my location at the far end. My finger tensed on the trigger, waiting for his slimy form to come well within range of my shaking hands. He parted the hedge in front of my face, and I filled his with the remaining rounds from the .38. The creature fell out one side of the hedge and I the other.

I had practiced loading the revolver on many occasions, but never with a heart full of adrenaline and a body filled with raw terror. I managed one round in the cylinder for every two I dropped to the dark grass at my feet. Having a go at 'Hello Johnny' in the tall grass while someone is being eaten alive a mere ten feet away can be a bit unnerving. At length I settled for the five rounds I had in the cylinder, swung it shut and brought the revolver up to eye level.

A blood-slicked talon parted a bit of hedge to the right of me, making way for that waggling snout and those menacing eyeless slits. I jacked the .38 hard up to its chin and pulled the trigger. The impact decorated the hedges with bits of putrid flesh and snout. Black talons slashed at the space I'd occupied moments ago, then disappeared.

I knew I had to stay on the move, perhaps find a down-wind location and stay put, but there was no discernible breeze, and I was down to four bullets and a single prayer. I crashed through the hedges saying the Our Father and firing at anything that dared to move. I got off two shots before the revolver was batted from my hand.

A flash of talons knocked me to the ground. Like razors, they dug into the meaty part of my back and ripped away bits of muscle and flesh, shredding it into long bloody strips. A second swipe rolled me over and caught me about the left temple, tearing out my eye. I groped about in the dark, searching for the eyeball like a child desperate to find a prized marble. One of the beasts flexed its talons and speared it up, savoring it like a freshly scooped melon ball. Blood filled the corners of my remaining eye, blotting out my vision.

Then, just as before, as quickly as it all began, it was over. The creatures were gone. There was nothing left of the woman to speak of, save for her purse and a shredded cotton dress, soaked to the full with blood. Had the creatures really gone or were they merely part of the cobblestone and hedges I now stood between? I couldn't say. I also decided not to find out.

I was rattled, but more so by shock than pain. The speed of it all, the appearance, the tussle, the attack, was taking a while for me to suss out. Having bundled my mangled face in the remnants of my shirt, I worked my way down Lennox Street, wedged myself through the transom over the doorway of Callihan's Baked Goods and hid out till daylight.

A month in hospital stuffed full of tubes and wires did little to settle my jangled nerves and relieve me of the shock of a wrecked body and a missing eye. The surgeon patched the wound as best he could, but with the condition of my face, he had little left to work with. Either the hospital staff assumed I had gotten myself into a bit of a go at one of the local pubs or was the victim of a merciless mugging by a heat of local thugs. They begged me to tell them which. Yet how could I?

I was not much to look at after that. I spent much of my time sulking about, angered by the whole wedge I'd found myself in. I stumbled round my flat, giving anything a toss that wasn't tacked down. The mirrors were the first to go. I cursed the creatures, myself, even my eye for seeing the bloody things in the first place.

After that night, I stopped partaking of strong drink, for I could never allow myself to become careless again. At any given moment, when I was most vulnerable and least prepared, they could appear. It may be at a street carnival, or between the loose joints of my floorboards, changing to suit their needs, or perhaps simply lurking about just within the shadows to amuse themselves by inducing panic in their prey.

Now that I had seen them, truly knew of them and what they were, they would be hunting me. That is why I despised the city. It distracted me, and I couldn't afford *not* to pay attention. Very close attention. For if I didn't, the moment my back was turned, or my eyes drifted to admire a brunette with a well-placed curve, I was done for.

With little support from the law, I took to relying solely on myself for protection. I set about the task of arming myself with every conceivable weapon short of cannon and grape. Knives and blades proved to be quite lethal. A well-placed blade removed the head with one smooth swipe, but this required me to get too close to avoid those coal black talons. With only one eye remaining, I dared not give them a close-in advantage. A blast to the snout with a high caliber handgun proved to be the surest method to incapacitate them. I couldn't actually say it killed them. Once attacked, they simply melded back into whatever they had appeared from.

The attacks came more frequently after that. A young boy with dreadful piercings and a shaven head, out to celebrate his eighteenth and final birthday; an auto mechanic from Brindall, off on holiday; and an investment banker looking to score a hot bit of property from an elderly couple for little more than a chat and a dance. I saw them all, each attack more vivid and vicious than the one before, as if the creatures intended it to be so. And me, horrified and helpless, unable to do anything but watch the carnage and blast away at odd bits of alien flesh.

Each attack played over in my brain, like a cinema feature on an endless celluloid loop. The eighteen-year-old, having drunk his fill at the Bull and Horn, staggered into a vacant lot across from my office at the same instant I locked up for the evening. He had scarcely hit the sod in his drunken stupor, when bits of turf began to rumble under him, churning in a rolling fashion. Then came the talons, thrusting up through the turf and straightway through the boy's chest cavity. In less than two minutes, twenty-one creatures erupted from the earth and began to feed. I got off three rounds, but the distance from me to them had me at a decidable disadvantage. I didn't want to hit the boy, though I doubt he would have felt it by that point. As I moved closer, they disappeared into the turf, taking the boy's remains with them.

The other two attacks were a bit of a combo. The banker was on his way to survey the prospective property when his auto chucked a wobbly. He limped it to the curb on Fenster Street and popped the bonnet to have a look. The auto mechanic, on his way to a pub crawl to soak up some of the local flavor and several pints, stopped to assist. That's when the whole thing went pear shaped.

The mechanic was busy fiddling with some greasy bit on the engine, telling the banker how fussy those German autos could be. I rounded the corner on my way to post a letter at the precise moment the entire auto fluttered and belched forth a snarling pack of creatures. The mechanic, instantly cleaved in two from groin to forehead, toppled to either side of the gleaming black auto with a sickening thud. The attack put the banker on high alert, but it was too late for him to react. The creatures split up, half of them feeding on the remains of the mechanic, the other focusing on the banker's meaty thighs. I'm sure they considered me a bit of a wally, charging round the corner with a handgun going on about some pack of man-eating creatures about to have at them with teeth and talons. I wanted only to help them, perhaps save them if I could. Instead, I only managed to boggle the whole sad mess, blasting away wildly as I dashed toward them. All that remained was a stalled German auto with a bloodied bumper, gleaming in the afternoon sun.

After that they came at me constantly. I began to see them everywhere. In the lift, at a park, on the motorways driving everything from taxis to rubbish trucks; they haunted my every step. They usually appeared in pairs like an alien strike force, tormenting me with those endlessly clicking talons, or scratching at doors and windows. I survived only by keeping my wits about me and learning to fight like a madman. I put my full faith and effort into it, losing my job in the process and going through my life savings like corn through a hungry swan. The creatures had terrorized me, maimed me and taken everything from me I once held dear. I vowed they would never kill me.

I took to the streets, living off bits and crumbs of whatever I could find. My flat was all but abandoned, empty of findings and furniture. I wanted to keep it, but I couldn't afford to be that predictable. I had to stay on the kip, moving about like a vagrant, first to Fort Wayne, then further south to Indianapolis, Richmond and Evansville. My instinct told me that perhaps this had all happened for a reason, my one chance to finally leave the city and explore the Indiana countryside. The changing of a habit starts with but a single day repeated.

The torture of it all kept me just this side of insanity. At length, they would retreat from the fight, reverting to whatever they were hiding in, becoming a piece of tin roof, a smoke stack, a railway platform, even the lampposts I leaned on to steady myself. When I moved on, they did as well. Hunting. Feeding. Blending into the background. And waiting. Waiting for that single moment in time when I would let down my guard. When that time comes, and I know it will, they will move out of the shadows, clicking those coal black talons and sniffing the air, ready to feed.

D. S. Scott

Frankie

"What ... did ... you ... do?" Frankie's mother spoke each word as an individual sentence.

Frankie looked down at the puddle on the ground and waited for the pain. Memories of this moment would be not of the pain that came next but oddly enough, the color of his mother's shoes. He looked down at the floor, his eyes drifting back to the pink slip-on shoes. After a minute of silence he raised his head and looked at her pale, peach colored dress, then at the white pearls around her neck, and finally at her perfect, golden hair. He had skipped her face on purpose but couldn't avoid it any longer. The look he saw there was the one he had expected - twisted, contorted hatred. Although familiar, it haunted him.

When their eyes met Frankie's mother spoke again. "I asked you a question, you little shit!"

Frankie was eight years old and already knew what shit was. It was him. At least that's what he imagined it was because it seemed to be his mother's favorite name for him. She called him "Shit" more than she called him by his name.

He started to speak but before he could begin, the pain came, swift and sharp. His mother's hand hit his cheek perfectly flat, producing a loud pop and causing a severe burning sensation. He cowered away and shuddered as she shrieked in fury.

"Look what you made me do!" she yelled.

Frankie recovered from the blow to his face and cautiously turned his head back to look at his mother. She was inspecting her hand, turning it this way and that.

"You made me break a nail," she yelled again. "Little shit ..." she added. "Your father will hear about this when he gets home from work, you know."

He began to cry uncontrollably.

"Stop that. I said stop it," his mother screamed.

He tried to quit but he just couldn't contain it anymore.

"I ... said ... stop." She raised her hand back and brought it down on the side of his head. The broken nail caught his ear and cut it. Screaming in pain and fear, he reached up to hold his bleeding ear. He cried in great harsh sobs that made it difficult to breathe.

"Stop it! Stop it! Stop it," his mother screamed. "Whiney little shit!"

Frankie watched as his mother's hand flew back again but this time he did not look away. He stared her right in the eye and waited. She seemed surprised but it didn't stop her for long. She hit him again and again. Each time he recovered from the slap, he looked back at her, staring her in the eye with defiance. This only enraged her more. This time she closed her hand into a fist and flashed a dark smile. He waited for a busted lip or maybe a broken nose. Her fist went back, and he braced himself for the punch. He closed his eyes this time and waited, but it didn't come.

He opened his eyes and looked to see a large hand wrapped around his mother's wrist. She was as surprised at her punch not landing as he was. She turned around to see her husband standing there, smiling at her.

"Now honey, what did I say about hitting the boy?" Frankie's father asked in a soft tone.

His mother looked at him and smiled. "You said you'd handle it."

"That's right, Babe. There's no need to get all worked up over a little accident, now is there?" He gave his wife a kind smile and let go of her wrist.

"No Dear, I suppose not." She turned on her heel and casually walked out of the room.

Frankie grimaced, not at his mother, but at his father—and what would happen now that he was home. No matter how horrible his mother was, it was safe to say his dad was worse. He was a violent man, and there was no stopping him.

His father stood in front of him, hands on his hips, looking down at the puddle. "So ... Frankie," he said in an overly cheery voice. "What have we been up to today? Hmm?"

Frankie had nothing to say. There was nothing he could say to save himself, so, instead, he stared at the puddle and sobbed quietly. His dad sighed. After a few seconds of silence that seemed to drag on forever, he spoke again.

"Frankie, we've been through this. Over and over again, son," he said.

"Dad--," he started to explain, to defend himself, to do something, anything in his favor, but stopped when his father put his hand on the back of his neck.

"Son, don't interrupt. It's rude."

He was silent. Standing there, he felt strong fingers drumming on his neck, rising and falling one at a time.

"Frankie. On the new carpet?"

He didn't even try to speak this time.

"Your mother and I work hard to support the three of us. We work to buy nice things and to keep our new house here in Indiana. Do you know how expensive it was to move here from California? We did it so we could start over. We put food on our plates and clothes on our backs. Do you realize how expensive all that is? I'm really not sure why we do any of those things for you, though. With the way you treat us and our home, you don't deserve any of what we provide. You were a fucking accident, son. One that we'll have to pay for the rest of our lives. Or at least the rest of yours. But we still put up with you. And how do you repay us?"

Before Frankie knew what had happened, his feet were swept out from under him, and he was slammed to the floor. His face was shoved into the puddle and held there. The stench was strong and sour in his nostrils.

"How do you repay us?" his father asked again, yelling this time. "You piss on the goddamn carpet," he screamed. His tone lowered as he spoke again. "The nice, new, white carpet your mother picked out especially for our new home."

He struggled against his father's hold on his neck, but he was too small to fight it. He flailed his legs and tried to push himself off the ground, but it was no use. He started to cry and took in long deep breaths through his nose, trying to catch his air. The stench of urine was overwhelming as it flooded into his nose and went back to his brain, giving him an instant headache. The struggle went on for another thirty seconds before his dad let go. He rolled over on his back and gasped for fresh air.

His father seemed out of breath too. He enjoyed what he did. He enjoyed it a little too much. Frankie noticed the bulge in the front of his pants and felt a knot growing in his stomach. After crouching over his son and admiring his work, he stood up straight and walked away as if nothing had happened.

Bruised and battered, he stayed on the floor for another twenty minutes before he was able to get up. When he did, he ran to the bathroom and threw up blood in the toilet. That's when he first heard the voice.

He turned his head to the side and listened. He could have sworn he heard someone say his name. He listened for another few seconds before he heard it again.

"Frankie!"

He looked all over but couldn't find the source of the voice. "Yeah?" he asked with caution. There was silence. Curious, he crawled over to the closet on his hands and knees, then placed his hand on the doorknob and paused. After gathering his courage, he swung the door open. There was nothing there except towels. "Hello?" Determined to find the source of the voice, he slid on his knees to the shower and pulled back the curtain. Nothing there either. "Who's there?" Finally, he heard it again.

"A friend, Frankie. A good friend."

"I don't have any friends. Mom says no one wants to be friends with me because I wet myself," he said matter-of-factly.

"Well, your mom's wrong. I'll be your friend. And I don't even care if you wet yourself sometimes. How about that?"

He smiled to himself. He'd never had a friend before. "Where are you?" he asked suddenly. "I can't see you."

"Don't worry about that, Bud. I'm here with you. That's all that matters, right?"

"Yeah," Frankie exclaimed. He was so happy he could jump up and down. He got to his feet and wiped the red vomit off his lip, planning to do just that but paused.

"What's wrong, Bud?"

"I'm not supposed to get excited. I'll wet myself again," he said solemnly.

"Says who?"

"Mom and Dad." Frankie grimaced thinking about them.

"Well, forget them. If you want to jump and run and get excited, you should."

He thought for a minute. "But I'll wet myself again. I already got in trouble today."

"How about this? If you go jump up and down and run around, but accidentally wet yourself, I'll take the blame."

"Really?" Frankie could barely contain himself.

"Really, really, Kiddo."

"Oh, wow! You're a great friend ..." He paused again. "Wait ... what's your name?"

"Well, goodness. I forgot to tell you my name, didn't I? Where are my manners?"

He grinned. "It's okay. I don't get angry like Mom and Dad about manners and stuff like that."

"Well, I appreciate that, Pal. It means a lot. My name's Nomed."

"Nomed? That's a weird name," Frankie chuckled.

"Oh yeah? How do you know? What if Frankie is a weird name and Nomed is the normal one?"

Frankie didn't know what to say, so he stood there in silence.

"Hey, come on. I'm just kidding around with you. My name is

pretty silly, huh?"

Frankie giggled. "Yeah ..."

Nomed laughed too. He had a good laugh. He seemed really nice. Good friends are always nice to each other.

"That's right. Good friends *are* nice to each other."

He could feel the grin come across his face as he spoke, "How did you know what I was thinking?"

"Hey, all best friends can do that. You didn't know that?"

"Oh, wow. No. But I know now."

Nomed laughed again. "You sure do."

Frankie started to laugh too, but Nomed cut him off.

"Hey. Aren't we forgetting something?"

"What?" Frankie frowned.

"Someone is supposed to be jumping up and down right now. And I don't see any jumping going on."

Frankie's face lit up, and he laughed some more. "Okay. Here goes." He crouched down on the floor and launched himself as high as he could into the air. For the first time in his life, he felt free to do what he wanted. "Wow! That was great, Nomed!" Then it hit him. He wasn't urinating all over himself. He couldn't feel a single drop and he couldn't put into words how happy he was at this moment. He almost felt like crying again. Only this time it would be from joy.

"What did I tell you? Forget those parents. They don't know stuff like me and you."

"You're right. Only best buds know best, right?"

"Absolutely right, my friend. Absolutely right."

Frankie was so excited he jumped and ran in place for ten minutes straight. This was the best day of his life. He couldn't have described how happy he was if he tried. After he was done, he sat down on the toilet seat and rested. He took in deep breaths of air and this time there was no horrible pee smell.

"Having a good time, Bud?"

"You bet! This is awesome," Frankie shouted in excitement.

"I agree. Totally awesome, my man."

"You're a good friend, Nomed. No, wait. You're a great friend," Frankie yelled again.

"Well, thank you. And guess what?"

He thought for a moment. "What?"

"You're a stupendous friend."

Frankie laughed. "What does that mean?"

"It means you're the best friend ever."

"Oh, wow! Really?"

"You betcha, Bud."

"Cool!" Frankie shouted louder this time. That's when everything came back. He heard a voice that cut through him like a knife.

"What the fuck are you yelling about?"

"Oh, no. It's Mom again," Frankie whimpered.

"Hey, hey. It's okay. Don't be afraid of her."

"But how? She scares me."

"Okay, let me think for a minute. We'll come up with something, okay?"

"You promise?" he smiled weakly.

"As your very best bud in the whole wide world ... I promise."

"Okay," he whispered. "Can I tell my parents about you?"

"No. Not yet."

"Why not?"

"They're not ready yet. But I promise you that too. You can tell them soon, okay?"

"Okay." He smiled a little more this time. He was feeling a little better about things until he heard footsteps coming toward the bathroom. "Oh, no. What do I do?" Nomed whispered something as the footsteps came closer. Frankie's mom opened the bathroom door with a look of fury on her face, but it soon turned to one of confusion.

"What are you doing? Why are you yelling?" she asked with suspicion.

He sat in silence; the only noise he made was the sound of his pee hitting the toilet water. His mother looked shocked out of her mind, and Frankie was surprised too. Instead of cowering away, he just stared up at her with a huge grin on his face.

"You're ... You ..." She fumbled with her words. "How are you ...?"

He kept smiling and shrugged innocently. When he finally spoke he was laughing. "Momma, I'm peeing in the toilet." He was so happy. Surely his mom and dad would be too. He waited for a response from his mother as he finished and zipped up his fly but it didn't come.

"Momma ... I ..." He got cut off with his mom's bitter words.

"I heard you, you little shit. Good for you. Now go clean up the mess in the living room, dammit."

He stared at her in horror. Why was she being so mean? Wasn't this what she wanted?

"Go." She pointed a threatening finger at him. "Now! And change your clothes. You smell like piss."

Frankie felt hot tears welling up in his eyes again. This wasn't fair. It was never fair. He lowered his head and walked out of the bathroom toward the living room. He hated his parents and wanted them gone. He wondered to himself if Nomed had any ideas about how to do that.

It took Frankie the better part of an hour of scrubbing to get the yellow stain out of the carpet. During this time his parents ignored him, which he was grateful for. He talked to Nomed the entire time.

They whispered back and forth and came up with a plan. Nomed was so smart. He knew just how to get rid of Frankie's parents. It was genius. Frankie wondered why he hadn't thought of it before.

"No worries, Bud. That's what best friends are for, right?"

"That's right," Frankie said, a little louder than he meant to.

"Are you done yet?" He heard his mother call from the kitchen, "It's time for bed."

"What about dinner, Momma?" Frankie frowned.

"Little boys who piss themselves and take too long to clean it up don't get dinner. It's time for bed. Now," she sneered.

He was angry. He had cleaned up the mess like she wanted. Yes, it took a while but it was only eight-thirty. Before he knew what he was doing, he stood up and yelled, "That's not fair!"

His mom growled before she spoke. "What did you say? What did you just say to me?"

Frankie was scared, but Nomed urged him on. That's what friends are for. And two friends are better than one mom. Quivering slightly, he said, "You heard me."

The look on his mother's face said it all. He was in big trouble. Nomed spoke as she stormed toward him.

"Don't worry about her, Frankie. She's not as tough as she seems."

"You sure?"

"Positive. Stick to the plan."

"Okay."

His mom ran through the kitchen and into the living room, her raised hand already in a fist. She stopped in front of him.

"Say it again, Frankie. Go ahead. See what happens. I'll show you fair," she taunted.

He closed his eyes, took a deep breath and let it out slowly. His mother began to say something more but stopped mid-sentence as he unzipped his pants. Her screams hurt his ears as he peed on the front of her dress. She stepped back and tripped on her now wet shoes, letting out a long, piercing shriek on the way down. He stepped forward and continued peeing on her but to his horror saw he was peeing blood. She tried to block the flow of red with her hands, but Frankie really had to go and didn't stop until he had finished.

"What the fuck is going on?" his dad yelled.

Frankie heard his father's heavy footsteps and jumped into action. He zipped up his bloody pants as fast as he could and ran for the kitchen. His mother tried to grab his ankles as he ran past, but her slippery hands couldn't hold on. She continued screaming as Frankie disappeared behind the kitchen counter and grabbed what he needed.

His dad ran past him and into the living room without even looking at him. When he had passed, Frankie headed toward his room. He could hear the fear and disgust in her screams. Now Frankie was a little scared too.

His hands were shaking and his heart felt like it would pop out of his chest at any moment. "What just happened?"

"You stuck to the plan, man. Good for you."

"Yeah, but the plan didn't include me peeing blood," he whined.

"Hey, don't worry about it. You're all good, Buddy."

"Are you sure? Blood isn't good. Am I going to die?" He shuddered at the thought.

"What? No. No way, Bud. You're fine."

"You sure?"

"Hey, would I lie to you? You're my best bud, Frankie. Not only are you fine, but you got your mom good. She totally freaked out. Isn't this great?"

"Yeah, I guess," Frankie said.

"You guess? Come on, Buddy. You wanted to get rid of your parents, right?"

"Yeah ..." he said, slowly.

"Then that's what we're going to do. We're gonna scare 'em. Then they'll leave you alone forever. I promise."

He grinned. "Forever?"

"...and ever."

Frankie's hands were shaking so badly he nearly dropped the knife he held. "What are we going to do with this?"

"You'll see."

"Okay," he said hesitantly.

"Okay, indeed. Everything's going to be okay."

"Okay."

He sat on his bed and waited. He could hear harsh sobs coming from the other end of the house. His mother sounded like she was hyperventilating. He changed out of his bloody clothes while he waited, looking up at the clock on the wall now and then. Half an hour passed and the sobs faded away. It was another half hour before he heard the shower come on. A couple of minutes later, he heard his dad's heavy footsteps stop outside his room. He held his breath, waiting. He jumped as the bedroom door burst open.

"Nomed ..." Frankie said.

The door hit the wall, and his dad stepped into the room. He stared at Frankie in silence for a full minute. Frankie shivered. He thought of the knife that lay under the pillow at the head of his bed.

"Frankie ..." his dad began.

"What?" He spat the word out like it tasted bad.

"Why in the hell did you do that to your mother?"

He thought of the words Nomed had told him to say. "Because she's a ..." he paused. "Bitch," he finished. He had never cussed before. To his surprise it felt good. It felt really good until his dad stood up and hit him on the side of the head.

"Don't you ever call her that," he trembled as he yelled with fury.

"Fine. I'll call you that," he replied, trying to recover from the blow. "Bitch."

This time was worse. The impact knocked him off the bed. His father turned and closed the bedroom door, then walked over to Frankie, picked him up off the ground and threw him on the bed.

"You're going to show me some respect, boy," he yelled. "And your mother's in the shower. She won't hear you yell. Not that she cares about you, anyway." He kicked his shoes off and began to take off his pants. He turned around to lock the door. "You're gonna get what's coming to you." He spoke again as he turned back around, "You're the bitch now, Fr-" but he stopped when he saw the knife.

Frankie thrust the blade into his father's crotch as hard as he could. Now it was his dad's screams that hurt his ears. "Frankie! What did you do? Shit. Oh, fuck. Oh, no. No. No. No!" He began to cry as he looked at the knife sticking out of his groin. Frankie jumped off the bed and followed his father across the room as he tried to back away. Falling backwards against the wall, his dad screamed again. "Oh, no. Oh, God. No, God. No!"

Frankie knelt down and looked straight into his father's eyes. When his gaze was met he whispered, "God's not here, Dad."

Somewhere in the depths of his body, Frankie watched in horror. He had no control of what had just happened. What *had* happened? There was so much blood. "Nomed?" There was silence. "Nomed? You didn't say anything about killing Dad." He waited for a reply, but none came. He wanted to cry but didn't feel like he could. It was like he felt numb and couldn't control his body anymore. He was terrified as he felt his hand go for the blade. He watched from inside as he yanked the knife out and carved something into his father's chest. His dad wasn't screaming anymore. His head was slumped forward, and he was barely breathing. Frankie stared as the knife carved a star in a circle on his dad's chest. Then he cut the number six all over. When he finished, his dad wasn't breathing anymore. Bile rose from his stomach as he realized his father was dead. He stood and took a step back before he threw up. He fell to his hands and knees as the bedroom door opened.

Frankie looked back up and saw his mother as a black, tar-like substance came out of his mouth. Her screams were as terrifying as the tar. It kept coming and coming, and she kept screaming and screaming. After another moment, her legs gave out, and she fell down hard on her butt. She tried futilely to back away from Frankie but didn't get far. Frankie stepped toward her with the knife clutched in his hand.

Somewhere deep inside, he heard Nomed say, "Don't worry, Frankie. I don't have a father either. He's dead to me. I'm a bastard like you. We'll be fine. We have each other now."

"Bill? Oh, God!" His mother stared at her husband and cried. When she looked back at her son she asked quietly, "Frankie, what did you do?"

Frankie felt a grin cross his face. He used the knife to point at the yellow puddle growing underneath her body. "No, Momma. What did you do?"

Lemmy Rushmore

The Brickyard Bleeds

ethanol fumes
and fans galore
the screams succumb
to engine's roar
amongst loud cheers
and rubber's scent
another life
lies fully spent
the flesh fled fast
from gleaming blade
with finished act
it's God I've played
a caution flag
then green they drop
I know I should
but I can't stop
a rolling start
the urge too strong
the picking choice
the race so long
high RPM's
and open wheels
I guide the knife
and hide it peels
on by they streak
each blowing past
'neath my skilled hand
the souls freed fast
as hurried crews
use all their tools
I rid the world
of useless fools
horsepower hums
I slice, I dice
no wasted stroke
each cut precise
I glide unseen
from kill to kill

the blood runs deep
as gallons spill
all eyes are drawn
the track the prize
it's sounds work well
to snuff the cries
gears are grabbed
the lead exchanged
as I proceed
with plans deranged
through stands I move
fulfilling needs
and on this day
the brickyard bleeds....

S.L. Dixon

A Great Hand

Looking at the right bower, king and ten trump-suit and two off-suit aces would usually put Breanne Lockstadt into a jittery fit trying to conceal her giddiness.

She didn't even pick it.

Hell, her partner didn't even pick it.

She was looking at a euchre and only three tricks away from victory, she and her partner Lizzy had another game in the bag. Breanne looked grim, didn't feel good. The cards unraveled and Breanne and Lizzy took the game, at least Lizzy was happy.

"What in the hell did you make it on?" Jerome asked his partner Freddy.

Freddy shrugged. He had a thing for Breanne, but wasn't that the point of the four of them getting together? You put four divorcees with adult offspring in a room eight straight weeks with the expectation that something will happen eventually.

Jerome and Lizzy tried their luck, went to bed twice, found themselves incompatible without a goodly dose of cognac, which meant the door was open should the group take to quicken the drinking during the shuffle.

"And you. Don't look so damn happy," said Jerome to Breanne. He'd known her since they were kids; he used to watch her sometimes when her parents went out on Saturday nights. It was Breanne's idea to get card games going, maybe find some matches along the way.

The cards were coming her way across the board; it was looking good, oh yes. But she was off in her own world most of the night and didn't see the fun, didn't notice much more than which suit to follow.

Jerome snapped his fingers, "Hey, wake up."

Breanne looked up at Jerome, "I'm going to ask you something, and I want you to be as honest as you can possibly be."

He smiled at Breanne, "Shoot. I could never lie to you," he winked at Lizzy.

"When you hit that kid with your car..."

"Whoa now," said Jerome, suddenly things weren't so funny.

"Just please, answer this."

He lowered his head. Lizzy and Freddy watched Breanne, enthralled.

"You'd been drinking. That's no secret although the cops didn't say anything; it was a different time. But you were masturbating while you drove. You'd just left Rosy Kisses. You'd had a lap dance and tried to pay the girl to blow you. She wouldn't. You offered her three hundred for a hand-job, but she just laughed. You got three more lap dances and left the building with hard on and only one option," said Breanne. She stared at the top of Jerome's head; he had a bald patch the size of a hockey puck budding on top.

He lifted his head, "I never told you that, I..."

"But I'm right, right?"

He dropped his head back down, staring at his wrinkled fingers; he wondered how answering the question might sour any future chances of getting into Lizzy's panties.

"I am right, aren't I?"

"How could you know?" He was sad. It was more than a decade earlier and he'd moved on. The kid didn't get to; the kid died, but accidents do happen, and it didn't hurt he was good buddies with the mayor and police chief.

"I saw it. I saw it back when you used to babysit me. I didn't recognize you at first, but I did later, and it all came back to me. I saw it. I never told anyone, but I see things, and I saw you. Now tell me, did it happen exactly like that? It's important," Breanne was emphatic.

Jerome considered his options; it was out there now. He nodded, a weak smile played on his lips, "I guess you're the only one who hasn't seen my dick, Freddy. Want a peek?"

"Well, that just about ends my night," said Lizzy, looking disgusted. She'd known Jerome only months and under the new light she thought she should be disgusted.

"Wait, we're not through," said Breanne, she sat Lizzy back into her chair with a firm hand across the table.

"Once is just luck, but I see things now and then, Lizzy. Promise you'll answer honestly."

"I have nothing to hide," said Lizzy, smug and certain.

"Fifteen years ago," started Breanne. Lizzy's wheels were already spinning in an unhappy direction. "You met a man named Earl after college. We hadn't seen each other for a couple years. You met Earl, and he knocked you up, it was all happy. Earl had a good job, and you stayed home getting fatter and fatter. You dated Earl out east. You knew he was married, but you thought it was done. At eight months pregnant, Earl explained that he had to get back to his real family and that he loved his wife. It was just a trial separation. That's what he called it a trial separation. I'm right aren't I?"

Lizzy's jaw dangled; she snapped it shut. Her eyes burned fire, but she didn't answer, didn't need to say a word.

"You got depressed, starting drinking like crazy. You wanted to kill the baby in your belly, but the baby came. You and Earl had that whole meatless, hemp clothing, hippie thing going and you had a midwife into your home. She helped you. She was Spanish, an immigrant. You and Earl thought you were helping the poor by hiring her. She came, and you delivered a boy. You saw Earl in his jaw and ears, in his nose and fingers. You saw him in those eyebrows threatening to bush right up even fresh out of the oven."

"Stop," demanded Lizzy.

"Wait, I'm right so far. I'm right. You lived in Melvin, out east; nobody had seen you in years. Out there with Earl and then with the baby. You fed the baby cough syrup until it didn't move and then you took your compost bin, filled a bag. Put the baby in the bag. You put four more bags over it and then you drove all night, north first. You put the bag into a Burger King dumpster, put it inside a bag of garbage to be sure and then you drove home. Here home. You came back. I'm right, right?" Breanne seemed sadder the more she spoke.

"I don't have to listen to this. It never happened. You're a liar and I don't care for it," said Lizzy, her show unconvincing.

"You got a tattoo on your hip. It's tiny, but it has the initials H.C. inside a heart."

"She does too. I've seen it!" it was Jerome's turn to revel in someone else's shame.

"So what? It means Hobart Carol, my great grandfather," said Lizzy.

"Why would you get your great grandfather's initials on your hip?" asked Freddy.

"She and Earl were going to name the baby Shine if it was a girl and Haven if it was a..."

"Heaven!" shouted Lizzy and then covered her mouth and fled from the room.

The trio listened in silence as Lizzy's engine roared to life and peeled away down the street. Breanne had created an impasse; she looked at Freddy, and he waited. She'd only recently met him.

"Well?" he asked.

"Yeah, what about Freddy?" Jerome was suddenly the most shameful in the room again.

Breanne shook her head slowly.

"Goddamn it," said Jerome. He stood and pushed his chair under the table. "If you two wouldn't mind, I'm going to drink myself into a stupor and try to remember how to live with myself, and I'd rather do it alone, so . . . ," he trailed with purpose.

Freddy shot to his feet; Breanne was reluctant but followed.

"I'm sorry Jerome," she said and then led the way out of the room.

Freddy had played the gentlemen all along up until that moment. Preoccupied, he didn't even consider opening the door for his date. They sat for a moment. Breanne took his hand, but he quickly pulled it away, afraid of what she might glimpse.

"Don't worry," she said, "I probably would've seen it by now, if there were anything to see."

"Just as well," he started the car and backed out onto the street.

They drove through town; Breanne lived on the north side, fifteen minutes from Jerome's bungalow. Tears flowed down her face, and she rubbed her hands on her legs continually. Freddy listened to her breathing and pulled over.

"Easy now, easy now," he said rubbing her back.

"I have to do something, and I need you to drive me. I'll lose the will if I have to drive myself. Please, it's important," she said after she'd finally managed to slow her gasps.

"What is it?"

"I can't tell you; I just need you to drive me. You need to drive me to Twenty-four Elgin Ave."

"But why? I need to know."

"I promise I'll tell you everything, but after."

"Who lives there?"

"I'll tell you after. This is important, please," she took his hand again. "Please Freddy, I need to go to that address."

He let go of her hand, looked over his shoulder and U-turned over the four-lane street. It was barren, as traffic usually was after dark in that end of town. Retirees rarely get up to shenanigans after dark.

The closer they got to Elgin, the thicker the traffic grew. "This one," said Breanne. She pointed at a home with chipping yellow paint on plastic siding and a roof with patches of moss growing over some of the shingles.

"This one?" Freddy stared in confusion at the slummiest building on the block.

"I'll be back in five minutes," Breanne said. Her voice quavered, and she leaned over to kiss him.

He watched through the passenger's side window. Breanne

walked up to the door, fished through her purse a moment and then opened the door. Then she was gone.

He sat up, a helpless manikin in his own automobile and looked out to the street, unblinking. He wondered what he was doing, what in the hell she could be doing. A few minutes later the answer came in two loud bangs. Lights ignited in neighbors' homes, and Breanne jogged out the front door.

She hadn't even gotten her legs inside the car when she said, "Drive, drive, damn you, drive."

"What did you do?" Freddy demanded, but he knew, it was all over her face, the message in the blasts. She sat with the tool of her crime still in her hand, black and shining under the streetlights.

He drove five minutes and then pulled into a dark parking lot running along the pier. "What did you do?" he demanded.

"I had to. I've known for years, but I couldn't do it until I knew. But I saw, and once I saw I knew. I saw the face, and it all clicked. I've known for thirty-five years he would do it, but I just couldn't, not until I was sure. Part of me weighed the values and no matter what, it couldn't match, I mean..." Breanne cried into her hands.

"What? Who?" He rubbed her back although he recognized her as a murderer.

"He was small when I first saw it and I didn't recognize . . . I thought maybe I was just imagining things. But, but then that man, the man with all the changes in mind, I can't remember his name. I'm all fuzzy; he's a senator or something." Her body vibrated from head to toe.

"Albert Milton?" Freddy asked. The man was the next big thing, Prime Minister someday many thought, but many people didn't like him, hated him in fact.

"Yeah, he was going to kill him, I saw it. I saw it when he was just a baby."

"Who?"

"My son, my Eric, my son. I thought if I did things differently over the years, gave him extra love, put him in better schools, put him first, put him before everything . . . It was why Walter left me. Eric needed me, but it didn't work, and I tried to say he wouldn't, couldn't. But he told me he was planning a trip and the memory, the vision, it clicked again. I saw the sign with name, date and time. Eric was taking a vacation, staying at the same motel and I knew, oh God I knew."

"Knew what, you're not making..."

"Knew he was going to kill Milton, my son, my little Eric was going to kill Albert Milton," Breanne lifted her head and tears streamed her face.

"So you...?"

"I had to; I had to, for the good of everybody. I killed him. He was bad; no matter what I did, he was bad. I tried, oh God I tried." Freddy had heard enough and pulled the car back out onto the street.

Breanne continued to wail while he drove. She recognized the area but didn't say anything. Heading downtown.

"I can't believe it. You're insane," he blasted at her as he drove, moving double the speed he had all night.

She had pondered that very idea numerous times over her life, but it just wasn't so. "I lied to you earlier. I saw something the day we met."

He turned to her, agog, "What, what?"

"It was like the others, and I want you to know I don't hold it against you. It's as much my fault as it is yours. Just move on after it happens, it's for the best for me anyway," she said as she rolled down her window and dropped the pistol onto the street.

"What are you talking about?" he stared at her, his foot to the mat, only a block from the police station.

"Just move on, it's for the best. I really liked you, you know?" she asked as Freddy missed an amber go red. While zooming through the intersection, a police cruiser crushed the passenger's side of Freddy's car.

Freddy survived.

Gary Murphy

Green Blue Skies

Frederick and his long-term, long-suffering live-in lover Anna watched the TV as the emergency bulletin streamed across the screen. The 32-year-old Frederick swore and cursed whilst the slightly older Anna paced the lounge nervously and explained that when the local nuclear reactor blew its top, it had sprayed radioactive material into the atmosphere and that they should get the fuck away fast. Even the sun could not been seen amidst the mess.

Anna and Frederick were simple village yokels who were just as entranced in the news bulletins as the next man. They co-habited Frederick's parents' summer home whilst the elderly pair travelled Europe.

"The roads will all be blocked," Frederick protested. "We should wait for orders from the military or the police as to what our actions should be. It'll be on the television – I'm sure of it."

In this small Russian village in rural surroundings, it was difficult to accept or comprehend how such beauty and scenic grace could be ruined forever. Nevertheless, Anna certainly had a point, suggesting they should escape instead of remaining to suffer.

Frederick warned, "We must wait, Anna. This is inland Russia. Our police and military are the best in the world. The authorities will not just leave us here and abandon people in danger, the people of Gorgon Valley."

Anna hissed vehemently, "Look out the window, Frederick...what do you see, you fool? Green – a green sky with a swamped, blotted sun. They have already deserted us and left us here to rot and die. We will surely die of radioactive poisoning."

"We don't know for sure it's radioactivity. We heard the explosion just twenty minutes ago..."

"The sky is fucking green!"

Frederick walked to the window and peered out into the fields of corn and barley on this unnatural day. There were no signs of life, only a vast open space of yellow plantation stretching for acre upon acre. "I think we should just wait, Anna. I've a fantastic idea."

"What is your stupid idea? I should have stayed in Sweden, instead of coming here."

"Let's fuck. It might be for the last time. Let's lick, kiss and caress every inch of each other's bodies, submit to lust and explore our sexual fantasies."

Although tempted by the notion, Anna said, "You're out of your fucking pathetic little mind."

She had short straight hair and appeared almost boyish in a raw Slavic sense. She was blond and blue-eyed with full red lips, perhaps a bit short in stature but athletically lithe. A temptress, you might say – a tease Frederick was lucky to have landed in the first place. If anything, his friends were justly envious that he managed to attract such a symphonic creature and keep her interest all this time. After all, Frederick was a fucking creep.

He placed his hands on her shoulders and grinned like a maniac of the first order. "Let's fuck like rampant wild dogs, Anna. What do you say? I know you want to, truly, really."

She brushed his hands off violently and backed off. "You're quite insane, aren't you?"

"The root of my cock is pulsating madly – ready to explode. I want to shower your tits with golden piss."

Confused, she frowned, "But, Frederick..."

Did she honestly expect him to say something else?

Why on earth would he want to piss on her?

Frederick unzipped his trousers and released the throbbing wee man. Anna gasped – she'd never seen it so big.

"Suck it," he demanded. "Take it in your mouth and suck it, you whorish slut."

Anna sighed and felt a tingling deep in her crotch as her pussy ignited.

She shouted, "I refuse, you bastard."

He walked closer to her as she retreated further. She knew he would rape her unless she kicked him violently between the legs. She had to attack this monster she thought she loved and would probably marry one day, a creature and disgusting pervert, and perhaps worse. Who could tell what this freak was capable of in these desperate times?

She laughed triumphantly as she unleashed the kick, landing it discreetly in his knackers, then turned and ran for the door whilst Frederick collapsed in pain, his mouth open wide and groaning as he clutched his waning swollen dick and dangly bits. The agony intensified as his knees hit the floor, causing his balls to ache and reverberate. "I'm sorry, Anna. Please forgive me!"

But Anna was gone – heading toward home in Sweden.

Frederick stood and staggered towards the open front door of the tiny cottage, hoping he might follow her. But she was an athlete, fit, strong and agile, already miles away. Yup – he'd blown it with his lovely Anna.

"Anna..." he murmured, as his eyes filled with pained tears.

There could be no response to his sorrowful, disgraced mutterings now. All he could do was watch her sprint away into the distance like a departed ghost, towards Gorgon Valley town centre.

Suddenly he remembered his flagging member and protruding ball-sack and staggered into the garden. Shortly, a long shadow was cast over him in the green-tinged area, perhaps made by a flock of birds huddled in a bunch as they traversed the sky, or maybe not. Maybe something wholly different.

Maybe not, after all . . .

Black creatures descended and landed on the drive, in the garden, and on the roof of the cottage, but these were not birds. They were of the like of creature Frederick had never witnessed or could not possibly identify. These things were a direct and absolute product of high-cost and wholly intensified radioactivity. Mutated, regenerated beasts, vile and bloodthirsty. There was no visible escape from this dark pack of brutes as they charged and covered his body.

The local tarantula population had transmuted and become huge black vampire-spiders with a taste for human blood – in particular, human brains once they had burrowed through the tough bone of the exposed skull.

Anna heard the screams in her wake but wisely didn't stop or even consider retracing her steps on a misguided whim to investigate matters, although she wanted to. Frederick was her man and partner, her knight in shining armor, her rock. But she had quickly exposed him for the self-indulgent, perverted bastard he was. She would be perfectly happy to live out her life without him, even though he had always been there with a shoulder to cry upon when crying shoulders were a rarity. And yes, he might have been a pervert, but in the sack so was she. When Sweden and Russia met in torrid lust, anything could happen and usually did. But to think of sex at a time like this was borderline insane, although it was actually a repulsive golden shower he had harped on in no uncertain terms, hardly sex.

She ran as fast as she could and wouldn't stop until she reached Gorgon Valley town centre. It didn't seem so far away.

All this exhausting running made her consider how much she smoked and drank and how drastically unfit she was for 39. Although on the cusp of 40 (and counting the months until then), she had still imagined herself more fit and durable than her heaving chest and aching knee joints indicated. She careened up the long deserted dirt track leading through the fields, with blasts of yellow plantation on either side and yearned for sweet little Sweden and its cosmos of sinners and saints. Russia had too many villains, too many dark figures which seemed to emerge from inside the shadows when least expected, or creep up on you whilst you slept, ready to kill or poison. A truly scary, secretive place, worse if you rubbed the people of its very private population the wrong way.

Darkness suddenly filled the heavens above. Anna faltered slightly in her stride as she paused to arch her neck and tilt her head to observe what seemed to be a vast swarm of crows escaping the vicinity and its pollution. Not crows, though – not in a green sky.

Yes, there was the pungent aroma of fetid chemicals and burning rubber when she finally slowed down and doubled up to rest and get her second wind. Again she cursed Frederick, "Damn you, I hate you," and wished desperately to turn around and run straight back into his warm and loving embrace...her Russian boyfriend, so tall and strong, and so damned cute.

"Anna," came the voice.

Bemused, she frowned as her heart pounded in her chest, and she looked around for the source, but there was simply nobody to be seen. Surely Frederick couldn't have run that fast from the cottage and caught up with her? He smoked 40 a day, for starters.

"Frederick, go jump off a steep cliff."

She said this, knowing his presence – although probably welcomed – was impossible.

Currently, the birds-or-whatever cast another shadow that shifted and grew across the green, lurid luminosity stretching across and covering the vicinity.

Finally, when the creatures dropped, she observed first with comic disbelief, then abrupt horrified certainty that these black crawling shapes had indeed come here precisely for her and her alone. She jerked and screamed when she felt the first two or three of the huge winged-tarantulas land on her person and scurry over her body.

But something other than winged-spiders was greatly afoot.

Frederick hovered and slowly drifted from above her head, until making a polite but terrifying touchdown before her on the road. It looked wholly effortless, yet the other creatures seemed to 'step back' and fall aside into the shadows, under the control of their master. A human-warrior sort, yet one that was deranged, and possessed a mind overrun by evil and perversion.

"Frederick?"

"I've come for you, Anna. I possess a great gift we can share and exploit. Just give yourself to me and submit. It's completely painless. Just biting, blood, gore and stuff, you cheerless slut!"

"No," she screamed, clutching her face with her hands and staring madly. "Please, don't do this. I'll do anything, anything you want me to, just let me live."

But Frederick wasn't exactly himself anymore.

Gone were the two arms and legs. All that stood before her now was a black, twisted and hairy, eight-legged devil - an abomination with Frederick's head sitting atop its body, supported by long blackened wings that protruded from its deformed back. His eyes seemed to glow neon-white, milky with the promise of impending doom for every living thing.

"You're not my Frederick," Anna protested, spitting her words. "You're a mutated beast." All the while, the 'smaller' spiders were climbing her body and exploring its curves and contours, biting her legs, her arms, her back, and the tender flesh of her neck. "It isn't so...none of this...I know it's an awful dream, I know it is...things like this don't happen in the world."

Frederick grinned as saliva drooled along his chin, "Too weird, eh?"

"Yes," she agreed quickly. "Too weird. I dream this shit every night and wake up, and everything is fine and hunky-dory."

As the vampire-spiders sucked her blood, thick bristle emerged from the wounds instantaneously as she transformed into one of them. It was here as she changed that her body began to vibrate and mutate whilst growing hair and sprouting many legs. It was an experience of painless pleasure. She was swept away in euphoric glee.

The two lovers met each other in the middle of the road as their scurrying accomplices gathered and awaited the spoken command from their newly-appointed saviour and leader.

This was just the start.

It heralded mankind's fall from grace and the revolutionary rise of the mutated flying arachnid.

This was the beginning of the end.

Anna and Frederick addressed the gathered crawling flock and rolling sea of blackness spreading across the fields in growing numbers. The spider-class had new leaders and understood the meaning of command – delivered from either the man or woman in their midst below. The swarm would obey everything they were told, just glad to have a purpose, a mission.

The young mutated couple lifted their arms and immediately began to levitate.

The spiders rose as well, flocking around the part-human couple's heads, willing to follow wherever they led. Frederick took Anna's right hand, and she reciprocated with a single kiss to the cheek, and together with the horde they took to the skies and headed for Central Europe and other destinations on land and overseas. As the radioactivity spread and polluted Europe, many changes would occur by way of obscene human transition and widespread grisly murder. Soon the tarantula-elite would be everywhere, and the skies would turn from green to black.

Tony Bowman

The Muse

She was his muse. It was that simple.

Rob watched Ann as she sat in the passenger seat, her bare feet with black-painted toenails propped on the dash. Her pixie face reflected in the window as the Indiana corn fields rolled by on a continuous loop of leafy green.

He couldn't remember when he fell in love with her – sometime in elementary school, of that he was certain, but everything else was hazy.

In school Ann had been the slightly off girl with the short black hair and eyes to match who might lapse into a conversation on the playground about a dead opossum she had walked past on her way to school. *Maggots, Rob, you shoulda seen them.*

Rob had been the tall, skinny kid with thick glasses. He loved her perspective, and turned her offbeat observations into stories. *What if it hadn't been a opossum, Ann? What if it had been a person?*

He saw the corners of her dark eyes turn up as she smiled.

"Keep your eyes on the road, Mr. Lovell."

"Hey, if you can admire the scenery, so can I, Mrs. Lovell," he said.

She stretched and yawned, "Yeah, but the scenery you want to admire will require us to get naked, and we're going to be late as it is. How much farther?"

"We should hit Kansas City by ten PM, barring naked trysts."

Ann laughed and opened the now ragged brochure she had been carrying around for two weeks, "Heartland Horror Convention, Kansas City Marriott – featuring best-selling horror novelist Robert Lovell, author of Moonlight Serenade."

"Best-selling author after a five-day free book giveaway..." Rob said.

"Silence. I'm reading - Mr. Lovell will be signing copies of his book..."

"Which he will be selling at a ninety percent profit."

"I said shush – Signing copies of his book Saturday and Sunday," she said and slapped him with the brochure. "Today is Friday – we should already be there, not touring Indiana corn fields. Would you please go back to the interstate?"

"Rural back roads are inspiring. I've come up with at least

three more novels in the last hour."

"Argh, you're frustrating," Ann said as she settled back into the seat and turned her attention to the passing countryside.

They passed an old dilapidated farmhouse, its roof sagging in the August sun.

"Did you ever wonder who lives in places like this?" she asked.

There she was: the muse. He could almost hear the gears clicking between her ears. "I don't know – farmers I suppose."

Her black eyes were reflected back, a ghost image in the Plexiglas staring at the old house and past it. "Sometimes I think nobody actually lives in places like this. No people, just ghosts. Spirits. The world has passed them by and forgotten them."

Rob would write down what she had said, turn it, twist it, let it ferment. And then he would give it back to her as something bleak, haunted, and wonderful. She fed him, and he fed her. Together they were much more than the sum of their individual parts.

He had opened his mouth to tell her this as the road around them exploded. The car shuddered and dropped lower to the road in a shower of sparks. They slid to the right with a squeal of metal, and then stopped on the gravel and grass shoulder.

"What... just happened?" Ann asked. Her small hands gripped the dash as she pulled her feet under her.

"I'm not sure. I think we had a blowout," Rob said as he opened his door. He looked down at his foot in time to slide it to the left: he had almost stepped on a crooked nail. "What the hell?"

The road was covered in nails that had been twisted together so that no matter how they landed, one point always extended straight up. Jackrocks his father had called them – they were designed to be thrown on a road to disable vehicles. "Stay in the car."

Rob kicked away the jackrocks and surveyed the damage. All four tires had been shredded, and the Ford was sitting on its rims. "Son of a bitch."

He looked around, surveying the waving rows of corn bordering both sides of the road. If there was anyone there, they were well hidden.

Ann rolled down her window and leaned out, "I can't get a single bar on my cell."

"Yeah, mine's been dead for miles."

She stared at the road, "What are those things?"

"Jackrocks. Somebody purposely wrecked us," he said as he walked around to her side of the car. He opened her door, "Come on, let's get out of here."

"Why? Shouldn't we wait for a cop?"

"No. Maybe this was just a bunch of kids playing a prank, then again, maybe not. Either way, I'd rather take our chances on the road than to just sit here and wait on whoever did this to come back."

Ann got out and shut the door, "Good point."

Rob looked down the road behind them, "What do you think, the farmhouse?"

"Oh, no. Farmhouses in cornfields? Children of the Corn, Texas Chainsaw, Jeepers Creepers, forget it."

"Well, there's nothing else back there for miles."

She turned and put her hands in her back pockets, "Guess we go forward."

No cars passed them as they walked down the road. The sun disappeared on the horizon, and they had still seen nothing but farmland.

"I spy with my little eye," Ann said.

"Corn," Rob said.

"That's not how the game is played. You're supposed to wait on me to finish."

"A gas station."

"Yeah, I wish."

"No, I see a gas station," Rob said, and pointed down the road, toward a space the size of a football field, cut from a cornfield and paved over, where bluish light from fluorescent bulbs illuminated a sign that read Martindale Gas and Grocery.

"Finally, civilization. Pork rinds, pickled eggs, and jerky," she said.

"And beer – God, let there be beer."

Moths buzzed around the gently humming lights that illuminated the two gas pumps. A small motel stood to the right of the cinderblock store and attached garage. An old wrecker sat between the buildings, Martindale Towing scrawled on the side. A double-barreled shotgun hung from the gun rack in the back window.

"Maybe they can tow the car in and get us some new tires?" Ann asked.

"Let's hope." Rob pushed open the glass door and cool air-conditioned air buffeted against them.

The store reeked of cigarette smoke and aging deep fryer oil. A small lunch counter took up the left side of the building. A middle-aged woman in lime green stretch pants stood behind the counter smoking a cigarette.

"So you mean we're stuck here?" a girl with blonde hair asked the old man behind the cash register at the back of the store.

"We don't have tires to fit your car, Ma'am. My brother can drive into Fortville and get some tomorrow."

"Gary! We have to stay the night," the girl called across the store.

"Aww, for fuck's sake," a voice answered. He appeared beside the counter: a tall, disheveled man covered in tattoos.

The old man behind the register glared at him, "We don't allow profanity in this establishment, young man."

"Sorry, granddad. It's been a long day."

Rob walked up to the counter, "Excuse me, were you in some kind of accident?"

The blonde girl shook her head, "No effing accident, man. Somebody covered the road in nails."

"Yeah, ate our tires like a fat kid on cake," Gary added as he dropped the groceries on the counter. "Where's your beer, granddad?"

"No beer. This is a dry county," the old man said.

"We ran over the same nails. Our car is about ten miles east of here," Rob said.

The blonde looked confused, "East? We hit them ten miles west of here. What the hell's going on?"

A man sitting at the lunch counter turned and looked at them. His greasy overalls had a name tag that read Odell. "Teenagers. Not much to do around here, so they act up. What kind of car do you have?"

Gary shook his head, "It's a rental. Some kind of Ford."

"Car or truck?"

"Car."

The old man behind the register shook his head, "We don't have tires for that either. We don't get much business – all we stock are truck tires. You folks will be needing a room as well." He nodded to the people at the counter, "That's my brother, Odell, and his wife Elizabeth."

Elizabeth, the woman in stretch pants smiled and waved.

Ann nodded and smiled, "Can't we just call into town? We need to get to Kansas City before tomorrow morning."

The old man smiled, "The nearest town is Fortville, and that's sixty miles. They roll the streets up at night. Tomorrow morning is the earliest we can get you back on the road."

She looked at Rob, "Your signing. We won't make it."

Rob took her hands, "Hey, it'll be okay. We'll call them in the morning and tell them we're delayed. We'll be there by tomorrow evening."

"Hey, I know exactly how you feel," the blonde said. "We were on our way to this epic party in Dayton – I am majorly pissed."

The front door opened, and a small Indian boy walked in.

"Joseph, go check on Trula for me, will you?" the old man asked. Then he smiled at Ann. "My wife, Trula, is an invalid."

The boy stared at Rob and Ann for a moment, then walked behind the register. He opened a door at the back.

Light flooded the room beyond. It was a bedroom – the lone occupant sat up in her narrow bed, propping herself on skeletal elbows. Her eyes were too large for her sallow face. An oxygen cannula snaked around her upper lip and connected to a green and silver cylinder beside her.

The boy knelt beside her, and together they stared out at the group of people in the store. The woman shook her head, then leaned close to the boy and whispered.

The old man held a key out to Gary, "We'll put you folks in Room One. That's the one closest to the garage."

Gary slapped the blonde's butt, "Hope you got some thick walls, granddad. Katy gets a little loud, if you get my meaning."

The old man nodded, "Yeah, I get your meaning."

Katy and Gary walked away from the counter.

The old man turned and looked at his brother, Odell. The man stroked his chin, then nodded.

Rob watched the silent exchange.

The middle-aged woman behind the counter laughed, "Hell, why not?"

The old man laughed.

Rob and Ann looked at each other, not comprehending what was clearly an inside joke.

The little boy left the old woman's side and climbed onto the counter by the register. The old man leaned down and the boy whispered something to him.

He looked back over his shoulder at the bedroom. "You'll adjust," he said.

"Something wrong?" Rob asked.

The old man smiled, "No. Just a little disagreement. I'm putting you folks in room ten, far end of the motel."

Ann looked out the window toward the road and the cornfield beyond, "I think we should leave."

"Leave? What are you talking about?" Rob asked her from the bed.

The room was clean but drab, the walls paneled in a pattern from the seventies.

"There's something wrong here. I think we should hike back to the car and wait there."

"Ten miles in the dark to sleep in a car on the side of the road?"

"Tell me you are not creeped out by this place?"

Rob got off the bed and rubbed her shoulders. She leaned back against him.

"Of course I'm creeped out. But these people are harmless – they just don't get out much."

She turned and wrapped her arms around his neck, "Rob, please. Can we just go?"

"But why?"

"The old woman in the sickbed, the way she looked at me. It was like she hated me – I can't put my finger on it exactly."

Rob sighed, "Ten miles in the dark, the things I do for you."

She smiled and kissed him.

Rob closed the door and left the key in the room, "You ready?"

Ann shivered, "Yeah."

They walked up the concrete porch that led past the rooms.

The door to Room One was open slightly; light spilled out on the grey concrete.

Rob stopped beside it and peered through the opening. The room was empty.

He whispered to Ann, "They're not in there."

"Let's go."

They walked past Room One to the rolling garage door. The door's windows were about five feet off the ground, and light shown through from the inside.

Light and sounds.

They paused by the edge of the door and peered through the dirty glass.

The old man and his brother Odell were standing at a workbench near the back. Odell's wife, Elizabeth, was sitting on the workbench laughing, a cigarette hanging from her lips.

She pulled the cigarette from her lips and went into a fit of coughing.

"This is why you burn through them so fast," the old man said.

The woman wheezed and gasped, finally catching her breath, "I like to enjoy myself."

"You desecrate the gift you're given," the old man said as he walked back toward the store.

She grabbed Odell by the lapels and kissed him, "What do you think, honey? We had some fun desecrating these bodies, now didn't we?"

Odell smiled, "We sure as hell did."

The old man came back into view, and Rob gasped. He was pushing a wheelchair in front of him. The blonde girl, Katy, was in it, her hands and ankles duct taped to the frame. Another piece of duct tape covered her lips.

She struggled against the tape as he rolled her to a stop in front of the workbench.

Elizabeth hopped down from the bench. She knelt behind the wheelchair and placed her face against Katy's, "Odell, you remember when I used to look like this."

"Hell, darlin', I remember at least three times when you looked like that."

The old man returned with Gary in another wheelchair. He left Gary's chair beside Katy's.

"Which one of you is first?" the old man asked. Odell and Elizabeth looked at each other.

"I'll go first. Damned smoker's cough is driving me crazy," Elizabeth said. She climbed up onto the workbench and leaned backward, her head hanging off the edge. She looked at Katy, "I'll bet she pees herself."

The old man opened a canvas-covered bundle on the workbench.

Rob leaned up so he could see better, and Ann whispered in his ear, "Should we do something?"

"Like what?"

The old man turned toward the door. In his left hand, he held a bowl about a foot across. It was ornate and appeared to be cast from solid goal.

In his right hand, he held a golden sword with a blade about two feet long and a handgrip made for two hands.

Rob and Ann watched in disbelief as the old man placed the bowl on the greasy floor, then turned and brought the blade down on the middle-aged woman's neck.

She was still smiling as her head rolled across the floor.

Rob turned and clamped his hand over Ann's mouth before she could scream.

He looked back to see the old man push the bowl under the headless woman's neck to catch the dark red blood as it poured from the wound.

When the bowl was full, he picked it up with both hands and nodded toward Katy.

Odell walked around behind her and tore the tape from her

lips.

The girl screamed, and Odell laughed, "Ol' Gary here did warn us she liked to make some noise."

"Tilt her head back," the old man said.

Odell clamped his big hands on the girl's jaws and pressed as his brother brought the bowl to her lips. She gagged and wretched as the blood poured down her throat.

Outside, Ann was hiding her eyes against Rob's shoulder.

Odell and his brother stepped away from the gagging woman.

Her body convulsed and heaved in the wheelchair, then went still.

Then, she began to laugh.

Odell smiled.

Katy smiled at them with blood stained teeth, "Odell, I swear I forgot how good it feels to breathe without tar in my lungs. Cut this shit off'n me." The voice that came from Katy's mouth was the voice of Elizabeth.

Odell leaned down and began to remove the tape.

Outside, Rob looked into Ann's eyes and whispered, "Okay, I've seen enough. Let's get the hell out of here."

Ann looked past Rob toward the motel and screamed.

There was a blinding flash of light, and a sound like thunder in his right ear. He tumbled forward, his face hitting asphalt as Ann fell away from him.

His vision cleared, and he realized he was looking at a child's sneaker below a dirty pants cuff. A crowbar clattered onto the asphalt beside him. The world went black as Ann continued to scream.

"Feist-a-mighty, Robby, don't get up," a voice said.

Rob recognized the voice; it was his best friend Toby from elementary school. They were ten years old, and Toby's mother had made him say stupid shit like "feist-a-mighty" instead of blaspheming.

It was annoying.

Rob's left eye was swollen shut, and his jaw ached. He had just taken a beating from a bully. He couldn't remember the fat kid's name, but he had about seventy pounds and six inches on Rob.

Ten-year-old Rob rose up on his hands. The reason for the fight was sitting on the asphalt about ten feet away: a girl with black hair and eyes. She had been talking about how ghosts were real, and the fat kid hadn't liked that. He had backed up his opinion by calling her a creepy bitch.

She had countered by calling him a fat fuck.

The fat kid had retorted by shoving her across the playground and onto her knees, which now bled bright crimson down her legs to her black boots.

She was crying and looking at Rob, whom she had never talked to in her life, but who had gone in swinging and come out looking like he had lost a fight with a meat grinder.

On the playground, Rob rose up to his knees.

"Don't, he'll just hit you again," Ann had said.

Rob Lovell had stood up and smiled at her.

Rob was on his feet in front of the garage. There was no smile on his face. The parking lot was empty.

His left eye seemed cloudy, and his entire left side felt 'dumb'. He raised his left hand and flexed his fingers. They didn't move quite right.

He looked down at his feet. The bend of the crowbar was stained red with his blood. He reached around to the right side back of his head and touched it gingerly. There was a deep bloody gash and a dent.

Even in his addled state, he knew a dent in your skull was a bad thing.

He reached down and picked up the crowbar with his right hand, seeing stars the whole time he was bent over.

He walked toward the tow truck.

There was a scream behind him, and he turned to see the woman who had been called Katy running toward him from the store, a butcher knife in her hand.

He brought the crowbar up in an arc. It hit her jaw and kept moving, driving bone and skin impossibly to the left side of her face.

The knife clattered onto the asphalt, and she went face first into the hood of the truck.

Rob brought the crowbar down on the back of her neck and heard the vertebrae snap as she collapsed to the pavement.

He turned to see Odell, presumably in Gary's body, emerge from the store running toward him.

Rob brought the crowbar straight up. The wedge on the crook disappeared under Odell's jaw, tearing through his palate and tongue before driving into his brain.

He stood, staring into Rob's eyes as his eyes glazed over.

Rob braced himself against the tow truck door and kicked out with his right foot while pulling the crowbar from Odell's head. His body fell beside Elizabeth's.

Rob turned and shattered the tow truck's driver side window.

"I don't like her," Trula said. She was sitting up in her bed, the gentle hiss from the cannula whispering in the dim light of the room.

"Trula, we can't be choosy at this point," the old man said as he placed the golden bowl on the floor beside her.

Ann was strapped into one of the wheelchairs near the foot of the bed. A metal apparatus with screws had been jammed into her mouth holding it open.

She glared at the two of them.

"She's mean looking. And too small. A strong wind would blow her over. Just kill her and then go down to one of the truckstops on seventy and find me something more suitable," Trula said.

"Just try this body for a few days. If you don't like it, we'll change," the old man said as he knelt beside her holding the knife.

Trula smiled, "All right, dear."

He pulled the pillows from under her and slid her over, so her head was hanging off the edge. He kissed her forehead and whispered to her.

She closed her eyes.

He raised the blade high over his head in both hands and brought it down.

Ann screamed through the metal frame as the woman's head rolled against the nightstand.

He pushed the bowl under the stump of her neck, "Can you see the writing on the bowl?"

Ann was hyperventilating.

"It says 'Espiritu en la Sangre'. That's Spanish. It means, 'Spirit in the Blood'," he said as the bowl filled. "I took it off a Spaniard in 1743, down in the Florida territory. He claimed to be two hundred fifty years old. Wanted me to cut off his head, catch his spirit in the blood, and pour it down somebody's throat. I did the first part for the old bastard."

Ann strained against the metal frame, trying to close her mouth.

"Didn't have the guts to try it myself. Just brought the bowl and sword home. Then when my daddy, Joseph, took ill in the winter of 1760, we tried it out. Damned thing worked," he said as he lifted the bowl reverently in both hands.

Ann was shaking her head back and forth.

"Now, don't you fret. Trula and I ain't like my brother and his wife. We take good care of the bodies that are donated. Why, we've been in these two hippies since 1968," the old man said as he walked toward her. "It doesn't appear to hurt, but when Trula's soul pushes yours out – well, it just dies. You don't go nowhere like heaven or hell. Sorry. But, like I said, it don't appear to hurt."

Ann screamed.

The old man stopped, his eyes on the bedroom door. He raised the bowl in front of him like a shield.

The shotgun blast in the small room was deafening.

The bowl was shoved backward, the shotgun having been aimed at it. The bowl's contents splashed across the old man's face as Rob fell on top of Ann, covering her face in the off chance that any of the blood spattered onto her.

The old man dropped the bowl and staggered backward sputtering and coughing.

His eyes focused on Rob, and he bellowed in a high pitched voice.

Rob raised the shotgun and pulled the second trigger. He had aimed for the old man's chest, but his bleary vision had caused the shot to hit lower, tearing out the man's guts in a shower of double ought buckshot.

The old man fell backward against the wall and slid down.

Rob ripped away the tape from Ann's ankles and wrists, and she wriggled into his arms from the chair. He gently turned the thumbscrews on the device wedged in her mouth until it was closed enough to remove.

She stroked the side of his face, her hands coming away blood red, "Oh, Rob, are you okay?"

"No, I don't think so," he said with a slur.

She helped him up, and they shuffled toward the door.

"He was almost three hundred years old," an old woman's voice said behind them.

They turned and looked at the old man. Trula's voice came from his lips, "I told him you were wrong. I told him you were mean. I didn't want somebody like you."

Ann leaned Rob against the door frame and walked up to the register.

She walked back a moment later with a plastic lighter in her hand. She lit the curtains beside the bed on fire, "Yeah, fuck you too, old woman."

They leaned on each other and walked out into the parking lot.

The Indian kid was standing by the pumps.

Rob stared at him, "You the one hit me with the crowbar?"

"I am," the boy said. His voice was old and raspy.

"You the old man's father?" Ann asked.

The old man in the boy's body nodded.

Rob smiled, "Well, Joseph. You weigh about sixty pounds. I figure Ann and I can break your neck and leave you for the crows if we want."

"I reckon so," Joseph said. He turned and walked across the road into the cornfield beyond.

Rob and Ann were almost a half mile away when the gas pumps exploded behind them. A red mushroom cloud lit up the sky.

"I almost lost you," Rob said.

"I was never afraid," she said. He leaned on her as they walked.

"When I was on the ground, I remembered when I met you. The fight, you know?"

Ann laughed, "Oh, I remember. You looked like hell. Then you got up, smiled, and kicked that fat kid's ass. That's why I wasn't afraid, Lovell. You always get back up."

Red flashing lights appeared in the distance, and siren wails filled the air.

"You know – in a horror story, this would be the time when that nasty little kid would come running out of the corn with the knife and bowl," Ann said, but the look in her eyes wasn't one of fear - the fight would have had only one ending.

She was his muse. It was that simple.

Gary Murphy

Witness in Spiritual Divine

Claudia Wong sat in a hotel room and witnessed her own murder from a mere two feet away. The monster – one of the new bright and intellectualized so-called zombies - began to feast on her dead flesh. It was Linker City, and the year was 1928, shortly after WW1 ran out of witless soldiers to kill on either side. England was engulfed in steam and pollution, and those who knew the elusive magic ruled the land. Claudia was a medium – a kind of Tarot reader and someone who channeled the dead at impromptu séances scattered mainly in the north where she lived. Linker City, before the war, was a coastal town called Whitehaven, casually situated alongside the disgusting, oily Irish Sea. Since the war, the fish and every other aquatic life, had expired in their watery beds and simply become dead and extinct. Fish was no longer on the menu.

Zombies were the outsiders and the solitary few destined to walk the earth in solitude and fend for themselves, since their only nutrition was human flesh and blood which nobody wanted to give. The living dead population was irreversibly expanding into towns and cities in every corner of the world. Like it or not, people had to adapt and accept, and then understand the zombies would always be there. In a world descending into shit, this was hardly a problem. Besides, most of these blood-drinking bastards had proved weak and flimsy staggering through polluted and poorly policed society, choking on the toxic waste in the atmosphere. They were easily tossed aside when they tried to accost the so-called 'innocent' among us.

A child could beat a zombie if they tried hard enough.

Well, maybe not a child, but perhaps a woman. The zombies – some, yes – could be as strong as an ox, but they just looked weak. These ugly fuckers were a handful at times, however. They would rush you when you least expected it, pick locks (some could do this) and creeping up on you during the night as you slept in your bed. In the mornings, there was little light in Linker City because the sun was obscured, blacked-out by the thick fog that seemed to have spread everywhere. People wore gas masks nationwide.

Claudia sat in a chair in the corner of the hotel room and watched herself sleep, astounded at the fact that one of the creatures had managed to pass the reception desk and ascend thirty floors unseen. She would never know. This was a fact.

It was a male monster, tall and shambling, his breathing slow and sluggish as if exercising the clogged lungs a bit too much. He just came sauntering inside, free as you will. Claudia thought, "It's the last time I come to this damned place."

The zombie could not see the sitting ghost in the corner, just the sleeping body on the bed.

Claudia protested, "You can just turn the hell around, and walk straight back out. There's no way you're feasting on me tonight."

Of course, the zombie heard nothing, although it did seem to harken to something as it tilted his head and listened. It heard something, but groaned in a guttural fashion, as if in dumb dismissal at whatever rude distraction held it back from its grub.

She cried but couldn't move, for she was rooted to the chair – a typical hotel wicker affair. It was politely cheap and decorative.

She screamed at the would-be consumer, "Fuck right off, you bastard!"

But when the zombie pulled back the bed-sheets, her body did not move, suggesting to Claudia she was already dead and wouldn't experience any of the pain of being brutally devoured in her sleep.

"Please," she protested, "don't do this. There are plenty of others in Linker City; why must you have me? I'm only 35 years old, you heartless bastard!"

The zombie's eyes bulged in ravenous glee as he observed the prize before him. It was enough sustenance to keep his rambling body going for days.

Unusually, it clapped its hands and seemed to laugh at its sheer good luck.

"Oh," Claudia commented sarcastically, "I suppose the sight of a potential kill overjoys you?" Tears welled in her eyes, and she yelled, "Please, I'm begging you, don't do this, there are lots of others..."

The zombie laughed a little more, even pausing to do a macabre dance on the wood-tiled floor. It swivelled its hips and twisted in joy – boy, would this creep enjoy this feast on the bed before it.

Claudia suddenly thought it might be one big joke, but the sight of her ripping flesh scuppered that idea. The fella went to work sinking its teeth into her naked exposed abdomen and tearing a teeming crevice in it. Blood issued forth in festooning spurts and presented a whole lot of intestines. It was here Claudia conceded she had previously died in her sleep. Her body simply didn't move...

"It's sickening to behold, isn't it?" a male voice from somewhere said.

A ghost stood beside her now, a ghost of stunning beauty and with a slight resemblance to the zombie.

She stammered, "Who...what...?"

He continued with the hint of a pleasantly warm smile Claudia found comforting, "The spirit cannot rest," he said, offering her his hand, "until the body rests."

Distracted from the horror, Claudia accepted the handsome stranger's hand.

As she did, she was able to stand and together the two ghosts watched as Claudia's other-being opened its milky eyes and rose from the bed, now a zombie herself infected by the virus sweeping Linker City and the entire planet.

"Where to from here?" she asked. The zombie took its new catch by the hand and led her from the hotel room into the lobby beyond as her innards spilled from her open guts and onto the floor.

Their mewling was obscured by the sound of flying cars outside the hotel window. Airbuses and levitating steam-trains took to the skies from the station below at ground level, where they roared their engines and galvanized into action. It was no wonder the entire population had no alternative or other safe option but to wear gas masks.

"We must follow until they expire. Then we will be free."

It was all that needed to be said; Claudia Wong understood completely. Like the stranger, she would follow her former self to the very end, until redemption and ultimately spiritual freedom.

Together they followed themselves from the hotel, into the crowded, polluted street, alive with zombie skirmishes and obtuse bloodshed of hapless and innocent city dwellers.

The undead were everywhere in force, sweeping the entire neighbourhood as they overlooked mass hysteria on a grandiose scale. Their swarms overpowered Linker City police officers out to contribute to the effort, as well as the military who were so penniless they avoided as much danger as possible, lacking decent weaponry to confront the freaks.

"What is your name?" Claudia asked the beautiful stranger.

"Esteban," he replied, "And you are Claudia, I believe?"

"Claudia Wong. Yes, that's right. How did you know?"

He laughed and stroked her hand, "When you're in the business of dying, intuition comes naturally – and also, you will discover, vast knowledge of life and death."

"Oh, I see." She gestured to their zombie selves shuffling ahead, "So we'd better try to keep up because we have to die eventually."

No words were ever spoken between Esteban and Claudia again. When they turned the next corner, a flying car careened into the zombie couple and the rotating, twisting mechanics in its base latched onto them, dragging them under and ripping their fetid undead bodies to shreds. No pain was experienced, since the pair had no feeling.

Timothy Frasier

The Bear

"Whack, whack, whack!"

Kathy Mobley tiptoed down to the cellar and peeked through the crack of the partially open door.

"Whack, whack, whack!"

She frowned as she watched Will striking the deer torso hanging from the ceiling with his machete. Her fifteen-year-old son frightened her so much that she was afraid to say anything when he brought the deer down to the cellar, which he considered his "training room." He'd shot the deer the day before in the back pasture. A weight bench rested in the corner next to his punching bag. Centerfolds of naked women from his favorite porn magazines decorated the wall on each side of a full-length mirror.

"Will," she called softly as she opened the door fully. "You need to get ready for school." Disgust registered on her face at the sight of the wet intestines on the floor and the gore covering Will's naked body. The room smelled of blood and shit.

Will stopped, tossed the machete to the side, and began flexing his muscles and posing in front of the mirror. He often commented that he'd been a bear in a previous life, which unnerved Kathy, because her late husband, Robert, used to claim that *he* was a bear inside. "Well, get me a towel; you'll get pissed if I get this shit on your precious carpet." He picked up his machete and placed it on the wall next to his other sharp-edged weapons. Most of his guns were upstairs in his bedroom.

Kathy rushed upstairs and grabbed one of her older towels.

"Turn the water on while you're up there," he shouted from below. It took forever for the warm water to reach the shower.

She stumbled on her way back down but managed not to fall. "Here's a towel," she said while holding it out for him.

"Wipe the blood off of my feet and legs." It was a command, not a request.

She swallowed, knelt down to his feet, and began cleaning. When she made it up to his thighs, she noticed his excitement growing out of the corner of her eye and quit cleaning. "That's good enough to get you to the shower." Her voice trembled. He was over six feet tall and well on his way to being heavily muscled like Robert. Unfortunately, for Kathy, Will had also inherited his father's bullying, sadistic nature.

Several masked men in the community had killed Robert when Will was still a toddler. Though never proven, Robert was the primary suspect in the disappearances of eight young women over a five-year period. The men shot her husband multiple times in the front yard of their secluded farmhouse and then beat him with metal pipes until he expired. Kathy had huddled under the kitchen table clutching Will, afraid she was next.

Will laughed and trotted off to get his shower.

Kathy glanced around the room with her nose wrinkled. The duffle bag in the corner caught her eye, and she walked over to it. It was open with some loose clothing stuffed inside. She pulled them out and recoiled when she saw a pair of bloody panties and bra. The other garments were ripped and blood-soaked. Guilt welled up in her as she thought about those poor girls all those years ago.

She rushed up the stairs and then went outside to the porch swing to smoke. It was going to happen all over again. How many poor girls would die before it ended? There was no way she could live through it again. Hardly a day passed in which she didn't think about them.

"Mom!" he shouted. "Get me my clothes!"

Kathy crushed out her cigarette, rushed in, and picked out his clothes.

"Drop me off at The Corner Burger after school. I have this hot bitch that wants my body." He slipped on his shirt and socks, saving his jeans for last. "Was Dad's as big as mine?" he said, as he grabbed his penis and pointed it at her.

She closed her eyes, but not all the way. "I'm your mother. It's not right, you acting like this. I'll be in the car. Hurry or you'll be late again." Kathy left the room.

Will went outside and got in the car next to her. She started the engine and pulled out, barely looking for traffic, as it was almost nonexistent on the rural, Indiana road. "Who's this hot bitch that wants your body?" Kathy looked at him and then back to the road.

"Trixie Martin." He glanced at his mom with his eyebrows raised.

"I know who she is. You were sitting together three times last week when I picked you up after school. Looked like one of the whores that chased your father. Are you going to fuck her?"

"What..." Will cleared his throat. "I've never heard you say that word before."

"All the whores want what's mine, expecting me to sit in the shadows while they wrap their nasty legs around my men. Do you think Miss Trixie is prettier than me?"

He stared ahead with his eyes wide.

"I bet you wouldn't think so now." She reached across the seat with her right hand and grabbed his crotch. He grabbed her hand and pushed it away. "You're nothing but your father made over. Just a fucking tease." She pulled over to the edge of the road. "I'm no tease! Get out of the fucking car!" she screamed. "Get the fuck out, now!"

Will got out of the car looking confused and frightened.

"And you're no fucking bear! Nor was your chicken-shit father." Her eyes bulged and the veins stood out on her forehead as she leaned from the steering wheel toward the open passenger-side door and whispered, barely audible, "I'm the only bear this family's ever known. I've always protected what's mine." She took off, spinning her tires. The road was lined with massive oaks that whizzed by as the car reached eighty miles per hour. Her nostrils flared at the coppery smell of blood, as the car suddenly seemed full of people. Bile rose in her throat as she looked in the backseat and recognized several of the girls she'd killed all those years ago. Kate Winslow's face peeked out at her from the back. Her face red—the lamp chord still tight around her neck. Angie Stills was next to her, the slice across her throat a brilliant crimson against her pale skin.

Trixie sat next to her in the front seat bleeding, still wearing the same shocked expression from the previous night when she hacked her to death with Will's machete. A quick glance in the rearview mirror revealed Robert in the middle of the backseat with his eyes, even the one drooping on his cheek, staring at the girls surrounding him. His head was knotted and bulging from the countless blows he received all those years ago. A chorus of voices filled the car with Robert's laughter dominating all, the same laugh he used every time she questioned him about lipstick on his shirt or his missing underwear.

"No more," she whispered as she picked out a large oak.

CS Nelson

Cornfed

(Editor's Choice Award Winner.)

"Hey, Jan-hole! You wanna get that?" Phillip yelled from his recliner, drooling into his laptop. He leaned toward the kitchen on one elbow, his hulk precariously close to tipping the chair into a mottled pizza box.

The opium lilt of "Blue Velvet" filtered down the hallway. It wasn't that Bobby Vinton's tinny vibrato sparked trips down memory lane; the alarm clock MP3 had been programmed to play random selections as a dinner bell three times a day. Nine months ago, someone's over-sized ass had knocked it to a single-song repeat cycle, locking it on the same track.

Janice sat at the kitchen table behind her laptop, lost in Sim Party.

He waved a meaty hand and snapped his fingers. "Hello? Yo, digitramp, it's your turn."

She exploded in place, ripping her ear buds out to a plate full of ketchup smear and slamming her laptop shut. "What!"

"Dinner!"

"Whatever, asshat, it's your turn." She screwed her earbuds in; "Gross," she said, and yanked them right back out to wipe off a sticky glob of ketchup.

"Blue Velvet" ended for a two-second, rebooted, then started again. Phillip hefted himself out of his tortured recliner and shambled past her, purposely bumping her chair mid-Sim Party dialogue and knocking her fleet fingers askew. She flipped him the bird and continued guiding her male Sim around the virtual penthouse where it interacted with unicorns, divas, and an elf aviator.

"Douche," she said.

Phillip backed up, ripped a squeaky fart, and pushed for a staccato extension before moving to the counter where a can of creamed corn sat half opened since yesterday.

A moldering soft batch cookie soared across the kitchen. The dough bounced off the back of his head with a satisfying thump, leaving a sticky wad of oatmeal raisin to dangle from the thick shelf of overlapping skin. Janice turned back to her open Sim prompt and suggested naughty things to the cyber party, squeezing a dry smile from her pudgy cheeks.

Phillip ignored his wife's attack and shook the last dollop of corn into the turkey baster.

"Hey, you check the mail yet?" he said.

"Yeah... No." Clickety- clickety-click.

"Lazy turd."

"Whatever, bitchboy. That's your turn, too—oh, you prick!" Janice pushed back from her cyber world, breathing hot and heavy, then leaned in, face screwed up with indignant determination. Her Sim's suggestion had been taken to a whole new level. Janice's $1200 avatar investment now lay spread-eagled to the unwilling receiving end of her idea.

Phillip laughed over her shoulder, "Haha! Oh yeeah! You got owned, dude. A unicorn, too, no doubt!"

"No shit," she said. "Okay, okay. I got a little something for that."

Her fingers flew over the keyboard and summoned the cheat engine that would allow her to maul and molest the virtual world to whatever her angry heart desired. Code poured out in green font across the black pop-up window. She typed RUN and closed the hack, sitting back with crossed arms to enjoy her handy work.

"Oh-ho! You are all kinds of scandalous, babe!"

The heavyset couple giggled at the digital ménage a trois now going viral in the virtual world of peeps, unicorns, and an interactive chainsaw. Sim Party penthouse turned into a meat grinder.

"...blu-ue... vel-vet... woah-woah-woah..."

Janice blinked and scowled up at her husband through wire-rimmed glasses. "Jesus, Phillip. Would you feed them already?"

Phillip snorted but shuffled back to the hallway toward the continuing warble floating from the farthest most bedroom of their almost-by-the-beach home.

The house itself belonged to Phillip's grandparents, his adoptive guardians since thirteen when his parents had died in a Hollywood ritual suicide involving all-natural carrot juice, yoga mats, and cyanide.

And faith, Phillip thought, can't forget the faith. Wonder how that's working out for them?

Perhaps it was his high school psychiatrist's so-called "emotional bruising" that made Phillip not give a crap. He visited one once at his Gramma's request, then spent a summer at a fat camp and all it did was get him access to his first experience with porno mags and a few connections to some sweet video game cheats. He was perfectly happy eating, sleeping, and living the big life on his big butt doing big-time couch-time. And he really didn't give a crap. Ooh yeeah.

But now with Gramma and Grampa Foley both too old to feed themselves, Phillip and his beautiful chunk-o-bride Janice —a product of other issues he really couldn't care less about—were full-time tenants of the Foley's Santa Monica home. Whenever the two ancient fart-factories finally decided to quit stinking up the house and died already, Gramma and Grampa Foley had arranged to put the estate into the hands of the Delaney Street Foundation and turned into a shelter for a bunch of lazy-ass homeless people and their stupid homeless kids. Until that day, Phillip and Janice had a good roof, good Wi-Fi, funky Sims, and steady Social Security checks to keep them going. And pizza every night, can't forget that. The lazy be-otches on Delaney Street could just wait. And Phillip and Janice could feed the gross oldies with a turkey baster as long as they needed. Ooh yeeah.

Ten feet from the door, Phillip jabbed the turkey baster in Janice's direction like a rapier and for the hell of it said, "Shut. Up." He pulled the knob and walked into the bedroom. The smell hit him like a blast of rotten green mist.

"Ohgod," he said as he covered his mouth to beat his gag trigger. "Ohgod, ohgod."

He threw the turkey baster to the chest of drawers nearest the door and backed out, sealing the odor in the room with a slam.

"What now?" Janice peeked around her laptop screen, bursts of crimson pixels reflecting in her glasses.

Phillip exhaled with enough theatrics to impress Shakespeare. "One of them went again, man."

"Ha!" She laughed and rocked her shoulders. "Kar-ma!"

"Screw you. I just farted. I didn't do all that."

Phillip returned to the kitchen to dig through a drawer until he found a dirty filter mask. He curled his thick lips up at the stained and worn paper before donning it.

"Go to the store and get more masks. This one's all groaty, man."

"Yeah sure, Sherlock. Just as soon as you find my keys."

"What? You don't got your keys yet? Ha! You're such a smacktard," he said, the bite in his voice reduced by the filter, making him sound more like a cartoon spaceman than the brute he was trying for.

"So? I don't need to go anywhere. You're the one that has to clean up your grandparents' diapers. I'm fine—shit."

Phillip bumped her again on the way back to the room, the last soft batch cookie smacking him in the ear this time. He didn't bother with the chemical warfare, though; enough egg and road kill oozed out of the closed door to render his little contribution invisible. He imagined a thick gathering of heavy gas, all wet and green, pooling up like thickening mire around his feet. He opened the door.

Phillip glared at the old couple lying in the filth of their bed.

"Disgusting," he spat. Armed with Febreze Lavender, air filter, and his creamed corn turkey baster, he resumed his grandson-ly duties of caring for old people. "Alright. Ladies first, Gramma. Open wide."

Soft blues eyes turned up to Phillip. He glanced down. Her delicate hand grasped Grampa's.

"Ahahhh. How sweet," he said, jabbing the baster between her lips. "Yegh."

Creamed corn slid down her throat. She swallowed slowly, tried to lick at the bits dribbling out of the corners of her mouth as best she could. In her peripheral, she could see her husband, her lover and best friend for over seventy years, gagging as Phillip forced the gruel into his mouth. Emma Foley gave a squeeze of her husband's hand, felt a shallow return pressure. She closed her eyes.

The grandson muttered, cursed, sprayed them both with liberal amounts of deodorizer, and left. Emma no longer felt the discomfort of the filth. There was a time, many months ago, when she fought hard for her pride. After a while, it became obvious that changing bed sheets, cleaning soiled clothing, giving baths, or any attempt at personal hygiene was too much to hope for with Phillip. He was a lost soul.

After the glutton she once loved as a grandchild slammed the door, Emma opened her eyes and tried to roll over to kiss her husband. He felt her movement, and they managed to meet in the middle. She smiled, as did he, but more with his eyes. It was enough. His lips said I love you. There just wasn't the breath to jingle vocal chords anymore.

"Well? Did you?" Janice said. She had moved to the couch, her laptop balancing on her wide, pasty thighs, feet propped up amongst the litter of the coffee table. The widescreen played a Cupcake Wars episode with the sound off. Janice's laptop counted down the seconds to a cyber-auction for her favorite anime action figure set, a Sailor Moon and Friends special edition. She loved Sailor Moon.

Phillip didn't answer. He leaned against the couch back, eyes undressing the television. She could smell the old people, now. It was gross. Like rotten ham and milk. Old people were gross in general, but especially when they ate like pigs and pooped themselves. Gross gross gross.

"Phillip?"

"God! Yes, I fed them. Do you still hear the stupid music?" His voice came through muffled behind the mask still secured across his face. He kept his attention on the bacon frosting cupcake arrangement.

She rolled her eyes. "No, dork. Did you check the mail? We're running low—YESSS!" Janice did a seated butt-dance.

Phillip pulled the mask up to rest on his forehead. "What is it?" He moved to shoulder surf.

"Oh cool, you won."

"Of course I won. I only need two more to finish the collection."

"Stupid dolls." He went back to his recliner where he had dropped his laptop. "Hey, I just thought of something funny. My grandparents eat like garden snails; I wonder if they fu— "

"Stupid?" she yelled, pushing up from the couch with tears building in her eyes. "Screw you, Phillip Foley!"

Sometimes Phillip could really say the wrong things. Janice could take just about anything from her husband's idiot mouth, but her anime collection was freaking sacred. "Go to hell, Phillip!"

"No problemo." He leaned back in the overstuffed chair, its metal frame screaming.

Janice snatched up the remote and raised the volume. It made her feel better. She threw it down, and it rebounded off the coffee table, skittering across the hardwood floor beneath the couch. Phillip slipped on his Beats by Dre and followed the bright red cord to his laptop's headphone jack.

Janice snarled her lips and plopped back into her couch crater. It was time to order pizza. For her, anyway. He could get his own or eat cream corned for all she cared.

Roger Foley held his wife's face in his mind even after the sun took the light from the bedroom. He didn't mind this. Once one of the kids had left the nightstand light on for two months, and that was hard. Sleep was already difficult with atrophied limbs, bedsores, and the state of muscular attrition they suffered. But the constant artificial lighting played hell with his mind. He could never tell if it was day or night. To make matters worse, the light was not the room lighting, but one of the grow lights his grandson had used for the plants he used to keep in the closet. Roger had a fairly good idea they were marijuana plants—or at least they were sold as such. Phillip wasn't the sharpest sausage on the link, but definitely the thickest. The Foleys lay exposed day and night to a garden-variety illumination that was supposed to make things sprout and flourish.

Then the girl cut it off. Now they had natural sunlight until nighttime. It was better, but he suspected, much too late.

Roger and Emma felt things growing beneath them, through the holes in their backs where flesh had long become tender mush from sub-dermal blood pooling and disuse. Tiny tendrils spread through their bodies, fusing them to the filthy mattress where their own fertilizer and dead skin cells fed a host of organisms that also longed for light.

But these creatures wanted the grow light more. Roger and Emma couldn't fight it.

It was only a matter of time before one of the kids, this time the girl, left the grow light on again. The little chunky punk cursed them for stinking, shoved food at them—weaving tendrils inside flailing at the excitation of light and nourishment—and then slammed the door on the way out. Light still on. That night , the Foley's own systems began to push back against the tendrils, weaves of capillaries and nerve webs following them down to the source, beneath the hardwood floorboards rotted through from human moisture and age.

Roger and Emma turned one last time to face each other, formed silent words of love and let their parched lips collide before they gave in to the growth. They lay in bed, smiling, clasping hands, and sprouting down as a single system into the soil before growing back up through the walls of wood and fiber that would one day be a home for those who truly needed one.

"Hey, Phillip?" Janice stood just outside the bedroom, the door still closed.

"No. Nuh-uh. It's your turn, Janice, and I don't care how bad it makes you sick. Just puke in there, dammit."

"No, Phillip. Something's wrong."

He looked up from his smartphone app. Janice stood outside the bedroom door, totally spooked.

"Well, what is it?"

"I really think you need to come over here." She sounded tiny.

He sighed and tossed the phone onto the coffee table's pile of pizza boxes, Diet Coke cans, and DVD jackets.

"What?" He got halfway before the smell hit him.

"Oh my God! What is that?"

Janice shook her head and covered her mouth. Overpowering and aromatic, wet earth mingled with raw flesh for a stew that hovered like a thick, persistent swamp gas. Plasma and mud, the metallic tang of infection mixed with the protein of night crawler.

Phillip looked down at the doorknob. Then back up at Janice who, for the first time in their marriage, turned helplessly to him for protection. She moved behind him.

He pulled on the knob and took one belligerent step into the room before he emptied his stomach with a violent heave, splattering the once beige carpet with sausage, pepperoni, and extra cheese. Janice didn't even make it pass the threshold before she too threw up.

Phillip broke through the clenched spasms of his gut with a high-pitched cry. Gramma and Grampa Foley lay holding hands in bed, the sheets no longer intact enough to cover their frail bodies. All along the edges of their naked forms, brown roots stretched down into the decomposing mattress, melding them together, one with the blossoming bed set. They both stared straight ahead, smiling.

Grampa's chest heaved. It distended even more. A rope of something not quite animal or vegetable snaked its way from beneath his bony pelvis and wriggled like a carnivorous worm toward Phillip and Janice. Then another. More came out of Gramma, lifting her off the bed. Grampa's chest burst open from thick braids of the woven flesh and vegetation, a wall of hungry tentacles groping in a whipping frenzy for Phillip and Janice.

Phillip threw Janice backward in his rush to save himself, slamming the door before the things could reach him.

"Get me a chair or something!"

The doorknob twisted in his fat palms. "Hurry!"

Janice backpedalled with remarkable speed, lugging a kitchen chair behind her. She shoved it against the knob and Phillip thumped back down the hallway, hollering over his shoulder, "Stay there and don't let them out!"

Janice whimpered but leaned into the door. It moved beneath her, pulsing, stretching. Pressing forward, one slow bulge with each monster heartbeat.

Phillip plowed his recliner in front of him like a steam shovel.

"Move!"

Janice jumped aside as Phillip shoved the recliner in place of the chair, the wooden seat and frame shattering beneath the weight of the heavier piece.

The door bulged twice, then settled.

They turned to each other, eyes wide and lips quivering. The scraping sounds of hundreds of centipedes scrambled throughout the structure - chewing, binding, fastening; feeding on wood fiber, feces, pizza crust, and creamed corn.

Phillip and Janice stayed away from the bedroom, though eventually the door burst from the weight within. By that time though, it was no big deal. Food came by delivery, the checks by mail, and no one cared if the trash made it out on Tuesdays. Oh, yeeah. They had a good roof, good Wi-Fi, funky Sims, and steady Social Security checks to keep them going. And pizza every night, can't forget that. Besides, they never did find the car keys... or the television remote, but Cupcake Wars was some good eats to watch.

Neither was sure when the front door fused closed or when the stuff started to grow out of the walls, but that was all right, too. They just stayed on the couch. It was mostly safe from the gross, old people thing.

Phillip and Janice sat staring at their laptops.

"Oh-ho, did you see that?" Phillip said, voice like a throat full of dirty filter masks.

"Whatever. Check this out," Janice sounded even worse, a gurgling, wet-paper girl.

They moved avatars around the virtual penthouse, interacting with medieval weapons at a cocktail party. Janice's Sim whomped Phillip's waitress avatar with a morning star, taking off half her face.

"You suck," he said. He tried to lift one of his sizable butt cheeks to fart, but just made a mess instead.

"Ha. Now you gotta sit in it," she said in her odd monotone.

Both had been sitting in it for quite a while. The clothes hanging from their flabby bodies tattered from stretch marks, the tendrils having long sucked the nourishing minerals from filth and fiber. And the extensions from Gramma and Grampa now penetrated Phillip and Janice, taking root within their soft and pliable systems. They couldn't have gotten off the couch if they had wanted to. Just as Gramma and Grampa Foley's roots run deep into the foundation of the old almost-by-the-beach house in Santa Monica, Phillip and Janice now started their own intermingling branch of vein and vine, reaching down through the couch cushions, past the lost remote control and Janice's car keys, through a pizza box ripe with wriggling mold and into the webbing of the Foley's foundation.

A solid foundation meant for those that needed a home.

Across the house, a chorus of angels floated out through the jagged gap into the bedroom, accompanying Bobby Vinton singing "Blue Velvet." Just in time.

DINNER

Mathias Jansson

A madman's memoirs

Blood is dropping
From the pages of my book
Dropping down in the white snow
Creating a kaleidoscope
A Rorschach pattern
From a madman's memoirs

In the snow I can see
Written with crow's feet
Flapping wings of black raven
Fear glowing in your eyes
A terrible screams trying to crawl
Out from your mouth
Chained and gagged I pull you
Up the sides of Hoosier Hill

At the top I pick up my rusty pen
The jagged blade lays familiar in my hand
Slowly I start to write the next chapter
In my bloody memoirs
With ink poured from your poor soul

Lemmy Rushmore

man's best friend

in cranial crevices
a carnivorous beast
if he's not taken for walks
it's upon me he'll feast

in the frailest of cages
he now paces the floor
maddest of dashes he'll make
through the first open door

with rabid inclinations
and the urge to destroy
the precious moments with him
are not times to enjoy

ever so loud is his bark
to say naught of his bite
he shall hound at the last bits
leaving scars from the fight

if he can't go for the throat
I'll be licked by the pain
urinating his vile way
on those places that stain

with his howl so constant
it is peace I can't find
ever gnawing and gnawing
on the back of my mind

he's a horrid rendition
of this me that you see
he's there panting and frothing
as he waits to be free....

Jon Wesick

System Failure

The old man was out there at 6:00 sharp. As always, he wore the same pair of sagging, double-knit pants. Marsden watched him through the kitchen window, nibbled toast that tasted like fiberglass, and wondered if the pants were the old man's only pair. Like he did every morning, the old man hobbled into his yard on his bum leg like some clockwork contraption, attached the flag to the halyard, and hoisted it to the top of the steel flagpole where it hung limp in the stagnant air. Marsden guessed he was a veteran. Probably hurt his leg in Vietnam. Even though Marsden and Susan had lived in that house for over seven years, he'd barely spoken to the man. Forty-three days earlier, during the September 11 attacks when strangers came together in common comfort, Marsden had avoided his neighbor. Something about the man's pale, freckled skin and thistle-like hair repulsed him.

Marsden sipped his coffee and spat it back into the cup. It had a strange smell not unlike the insecticide he used on the plum trees. He looked for the expiration date on the carton of cream he'd bought the previous night. If Susan were there, she'd make him use skim or soy. That's the problem with being married to an M.D. She was always after him about his health but with her in D.C. for a meeting, Marsden could bend the rules. He looked at his watch and poured the coffee out. He'd stop at Starbuck's on the way to work.

That didn't work out either. The kid behind the counter had a cough that echoed like he was in need of a chest x-ray and six months of potent antibiotics. Resigned to drinking the swill at the office, Marsden got back in his Lexus, switched on the radio, and punched the tuner to WBNZ.

"We ought to turn the whole damn country into radioactive slag," an unfamiliar voice said over the speakers. "I mean, why have all those missiles if we're never gonna use them?"

Marsden changed the station and got on the West Shore Parkway heading toward the Verranzano Narrows Bridge. Traffic was heavy but kept moving. The air over Manhattan was gray with smoke. Even when running on recirculate, the air conditioning couldn't keep out the smell. He spat out the window but couldn't get the metallic taste out of his mouth. He got off

FDR at 42nd Street and thought he saw a human skeleton on the corner. He looked again, but it was only a homeless man with dark sunglasses resembling a skull's empty eye sockets. After a forty-five minute drive, he parked in Midtown in the Ferris Building's underground garage and took the elevator to the Morris Detweiller Associates office on the twentieth floor. Jack Taylor ambushed him on his way to the lunchroom.

"Got a minute? I need to talk to you about your tech company rankings."

Marsden followed Jack into his office where the air had a sour smell from discarded gunpowder tea leaves Jack had brewed, the drink he swilled for his prostate.

"You did some good research." Jack threw himself into his leather chair, tossed Marsden one of the apples on his desk, and bit into another. "I think you scored OmniDyne too low, though."

"If you look at the price-to-earnings ratios..."

"I know but sometimes the numbers are misleading. Stock recommendations are a judgment call after all. And after the World Trade Center, defense can only go up." Jack handed back Marsden's report.

Marsden set down the apple and located OmniDyne on the last page. Jack had been pushing that stock on his clients for months despite the crappy numbers, but arsden knew it was futile to resist.

"I'll factor in some adjustments."

"Great! If things turn out like I expect, there'll be a nice surprise for you at Christmas."

Marsden stopped in the lunchroom and poured himself some coffee. It had the same chemical smell as at home. This time it brought back memories of fetal pigs and high school biology. The smell wasn't insecticide. It was formaldehyde.

He worked through lunch to find some justification for Jack's changes, had a sandwich brought in, and e-mailed the revised report. He left at 5:15, made it home by 6:00, and went out to the patio to indulge in his secret vice, a fine Dominican cigar. Before he could light it, the doorbell rang. He set the cigar down to answer the front door and found two men in suits on his doorstep. Both had weightlifters' builds. One was an albino. The other had a pencil-thin mustache and brown skin that darkened to almost black under his eyes.

"Mr. Marsden?" asked the albino. His breath smelled of rotting meat.

"Yes."

"There's been some trouble with your wife, sir." The second

man, the dark one, showed a badge. "FBI. I'm Special Agent Briggs, and this is Agent Cooper. May we come in?"

"Is she okay?" Marsden stepped aside to let the agents enter.

"She's missing, and we're afraid there may have been foul play," Cooper said. "Do you know anyone who would want to harm her?"

"There was a professor she accused of sexual harassment but that was years ago." Marsden led them into the living room.

"We'll need to get his name just in case." Briggs took out a notepad. "Did you notice any changes in her behavior lately, any unexplained absences or new acquaintances?"

"No."

"Did she leave any letters or documents behind?" Briggs kept his gaze on his notepad. "Something that might give us a clue of her whereabouts?"

"No. Nothing like that."

"Do you have a safe deposit box?" Cooper asked. "Could she have left something there?"

Marsden turned from Cooper to avoid the stench coming from his mouth. "The bank's closed but I can check first thing tomorrow. Do you have a card?"

"You wife's work has national security implications." Briggs set his business card on the coffee table and stood to leave. "Don't discuss this with anyone for now."

"I know this is pretty upsetting, sir," Cooper said, "but we've dealt with these things before. Let us do our job and we'll get your Susan back safely."

After the FBI men had left, Marsden dialed his wife's cell phone and got her voice mail with the recording of Susan reading a Pablo Neruda love poem that had formed part of their wedding vows. Even two shots of single-malt whiskey could not get him to sleep that night.

He was red-eyed and awake for the flag-raising the next morning. He brewed and drank the coffee that smelled of formaldehyde. He needed it to get through the day. When he got to the bank a few hours later, his safe deposit box was empty. Their passports, gold coins and stock certificates were all gone as were the car titles and deed to their house. He stepped out of the privacy booth and motioned to the bank teller.

"Something's wrong." He lifted the notebook that held the signatures of customers who'd accessed their boxes off the cabinet.

"Sir, you're not allowed to see those." The teller snatched the notebook away.

"Just tell me who was last in my box."

"I'm not supposed to." The teller flipped the pages. "Here it is. Susan Dunlop-Marsden. Yesterday at 4:00 PM."

"But that's impossible! She's..."

"She's what?"

"Never mind. Thanks." Marsden hurried through the bullet-proof doors and out to his car.

On his way to the office, he ran a red light and nearly collided with a minivan. The driver laid on her horn and shook her fist. Marsden picked up a roast beef sandwich at the deli in the lobby and dashed into the elevator. By the time it reached the twelfth floor, he realized he'd left the FBI man's business card at home. Once he got to his desk, he looked up the number of the local FBI field office and dialed.

"I'd like to speak with Agent Briggs, please."

"I'm sorry, sir. There's no Agent Briggs at this office."

"Agent Cooper?"

"We don't have an Agent Cooper either. Maybe someone else can help you. What the nature of this call?"

"Sorry. Somebody must be playing a joke on me." Marsden hung up and tried Susan's cell phone again but only got her voice mail.

He went to his office window and looked at the traffic below, the automobiles like toys and the city a board in some giant boy's game. Should he call the police or would that get her in more trouble? Susan must have emptied the safe deposit box after all.

"Where have you been?" A colleague said after sticking her head into his office. "Detweiller's holding an emergency meeting. Everybody's been looking for you."

Marsden followed her into the conference room, and everyone sitting at the mahogany table turned to stare.

"Sorry I'm late."

Frank Detweiller nodded and Art Finklebaum, the lawyer, continued his briefing. He spoke another fifteen minutes of incomprehensible legal jargon before wrapping up.

"I wouldn't panic." Finklebaum closed his briefcase. "The SEC feels the need to flex its muscles from time to time. As long as you have records showing your rationale, you'll be fine."

"I have total confidence in our analysts," Detweiller said while staring at Marsden.

Marsden cornered Jack after the meeting broke up.

"What's going on?"

"Oh, some investor got her panties in a bunch and complained to the SEC. It'll blow over."

Marsden returned to his office and checked that his original report was in the file cabinet and that he'd saved an electronic copy on his computer. He lost track of time organizing his records and didn't realize he was hungry until after 1:00. Unwrapping his sandwich, he noticed something white wiggling on the cellophane. He pulled the bread apart and found dozens of maggots on the meat.

"Damn it!"

He took the elevator to the lobby and tossed the putrid sandwich on the deli's counter.

"What's wrong with you selling this kind of crap? I ought to report you to the health department."

The clerk turned away and began slicing tomatoes as if he wasn't there.

"Hey! Do you speak English?" Marsden shook his head and walked away muttering, "Immigrants."

He left the office late and found an orange detour sign on his usual route through Brooklyn. The unfamiliar streets seemed menacing in the darkness. After several wrong turns, he lost his bearings and ended up in a deserted warehouse district of bad smells, broken windows, and sooty brick facades.

He paused at a rusty stop sign before taking a right turn. A crowd danced around a smoky, red light ahead. When he got closer, he saw the flames were coming from an overturned taxi. Two thugs held a turbaned man's arms behind his back while a third swung punches into his midsection. Fearing for his safety but unwilling to do nothing, Marsden laid on his horn. A brick hit the windshield leaving a spider web of cracks. He hit the gas and fishtailed around a corner leaving cursing and gunfire behind.

At home, he found a CD in his mailbox. Once inside he slid it out of the unmarked envelope. It was by a band he'd never heard of, Neutral Milk Hotel. He slipped the disc into his stereo. The discordant horns reminded him of a New Orleans funeral or a documentary he'd seen about Tibet. Involved as he was in the music it took him minutes to realize the phone was ringing. By the time he made it to the kitchen, the answering machine had picked up.

"Marsden, it's Susan. You have to get out of there."

He dove for the phone and yanked it off the hook.

"Hello. Susan."

The line went dead. Marsden started to dial her cell phone, but the doorbell rang. It was the two phony FBI men.

"You didn't call me about the safe deposit box," Briggs said as

Cooper stepped past Marsden.

"It was empty," Marsden said.

"Heard from your wife?" Cooper asked.

"No. Now if you'll excuse me, I have some things to do."

"We need you to come downtown and answer a few questions," Briggs said.

"The FBI has never heard of you two." Marsden stepped to within an inch of Briggs. "I don't know what your game is, and I don't care. But if you don't leave now I'm calling the police."

Cooper grabbed Marsden from behind. Marsden opened his mouth to scream, but before he could get any words out, Briggs covered his face with a foul-smelling cloth. Marsden sucked the fumes into his lungs as he struggled. It was the same smell as in the coffee, the smell of dissections in high school biology.

He woke up on a steel table. Wearing a blood-spattered apron, Briggs was holding someone's liver in his gloved hands while Cooper cut away at Marsden's arm with a hacksaw. Marsden opened his mouth to scream but how could he scream with his lungs in a bucket by his feet?

He woke up with a pounding headache at home and found his living room gutted. Books lay strewn across the floor like dead birds, and the couch had been slit open and emptied of its stuffing. The CD was gone. He dialed the police from the kitchen.

"Nine-one-one, emergency."

"I've been assaulted and robbed."

"Hello. Is anybody there?"

"I said I've been robbed."

The phone went dead. He dropped the handset, leaving it to swing from the cord, and dashed outside as his neighbor was raising the flag.

"Did you see two strange men at my place last night?"

"Do you know the price of freedom?" the old man asked. "It's blood. Pay the price, son."

Marsden walked away muttering, "Crazy old bastard."

Craning his neck to see around the opaque spot in his broken windshield, he drove to work. Detweiller cornered him as soon as he got in the door.

"In my office!"

Marsden followed him into a suite with a view of the Manhattan skyline. The CEO's face glowed with rage like an electric heater element set to high.

"Jack told me about the shenanigans you played with the OmniDyne stock," Detweiller said. "I'm very disappointed."

"It was Jack. Not me. I have the report to prove it." He dashed to his office.

Detweiller followed like a steamroller that had already made up its mind.

"Right here." He opened the bottom drawer of his file cabinet, pulled out the last folder, and found it empty.

The floor seemed to crumble beneath his feet. He flailed for anything that would stop his fall.

"I have a backup on my computer." He flew across the room and punched the power button on his PC.

Detweiller crossed his arms over his chest and tapped his foot. The computer groaned and displayed a blue screen with the words "System Failure."

"You're lucky I don't send you to jail. I want you out of this office by noon." Detweiller turned and walked away.

An hour later, carrying his effects in a copy-paper box, Marsden ran into Jack Taylor in the lobby.

"Why'd you do it to me, Jack?"

"Because it wouldn't hurt you."

"I'd say it hurt me pretty badly."

"Think about it," Jack said. "Where were you on the morning of September 11?"

"Here in the office."

"No, you weren't. You needed to talk to Meacham at Smith Caldwell. Remember? You were in the Twin Towers when the planes hit."

It came back to Marsden – how the floor shook when the plane struck, smoke, panic and flickering emergency lights in the crowded stairwell, the old woman who fell, and how there was no time to go back and save her.

"Sorry about ruining your good name, Marsden, but I couldn't go to jail. You need to move on."

Marsden left the Ferris Building and wandered south until he arrived at the smoking hole that was once the World Trade Center. Ashes everywhere. A thousand smoldering fires. The policeman in a dirty filter mask who guarded the barricade didn't notice him walk past. Rescuers with body-sniffing dogs searched the ruins while workers in grimy coats cut twisted steel with welding torches. A comfortable place called to him, and he lay down next to a pile of bricks.

He closed his eyes and prepared to give it all up, but something wasn't right. He had other memories, memories of envelopes of white powder that had arrived at millions of households. He recalled fevers and coughing, a crowded emergency room that couldn't cope with the plague, soldiers in gas masks firing on crowds, and nuclear missiles looking for someone to blame. He didn't die on September 11. He died in the aftermath.

Marsden made it home in time to see uniformed men in ski masks pulling his neighbors from their houses. The old man who'd raised the flag every morning was the first to get a bullet in the back of the head.

"You couldn't leave well enough alone. Could you?" Jack said as he poured gasoline over the bodies and lit a match.

The stacked bodies ignited in a macabre campfire of death. The old man's face grinned in the flames as the fire burned away his cheeks.

"Let's go!" Jack called to the uniformed men.

The death squad piled into trucks and drove away leaving Marsden behind. Marsden began walking. He abandoned the neighborhood and wandered his ruined country, mingling with the rich in their walled compounds and with the working poor. Fueled by the thought-energy of denial, the ghost of America lingered on the landscape of its former greatness. While democracy descended in a death spiral of secret prisons and blood-stained interrogations, its citizens dreamed opium dreams in the blue glow of their TV sets. Most didn't even know they were dead.

John D. Stanton

Judith Skillman

As Before Sickness

The fabric of infection—
how well it absorbs sound.
In a fever a thousand lifetimes.

Like silk organza, how delicate the skin
        though we pretend
to be headstrong little women.

Instead of confidence
oh Mary fetch a pail,
we remember what it is the cherubim left

when their wings broke,
when they stroked the air
with the hot breath of peppers.

A nostalgic rain comes to the garden. Mother
returns to the kitchen to make toast.
Blue glass objects line the sill—

bottles, cups, neck of Rilke's swan...
They'd left their childhood.
Even the stove with its open-mouthed darkness,

its velvet fingerlings of heat
inclines toward the saying
of omens and portents.

John Ledger

Father

Today is my father's birthday, and if he were still alive, he'd be fifty-five years old. I celebrate his birthday every year even though nobody else in my family does. Nobody else understands though, what a great man he was. They only believe what they hear. Of course, what they hear is that my father was a murderer; a serial killer if you want to get technical about things. I never saw that side of him though, never got to know his dark half. My father showered me with love and affection my whole life, working hard to put food on the table for his family. Evidently, though, he worked just as hard at living a double life Mom didn't know a thing about. She found out though, and that was when the shit hit the fan. When Mom found out about Dad's dark secret, that was the day that would change my life forever.

My brother Carl was living across the river with his girlfriend and nobody ever heard much from him. My sister Chelsea was off to college at Penn State, and we got to see her only on the holidays and during spring and summer break. I was in my sophomore year of high school at the time and my little sister Lucy was in seventh grade at the junior high school down the road. Every year Dad requested off work for his birthday, and Mom did too so she could spend his special day with him. Dad's 48th birthday wasn't a very special day though; February 15th, 2006 was the end and the beginning of a nightmare.

I walked home from school that day, stopping at the pizza shop on the way for a slice and a coke. I picked up a pack of smokes from the mini-mart next door afterwards. This had been our favorite store ever since my friends and I had discovered the Amish-looking guy who ran the place was weird as hell but didn't card us and that was all that we cared about. I was headed home, and I took a longer route than usual so I could burn a Camel or two on the way.

As I got close enough to see my house, my heart dropped in my chest as my cigarette fell to the ground. The first thing I noticed was the red and blue flashing lights, and I immediately wondered if they were at my house or not. They were, and there were a lot of them. Five police cars to be exact. I walked faster, almost picking up into a slow run down the hill towards my home. I got closer and noticed my mother and my sister Lucy were both out in the street with the police. The cops had their guns drawn and were aiming at my house. I got close enough that a police officer approached me, intending to intercept me as I heard my mother and sister yelling my name, calling me over to them. That was when I saw him on the porch, just sitting in his rocking chair with a shotgun in his hands. He looked completely defeated and old. The gun was pointed under his chin and I couldn't fathom what was going on. Why was my father about to kill himself?

I ignored the cop, walked across the front lawn and up to the front porch. I didn't get to say a word before my father spoke to me, "Lucas, I love you. I'm sorry. Now turn around."

"But Dad," I responded before he cut me off.

"I said turn around boy!" I did as I was told and began walking away. That's when I heard the blast. My father blew his head off right behind me in front of the police, my mother, my little sister and all the neighbors that had gathered to watch. I passed out in the front lawn. That was seven years ago. Things have never been the same.

My father's funeral was a joke. Nobody was there other than immediate family. Carl and Chelsea both showed up to make sure he was dead. "He was no father of ours," they both announced and my mother mourned and wept for herself more than anything, cursing his name in the funeral home. My sister Lucy was pretty traumatized from seeing him kill himself, and we all avoided telling her as much as we could, but that wasn't so easy. My father made the national news, not because of his death but because of who he was. Dubbed the "Keystone Killer," my dad was responsible for the deaths of 31 women across the state of Pennsylvania they said.

Earlier on the day of his suicide, my mother went to the garage to tell him lunch was ready. When she entered the garage, she saw he wasn't there and figured he had made a run to the beer distributor. As she left, she noticed the hatch to the attic in the garage was open. A ladder was set up beneath it, and she recognized an old army trunk sitting open on the floor. She walked towards it to look inside. My mother's mind entered a state of shock as she saw various items including multiple pairs of women's underwear and clothing along with sunglasses, jewelry and other things of that nature. She picked up what was obviously a journal and began reading very detailed accounts of what my father had been up to in his spare time. A few moments later, he walked in, crying. Mom turned to look at him as she asked him, "How could you?" Without speaking a word he grabbed his shotgun, went to the front porch, and camped out in his chair. My mother called the police and ran into the house to get to my sister Lucy whom she stayed inside with until the noise of sirens filled the street outside.

After all was said and done, there was the awkward funeral, then the awkward home life between the three of us. They don't understand why I don't hate him like they do. Maybe they never will. I refuse to look at him as anything other than my father, a man who loved me. The media has interviewed everyone from my siblings to relatives I don't even know from my father's side of the family. I've refused to be interviewed time and time again and I always will. I won't be a part of their circus. I do, however, know something nobody else knew on that fateful day.

There was another journal stashed away in the basement of our house that I retrieved later that night. All 31 women and the story of what happened to each of them was detailed inside it, just like in the journal the police had taken. Unlike that journal though, this one had four more names and pictures along with information about each of the women. These were supposed to have been the next four victims. The mission was never completed.

In the past seven years, a lot has happened to fuck with my head. My mother barely speaks to me, and she looks at me like I'm my father. Chelsea and Carl hate me for loving him, and Lucy is afraid of me. I still do my best to look out for her though; she's a little angel and she never should've had to witness his suicide. Maybe I should've told someone about the other journal, taken this weight off my shoulders. The problem is I couldn't bring myself to break the secret. Things have gotten so strange though I don't know how much more I can take.

In 2008, Jillian Henderson was found strangled to death in her apartment in Harrisburg. She was number 32 on the list. In 2009, Libby Watson was found strangled to death in her home in Marysville. She was number 33 on the list. In 2010, Jessica Foster was found strangled to death in her car in an Applebee's parking lot, also in Harrisburg. She was number 34 on the list. For three years now, the killing has stopped, and the cops have given up on their copycat theories and conceded to the notion that these three murders must be unrelated and coincidental.

Now here in my car, here in the present, on my father's birthday I think about that, and I think about how wrong they are. They were wrong to begin with, and they're wrong now. There is no copycat, and there are no coincidences. The killing hasn't stopped, and it never will. I think about all of this as I light up a Camel and I watch the world around me.

I think about my father, and how you all could never understand him. You could never understand true power. For what you all witnessed on the porch that day wasn't the end but only the beginning. My father didn't die that day, in fact, his spirit lives on stronger than ever, and he shall live on forever. The suffering will never ever end, and I am now responsible for fulfilling destiny. It's a lot to take in, and I think hard about all of it as I start my car and follow the red mustang that just pulled out of the lot. Inside that mustang is Samantha Kendrick. She's number 35 on the list. I think about my father on his birthday as I follow this woman home. My father never killed anyone; he simply loved his son.

Stuart Keane

Wet

The door closed behind Sophie with a soft clunk.

She breathed out.

Placing her heavy rucksack on the floor, she removed her damp coat and dropped it at her feet. It hit the carpet with a thud, keys and coins clinking as they bounced in the pockets. She shook her arms and arched her head upwards, her eyes focusing on the cream-colored ceiling.

She screamed.

And smiled.

That's better, she thought.

Another day, done.

Same shit, different day and all that malarkey.

Stepping away from her crumpled coat, she turned, bent down, and collected it from the carpet. She hooked the coat onto her hat stand and walked into the kitchen on her left. Turning around, she listened.

Silence greeted her.

"Henry? You back yet?"

No answer. Her husband wasn't home.

Sophie sighed again.

Out with the boys. Again.

He never has any time for me anymore.

With a flick of a switch, the kitchen lights came on.

Sophie tapped the button on the kettle and after a few seconds, the familiar hiss of boiling water filled the room. Opening a cupboard, she retrieved a teabag and dropped it into her usual cup, which sat waiting on the work surface. Leaning on the counter, she sighed, flexing her muscles and trying to remove the stress of her day. Her muscles creaked and groaned during her basic yoga stretches. Her mind remembered the stress of the day. She sighed deeply.

This day has been an absolute shit storm. I don't want another like it.

Comes with the job unfortunately.

You need a new job then.

I wish we could move already.

Paris or Rome. That's what Henry keeps saying.

It would be amazing. Paradise.

Better than Indiana.
Way better.
The love of my life and a romantic city.
Living the dream!
If only he were home more.
The grind of the day, straining our marriage.
No other choice.
Until then, the shitty job pays the bills.
Shitty job!
Forget that. Have a relaxing evening. You're off the clock.
Sophie placed her arms behind her back and yawned.

A bath. That's what you need. With plenty of bubbles and salts. Suddenly, Sophie felt alive, encouraged. The thought of a bath made her feel human again. Leaving the kettle to boil, she ambled out of the kitchen and across the hall into her bedroom. The door to the master bathroom stood open.

Sophie started to undress. The buttons on her shirt plinked as she unclasped them. Within seconds, her shirt—creased with daily sweat and moderately expensive perfume—lay on the bed. She unclasped her bra and held the cups in place with one arm across her chest as she closed the curtains. She glanced at the neighbor's window straight across the alley.

That's all Mr. Koontz needs. An eyeful.
You'd give him a boner or a heart attack. Or both, in that order.

A cheeky smile spread across Sophie's face.

In a playful manner, she removed her arm and stretched both limbs outwards, and the bra fluttered to the floor. The cool air on her exposed breasts and the sweaty strap marks left behind from the brasserie was heavenly. Her nipples started to stiffen. She stood like that for a moment before moving to the bathroom.

She tugged the cord to turn on the bathroom light then reached for the taps and twisted them. Within seconds, hot water started to fill the bath with a dull roar. She tested the heat with her fingertips and adjusted it. Once right, she smiled and walked back into the bedroom.

Sophie unbuckled her belt and dropped it on the bed then unbuttoned her trousers and slid them down her lithe, muscular legs. She folded them neatly and placed them across her dresser chair before slipping her panties down and tossing them in the hamper.

Sophie stood there, naked and exposed.

Moving to the bed, she sat down on the soft mattress and opened her bedside drawer. She rifled through the contents, picking out a black book, before realizing it was Henry's side of the bed. She shook her head and smiled at her error.

What is wrong with you?

You need a decent night's sleep. Or a good fucking.

Sophie blushed, closing her legs.

It has been a while.

She thought about her 'friend' in her bedside drawer. He spent his time tucked under her best underwear. Victoria's Secret and Ann Summers were his companions. In recent memory, he paid more attention to her than Henry did.

Sophie realized she was still holding the book. It was old and battered. Henry's makeshift address book, his little black book of clients.

She snorted.

She started to open it and remembered the bath was running. She placed her feet down on the soft carpet and stood up, dropping the book on the bed. It opened to a bookmarked page, but she didn't notice.

The sudden realization that she was naked made her teeth chatter.

Folding one arm over her breasts, she scooped her dressing gown off the bed with the other, wrapped it around herself and returned to the bathroom.

The bath was a third full.

Plenty of time.

She stroked her calves. *Still smooth, no need to shave tonight.*

She dropped a spherical bath bomb in, and it started fizzing.

Sophie returned to the kitchen and picked up the kettle, poured the water into the cup and let it rest. *Where was Henry?* She plucked the lid off the Batman biscuit barrel on the counter. After a second, she removed an Oreo and placed it in her mouth. Her teeth crunched down, and she closed her eyes. The chocolate goodness seeped into her taste buds. The creamy sensation that followed made her realize why she couldn't stop eating them.

The little things really are the best.

Grabbing Batman from the worktop, she picked up her cup and returned to the bathroom.

She checked her watch. 8:02.

Henry could be a while yet.

The bath was a massive structure, a ceramic teardrop latched into the corner of the room. The lining of the bath created makeshift support shelves, which held bottles of shampoo, shower gel, moisturizer and a razor blade with a pink handle and purple heads. A rubber duck sat lonely on the edge of the bath, its yellow hue faded from years of use.

Sophie placed her hot tea and Batman on the side with the toiletries.

Twisting the water off, she stood up and dropped the robe. The sudden silence in the room was strange but welcome. She breathed out. She looked at the purple bath water, the bomb still slowly fizzing into nothing beneath the surface.

She grinned. "I'm going to enjoy this."

She lifted a leg over the rim and climbed into the bath, the hot water scorching her leg. She hissed as her calf adapted to the heat that enveloped it, and placed her left foot down gently to secure her balance. The right leg followed and again she composed herself, both legs calf-deep in water. The heat rose, pricking sweat droplets from her open pores. Slipping a hair tie from her wrist, she tied her brunette locks into a small ponytail. She stood there for a moment, savoring the warmth, and started to sit down.

The telephone rang, and she flinched, surprised by the shrill noise in the sudden silence. Her left leg gave way, and she slipped backwards. Forcing the foot down again, it stepped on the slimy bath bomb, and her feet squeaked on the base of the bath. Both legs upended, and she jackknifed. Her head flew back and smacked against the edge of the bath. Water splashed out of the tub, splattering the white tiles. Her neck cracked, and a blinding pain flashed along her spine. Her eyes fogged over, and she slid, her body sliding into the water, the warm water swallowing her body, her torso easing into it.

Her right leg stopped her, bent beneath her rump, her body propped against it. Her head came to an uneasy rest on the rim of the bath. The water was a few inches below her chin, lapping against her neck.

She groaned in pain.

The smell of lavender—presumably from the bath bomb— slowly stirred her awake. Her eyes cleared, and she came to, slightly disoriented. Her head turned from side to side groggily. She gazed forward. Her eyes slowly began to focus.

Her left leg was floating beneath the water. Her toes were poking out of the murky, purple liquid. She noticed blue glitter in the water; it sparkled in the light. Her belly also broke the surface, as did her slick, rounded breasts.

"Help."

The words came out strangled, barely noticeable, almost a whisper. Her throat ached. The back of her neck throbbed, its proximity to the enamel tub amplifying the sensation. She tried to move.

She couldn't.

Don't panic. You took a nasty bump. Try again.

She did.

Nothing happened.

Sophie couldn't move.

Try again.

Sophie tried again.

Same result. Her body wouldn't move.

She looked left, at the bathroom around her, and glanced right at the blue tiled wall. A white bottle of shampoo sat beside her. She gazed forward and moaned.

"Help."

Again, the words barely escaped. A tear rolled down her face.

Her body was immobile.

You hit yourself pretty bad. You'll recover soon enough.

What if you don't? You might be a cripple.

Don't think like that. It won't get you anywhere.

It's a possibility though.

Your body is just in shock from the fall.

That's bullshit.

No, it's not.

Shut up!

"HELP!"

The words were forceful this time, vehement. They echoed around the bathroom. Sophie tried to shift herself again, and nothing happened. Her body was rooted to the slippery base of the bath.

She remembered the bath bomb.

Her brain was foggy, but it was trying to alert her to something. The thought wouldn't come. She looked down at her wet torso, wishing she could cover her modesty. Her nipples were erect and the water in the bath was slowly rippling along her chest. Her toes still bobbed in the water. Her neatly shaved pubic region waved beneath the murky water.

Normal bath activity. Except for one thing.

She *couldn't* move.

She sniffled. The pricking of tears burned the backs of her eyes.

Why can't I move?

Normally, her leg would shift and jolt and slide out from beneath her. It was a reflex action, provided by moving her body and having her skeleton react to the brain synapse. She even may slip and slide a little. In this bath, on this rainy evening, her leg remained immobile.

Shit, she thought.

Sophie glanced around. She tried to lift her arms and couldn't. Like her leg, they remained dead in the water beside her, their palms upturned, pale white under the lights' glow.

What was it about bath bombs?

Her brain was trying to alert her to...something.

Dammit, think!

Why can't I feel the water?

The warmth. The hot water surrounded her. She could see the steam rising as it rippled and distorted the air before her. She could smell the heat, its aroma usually relaxing. Now it was concerning.

How come I can't feel anything?

It burned my legs before and now...nothing.

She looked at her left leg. The skin was turning pink beneath the water. It bobbed up and down gently, breaking the surface before slipping beneath once more. Her skin was burning beneath the water. She checked her chest, and the skin surrounding her nipples was pink too. The crevice between her breasts formed a dark pink valley.

However, she felt nothing.

No sensation whatsoever.

Crippled. The word snaked across her brain. She didn't notice the gooseflesh prickling her soaked body.

"HELP!"

She screamed, and the noise reverberated around the bathroom. The noise was clear and precise, and bounced around several times before diminishing.

She thought about her neighbors.

Mrs. Smith lived downstairs, ancient and deaf. The stench of urine and cabbage were her only friends. Her hearing required the TV to be on full blast every day. *No use. She wouldn't hear a bomb drop.*

Bomb?

She eyed the last few drops of the bath bomb as they separated and spread out across the water, finally completely dissolved. *Think, brain, think! What were you trying to tell me?*

What about James across the hall?

Doesn't he work nights?

Sophie nodded as if answering her own question. He'd be starting his shift right now. Maybe you can call the super?

He doesn't work past five.

He lives in, though. *Yeah, good luck disturbing him at this time. He'd sabotage your heating or something. Stupid fat prick.*

You're forgetting one simple thing.

You can't fucking move.

You're stuck here. Unless your neighbors are nosy or psychic, you're not going anywhere.

"HELLO! ANYONE THERE? CAN ANYONE HEAR ME?"

Silence replied in startling, heavy fashion.

She moved her head and looked at her gown on the floor.

Searching for something...anything.

Right, this could work. You read about it in some magazine.

The one in the airport? Yeah, I remember.

I remember the article, not the magazine.

Please don't let it be Cosmo. Please be true.

Sophie closed her eyes. She breathed in and counted to ten. She breathed out.

Opening her eyes, she tried to move and couldn't. Her body remained inert.

"Shit." She stifled some tears and sniffed.

Bath bombs. That's it!

Remember to clean the bath out afterwards.

Helpful, thanks!

Why are you telling me...?

Sophie felt her weight shift beneath her. Her leg moved, slipped and idled away from her rump. She saw it rest against the side of the tub.

She noticed her buttocks sinking lower.

As were her chest and legs.

And her chin.

The water rose an inch, touching the underside of her jaw, swallowing her neck.

Her eyes widened. *Fuck.*

Bath bombs are slippery.

No shit, Sherlock.

It's why we're in this position.

You're going to slip into the water.

She realized her predicament. As the bath bomb continued to spread, the enamel became slippery and slick.

"HELP ME, PLEASE, HELP MEEEEEEEE!"

She couldn't feel the tub against her back, legs or arms, but she could see her body sliding slowly, lowering, the water bobbed and waved as her body immersed itself. She could no longer see her pubic region, hidden beneath a cloud of blue glitter, dirt and bubbles.

She paused for a second. Her body settled once more.

For now.

I've gotta get out of here.

How are you going to do that? You're lifeless in a bathtub full of water.

There has to be a way.

She watched her leg slide a little farther. The water rose another couple of centimeters. The purple liquid now lapped against her chin, below her lips.

If you don't get out of here, you'll drown.

Do something.

An idea slipped into her head. Sophie considered the option carefully. It might be her only chance.

It could also kill you, push you further into the bath.

You're going to drown otherwise.

Worth a shot.

Sophie calculated that the water wasn't too deep.

She arched her head upwards, and her neck sent a shot of pain into her brain. She grimaced in agony but continued. Her face rose, her chin slurping out of the water with a plop. The cooling sensation of humid air on wet skin licked her face.

Her head was facing up, away from the water. The back of her skull was balanced on the rim of the bath behind her, giving her a little pushing leverage. She couldn't feel anything below the neckline. Her movement was purely a balancing equation. Her skull pushed off the bath rim, using it as a platform. A constant throbbing, now isolated away from the enamel, made her gasp.

You hit your spine.

This isn't good.

She gulped; tears slipped from her eyes and coursed down the side of her cheeks. They rolled off her face and plinked into the water below.

Sophie felt her neck muscles tightening, a pressure building.

How long can you keep this up? What if you sink lower? You could go under.

I'll do it slowly.

Stay here. You'll be safe. Less risk. Henry will be home soon.

What if he's working and forgot to tell me?

You can't wait.

It's either this or drown.

She began to shake, and her skull began to ache. She closed her eyes.

Lower and then push up again. Keep doing it. It gets you away from the water.

On three. One, two...

Sophie's leg squeaked along the bath and slammed against the corner. The leverage holding her up, poised by her balanced body, was lost, and the weight of her prone body pulled her off balance.

She dropped into the water with a loud splash.

Water splattered the tiles and the floor as she dropped onto the base of the bath and bounced off the slick surface with a muted thud. She closed her eyes but was a little late with her mouth. Warm, bubbly water sluiced between her lips, pouring down her throat, choking her. She spluttered and coughed. The water dipped, allowing her breathing room until the miniature waves lashed back and slammed over her head, engulfing her in purple, hazy water. Sophie shook her head from side to side, fizzing up the liquid.

A gargling noise erupted from beneath the waves, and her face broke the surface.

She gasped, breathed, and gulped for fresh air. Water spilled from her nose and mouth, the stinging sensation on her throat telling her she'd swallowed some of the tub's contents. She coughed, spewing water and vomit into the bath water. The yellow bile blended with the purple to create a brown mixture of blue glitter, stomach lining and dirty, stagnant water.

The acidic stench of vomit pierced the lavender smell and soiled the air in the bathroom. She let her body bob in the water, and her body slid back to its former position. She arched her head back against the rim to balance herself.

After a moment, the water settled and all was back to normal.

Close one, she thought.

Sophie lowered her eyes. Small red lumps of stomach lining floated around her body, sticking to her skin. One sliver rested against her nipple. The water was tepid now, cooled by the activity in the tub. Wet hair matted to her forehead, a few strands coming loose from her ponytail. She flicked her head from side to side in an attempt to move them. It failed.

You need to get help. You're going to die in here otherwise.

She swallowed; her throat stung, making her flinch.

Impossible. I can't move.

"Sophie?"

She flinched. At first she thought her ears had played a trick on her.

"Sophie? You home?"

Henry!

"HENRY!"

"Sophie?"

"BATHROOM. QUICK!"

She angled her head so she could see the door. Faint footsteps grew louder and within seconds Henry appeared. He came through the door and slipped on the wet floor. He regained his footing and ambled into the bathroom carefully. His stark, blue eyes settled on his wife.

"What the fuck?"

"Henry, help me, please!"

"What did you do?" Henry took his shoes off and threw them into the bedroom behind him.

"I slipped and fell. I bashed my neck and I can't move. I can't move, Henry. I can't fucking move..."

"Okay, okay, calm down. You'll be fine. We need to get you out of that bath."

Sophie smiled at her husband. Her knight in shining armor.

He stood still, surveying the situation.

"Henry?"

"What?"

"Take the plug out. It'll solve the problem. At least that way I won't drown."

"I'm trying to figure out how to get you out without injuring you further."

"Well, pull the plug and we can take our time. I can still drown like this."

"Good point."

Henry stepped over to the corner of the bath towards Sophie's feet. The bath had a latch plug that opened via a lever behind the taps. His hand touched on it and paused. He withdrew and narrowed his eyes, looking at his wife.

"What are you waiting for?"

He frowned.

"What?" she asked as her body started to slip again.

"I didn't mean for this to happen."

"What? This?"

"Yeah...I mean no. No."

"This was an accident. I slipped in the bath. This wasn't your doing."

"I don't mean this."

"Well, fucking spit it out. I'm not in the best position..."

"You found my little black book. It's on the bed out there." He pointed to the doorway and bit his lip.

"So?"

"You found it."

"And?" Sophie was becoming exasperated.

"You weren't meant to."

"It's an address book, not secret FBI documents. And you didn't hide it very well."

"You weren't supposed to find it. Or read it. It's my private life."

"I didn't read it." She lowered another inch.

"Liar."

"I didn't! Anyway, what's so important about it?"

"Stop pretending. Stop putting it off..."

"I don't have a clue what..."

"Don't lie!"

"Henry...I don't know what you're talking about. We can discuss it in a minute. Okay? Until then, get me out of this *fucking bath*!"

"You shouldn't read about my private life."

"We're married. We don't have secrets." Rage burned Sophie's face.

"Well...I do."

"What?"

Henry said nothing.

"Henry?"

"I'm sorry, Sophie. Really I am."

Sophie frowned. Something changed in Henry's eyes.

She couldn't move.

It didn't matter.

He lunged forward, clasped Sophie's head, and forced her beneath the water. As she slipped beneath the murky surface, her eyes widened in surprise. Her mouth opened and Henry held his wife's head under the water. "I'm sorry, Sophie. I really am. I can't, and won't, be married to a cripple...and I can't be married to you anymore. This marriage has been stagnant for some time."

He spoke calmly as his large hands easily held Sophie down. Bubbles erupted from her mouth as he drowned her, her useless body unable to fight back. Strands of her hair tangled around his fingers and surfed the water's surface.

"It's best for all involved. I did love you, Sophie. This opportunity is perfect for us. I get to start again. You get to die in peace."

Her eyes closed as her oxygen diminished. A jet of urine sprayed into the bath silently. Sophie shook her head violently, futilely. Henry was just too strong.

A smile crossed his lips.

"You found out about my affair. I knew you would. You're a clever woman. It's best that you knew anyway. At least this way

I'm being honest and upfront with you. I can't be the man who divorced a cripple...I couldn't stand that, and it wouldn't do my career any good. I can't have you taking me to the cleaners, Sophie, I just *can't*."

She ceased moving. Her limp body floated in the dirty water, her eyes slowly closed, her lips and skin a glittery blue and purple.

The stench of hot urine and stale bath water filled the bathroom.

Henry released his dead wife and stood up, wiping his hands on a towel. He looked around and walked out of the bathroom. After a second, he stepped forward, pushed his hands into the water once more and rolled his wife over, turning her face down. Out of respect.

Respect, thought Henry. *Funny word considering*.

She floated under the water. Her body bumped against the side of the bath. Once again, Henry wiped his hands on the towel.

"Bye, Sophie." Henry walked out of the room. As he went, he turned off the lights and closed the door.

"Well?"

He spun around and smiled at Katrina, his new girlfriend. He closed the door behind him and leant against it. Katrina sucked on a lollipop and smiled. "I got bored of waiting outside. Hope that's okay."

Henry nodded.

"You have a nice home." Katrina stepped out into the hallway.

"It's not mine. This is the wife's...now. Like I told you, I'm leaving her for you. She'll understand."

"Is she home?" Katrina seemed startled.

"No, she must have gone out." He noticed Sophie's clothes scattered around the room and walked towards Katrina, distracting her. "Let's say we get out of here. There's nothing keeping me here anymore. Where shall we go?"

"A hotel?"

"I was thinking Paris or Rome."

"Oooh, how romantic."

"How would you like to live there?"

"You're joking, right?"

"I never joke about Paris or Rome."

"What, just up and go?"

"Why not?"

"It's a hell of a decision."

"We're actors. We can go anywhere."

Katrina smiled. She rubbed her chin thoughtfully.

Henry ushered her out the front door. He closed it behind him but didn't secure the latch. *They'll think someone broke in.* He smiled again then placed a hand on Katrina's rump. "So, what will it be?"

"I can't decide. Paris or Rome?"

"Let's do both."

"Really?"

"What's stopping us?"

"Nothing."

"So?"

Katrina chuckled. "This is insane. Yes."

"Yes? Excellent. We can buy clothes on the way."

"How exciting. Shopping and a holiday. Are you a catch or what?" Katrina leaned in and kissed her beau on the lips. Henry reciprocated. He pulled away and smiled, his blue eyes mesmerizing her. "Shall we?"

"Yes, let's go."

Within moments, Katrina and Henry climbed into the BMW at the curb. The car scooted off into the night. Then, all was silent. The night was crisp, damp with imminent rain.

In the bathtub, Sophie opened her eyes.

Roger Cowin

The Pumpkin Man

Come the Fall of the year
When the harvest moon reigns o'er the autumn sky,
Scarecrows form their crosses alight
To play mischievous games
   Of peek-a-boo and I see you
All across the October countryside.
"All hail!" The Pumpkin Man, they sing
As he rises from the field, the Harvest King.

Allamagoosalums and jump-a-bodies
Lurk aside many a dark and chary path,
Ready to pounce out and grasp
Any stranger unwise enough to trespass
   Upon their nocturnal lair,
But pay no mind to such jocular scares,
Even the devil's imps give way
When The Pumpkin Man holds sway.

Ghosts and goblins and ghoul girls too,
Cavort and prance beneath a ghastly moon,
Skeletons arise from their graves
To rattle their bones in a Halloween jive
   And dance a grim fandango
At the Midnight Monster Rave.
But the party doesn't really begin
Until The Pumpkin Man waltzes in.

Born of demon seed, sowed in the blood
Soaked soil of the desolate Midwest,
He haunts the October Country,
Hiding behind night's façade,
   The laughing, malevolent Jester,
The King of the Goblin Masquerade.
Come one, Come all, creatures both great and small
Attend thee now the Pumpkin Man's Grand Ball

Roger Cowin

The Legend of the Crying Woman

1.

The Heacock Road lay just north of Dublin, Indiana off US 40. The road is still there but closed to traffic after the road and its infamous bridge fell into disuse during the 1970's. Brush and weeds have taken over much of the road that was never more than a narrow, graveled lane barely wide enough for two cars to pass. Surrounded by old growth woods on both sides, the trees grow so close together that even at high noon the sun barely penetrates the dense canopy.

The road crosses Symonds Creek, a shallow stream that routinely overflows its banks during the spring thaw but has dried to a muddy bog by the time the hot, sticky dog days of late August roll around. An old wooden bridge offered 19th-century travelers passage across the stream for over a century until iron rails were added as a safety measure when automobiles became commonplace. The bridge is mostly gone now, only a bit of iron remains and a few well-weathered, wooden planks. But in the 1950's and 60's the bridge was a popular parking spot for local teens wanting to watch submarine races or simply spook each other with ghost stories.

Legends surrounding the area date back to the Native American tribes who occupied the land centuries before the coming of the white man. Tales of ghostly apparitions and strange creatures convinced the Delaware and Miami tribes that the area was cursed and despite the rich, fertile soil that made it ideal for cultivation, was neither farmed nor hunted until the pioneers settled the region in the early part of the 19th century. Even then, the immediate vicinity surrounding Symonds creek remained surprisingly sparse of habitation.

The present day legends of the Heacock Road Bridge, later known as The Cry Woman Bridge, can be traced back to an incident in the fall of 1948.

The war was over, and it looked like good times had come around again. The economy and the housing industry were booming, new cars were rolling off the lines in Detroit and soldiers, just back from Europe and the South Pacific, were settling down to the real business of raising families and building the most powerful nation in the world.

East central Indiana was no different than the rest of the country; the factories ran 24/7, churning out suddenly in-demand consumer goods, and the Datlows were no different than any other young couple in America. Frank Datlow had spent the war defending his country from the Japanese menace and had come home with a chest full of medals and a powerful hankering to serve the Lord, who he credited for his surviving the war. After mustering out, Frank returned to his home in Knightstown, Indiana, promptly married his high school sweetheart, Mary Ellen Finster, and set about becoming a Baptist minister.

It wasn't long before he was ordained and he and Mary Ellen had become the proud parents of a chunky, cheery baby boy they named Harry Winston, after Truman and Churchill respectively. Then in March of '48, Frank was offered the position of pastor at the First Baptist Church in nearby Dublin.

Frank immediately set about charming his new congregation and increasing its membership with his jovial, youthful charisma. Mary Ellen was the perfect wife; smart, sweet, and pretty, with long blonde hair and a pair of kewpie doll eyes. Their future seemed assured, but this happy existence would only last a few months before coming to a cruel, crushing end. It was late October, Mary Ellen and little Harry were visiting the Kolger's farm out on Wagner Road while Frank finished some work back at the church. Mary Ellen and Linda Kolger had become good friends over the past few months; both were mothers in their early twenties and enjoyed their weekly visits. They could get lost for hours discussing local gossip and the trials of *Stella Dallas,* their favorite radio show. It was almost full dark before Mary Ellen realized she had lost track of time, and Frank was probably done with his work. She knew he'd be waiting for her to pick him up, checking his watch every few minutes and tapping his foot impatiently. Phones were not so common in rural Indiana back in those days, and neither the Kolgers nor the church had one.

Hastily, Mary Ellen made her goodbyes, promising to see them at Sunday services, and climbed behind the wheel of her Mercury. Placing Harry on the front seat beside her, she gave the sleeping infant a quick peck on his forehead. The year-old Harry had gone to sleep earlier, and Mary knew he would stay asleep until Frank was in the car; then he would insist on waking him up to play with him on the ride home.

Dark, angry clouds rolled across the sky; lightning flashed in the distance and the low, ominous rumble of thunder announced an impending storm.

"You be careful Mary," Linda warned, "especially going down Heacock. It can get pretty slickery, and it's always washing out."

Mary Ellen promised she'd be careful, put the car in reverse and backed out onto Wagner Road. Despite her promise, Mary soon had the car up to fifty, her anxiety over reaching Frank before the storm hit outweighing her usual cautiousness. In fact, she would have missed her turnoff to Heacock if a sudden strobing flash of lightning hadn't momentarily illuminated the road. She took the turn too fast, spraying gravel and slaloming dangerously toward the ditch before regaining control. Relieved she hadn't wound up in the ditch, she slowed her speed as she passed the lone farmhouse on Heacock. After that it was just woods until she hit the outskirts of town. Luckily, the road wasn't a long one, and she figured she could make the church in ten minutes, less if she nudged the gas just a little. That was when the sky unleashed a furious deluge of rain and hail.

Mary Ellen flipped on the wipers, goosed the engine just a little more and chanced a hurried glance at Harry just to make sure he was still sleeping. She looked back up just in time to see she had drifted to the left side too much; suddenly the Heacock Road Bridge was filling her windshield. As another burst of lightning lit up the night, she slammed into the iron railing, crumpling the Merc like tinfoil and crushing Mary between the dash and the steering wheel. The last thing she saw before her spirit fled her body was little Harry being propelled through the windshield.

The sound of the crash could be heard all the way to the Johnson farm back at the intersection of Wagner and Heacock. Ralph Johnson threw on his slicker and rubbers, jumped into the cab of his old '37 Ford pickup and raced to the site of the wreck. Keeping his headlights aimed at the destroyed Mercury, he grabbed a torch from the seat and ran into the rain.

"Lord, oh Lord! They's dead for sure," Ralph muttered as he shone the light into the car.

One look and he knew Mary Ellen was dead; she looked like a bloody rag doll. Her head was laying on the steering wheel, eyes opened wide in shock and horror as if she had seen something so awful that even death could not erase the memory. As he walked toward the front of the car looking for anyone who might have been thrown from the vehicle, he felt his boot sink into something soft and small. He looked down and promptly puked up the chicken and gravy he had been having for supper. He had stepped on the broken, ravaged body of baby Harry. What really struck Ralph, what haunted him the rest of his life was that above the neck, there was nothing; Harry's head had been ripped completely from his body.

2.

"They never found his head, and ever since that night the ghost of Mary Ellen walks up and down the creek, carrying her baby's body, searching for his head." Steve knew he had told the story well by Beth's body language. She had pushed close enough that he could feel the gentle push of her breasts against his chest. He could feel his dick hardening in his jeans, and he only hoped tonight wouldn't end with another case of blue balls.

Steve and Beth had been going steady since the end of their junior year of high school, and Steve had diligently spent the summer trying to get past first base. It was now October of 1971 and they were both seniors, but Steve was no closer to breaking Beth's resolve than he had been on their first date. They had been parking on Heacock Road plenty of times, but their heated make-out sessions had always ended in frustration, with Beth pushing him away while insisting that she wasn't that kind of girl. Steve had begged, pled and even said the L word in an attempt to persuade her to go further, but to no avail. He had to be content to go home alone, horny and confused, where he would masturbate bitterly while thinking about her breasts, how they would feel in his hands, how her hands would feel wrapped around his cock.

Tonight though, he had been a gentleman. The Lincoln High School football team, which Steve quarterbacked, had destroyed nearby Hagerstown. After the game they had gone to the Friday dance, then to the Pizza King before Steve had convinced her to go with him to the Crying Woman Bridge. They pulled off the road as far as they could without winding up in the woods. The headlamps of Steve's '57 Bel-Air lit up the bridge, the harsh light casting an eerie, haunted glow on the old iron. The trees, many already shorn of their summer foliage, looked shrunken and misshapen, like twisted, demented giants, their gnarled limbs reaching out, ready to grasp any unwary traveler.

He was surprised to find they were the only couple parking at the bridge. Usually Friday nights would find any number of cars parked alongside the road, as the local kids looked for a quiet place to mack with their honeys, drink beer or hold impromptu ghost hunts for the Crying Woman.

He shut off the Chevy's lights, leaving them in inky darkness. On the radio, The Temptations were singing *Just My Imagination* as he slipped his arm around Beth's shoulders, pulling her close. He sighed as he felt her tighten up. Damn she could be such a cold fish. He remembered his buddy Dennis telling him the best way to get into a girl's pants was by scaring them a little, which was why it always better to take a girl to a horror flick than a comedy or drama.

"You know why they call this the Crying Woman Bridge don't you?" Steve said.

Of course, Beth knew. Every kid who grew up in Dublin or Cambridge City knew the story, but if it would postpone Steve's fumbled groping and clumsy attempts to touch her boobs then she was more than happy to play dumb. It wasn't like she wasn't attracted to him. He was tall, blonde, athletic, intelligent, and Beth rather fancied he looked like Robert Redford. A dozen colleges were already trying to recruit him to play football, but Beth had been raised to be a good girl. She would never dare show it, but she was just as revved up by their makeout sessions as him. When he dropped her off at her door after a night of particularly heavy necking, she would rush inside, slam her bedroom door, throw herself on her bed, wriggle out of her soaked panties and use her fingers to bring herself to one shuddering orgasm after another. Afterwards, she would feel guilt and loathing; certain she was a whore and headed to Hell for sure.

"Something about a woman being killed here and her ghost haunting the bridge," she replied innocently.

Steve smiled, and in the scariest voice he could manage he recited the legend of the Crying Woman. When he was done, and Beth was pressed so sweetly against him, he let his hand drift back to her breast. This time she didn't immediately remove his hand. Instead, she pressed against him harder as his tongue slipped inside her mouth. He could taste pizza and Juicy Fruit on her breath, but he was far too excited to care. She placed her hand on his thigh, close to his erection, yet not quite touching it which made it, maddeningly, all the more exciting. Then from the back seat came the sound of a baby crying.

Steve felt his heart leap to his mouth. Beth's eyes went wide, and her face turned white as the blood rushed from her head. Both clinched each other tighter as the baby's cry came again.

"Mama," it cried, a small, weak voice.

"Oh my God! Steve it's her baby. Oh my God! Oh my God!" Beth was screaming hysterically.

"Oh shit!" he said. Horrified by what he might see if he looked in his back seat but sickly compelled by the need to face his fear, he turned, his eyes bulging in terror. Suddenly, he burst out

laughing.

Beth looked at him like he had lost his mind as he leaned into the back seat and picked up a baby doll with a plastic head and soft body. Beth recognized it as a Baby Tender doll.

Steve dropped back in his seat, holding the doll with one hand and still laughing. "My little sister's. She must have left it when I took her to her dance class earlier."

Beth joined him in relieved laughter as the doll, obviously broken, again cried out "Mama, Mama."

Steve punched the doll, shaking his head and prepared to toss it back into the rear seat when Beth went bug-eyed and began shrieking.

"Beth, it's just a stupid doll. What...?"

She had slid all the way back across the seat, her head pressed against the passenger side window and was pointing wildly at something behind Steve. Bemused, he turned around to see what had freaked her out so badly. Probably just jumping at shadows at this point, he thought.

Once again, his heart lurched but this time it didn't come back down. Pressed against the driver's side window was a grey, mottled face, its mouth twisted in a blood-caked, grisly leer, milky eyes devoid of pupils, and wrinkled skin that sagged as if submerged in water for weeks. The thing's damp hair hung in unruly strings caked with algae. She slapped the window with her malformed hands, and Steve could see her nails had continued to grow after death into loathsome, yellow talons.

He was vaguely aware he had pissed himself. He knew they should be going, but he was beyond rational thought at that point. He was reduced to just staring into the gruesome face of the Crying Woman, a strange, little hiccupping whimper strangling his throat.

"*MY BABY, WHERE'S MY BABY?*" The Crying Woman croaked in a raspy, watery voice. "*I HEARD HIM CRYING FOR ME. GIVE HIM TO ME.*"

"*Steve, would you drive goddammit?*" Beth was screaming.

Like a zombie, he tried to obey. Still mewling pitifully, he tried to put the car in gear and promptly killed the engine. He reached down and turned the key, pumping the gas pedal furiously in his panic. The engine hitched but wouldn't turn over. Again he cranked the ignition, wincing and cursing at its stubborn, grinding growl.

Beth continued screaming at him to hurry up and start the *frigging car already*. The Crying Woman continued to beat at the window, shrieking and pleading for them to return her baby.

As her attacks became more violent, Steve became certain she would break through the window before he could get the damn car started.

"COME ON! COME ON YOU BITCH!" he cried in frustration, bashing the steering wheel with his palms in an impromptu tantrum that did nothing to coax the car to start.

Just when he was certain he had flooded the engine, the window crashed in and a pair of icy, clammy hands found his face. he screamed, a combination of fear, anger and desperation, depressed the clutch and turned the ignition hard.

The car roared to life. He slammed it into gear and sped away in a spray of gravel and smoke. He felt the dead woman's fingers slipping from his face as he pulled away, but her nails scraped across his skin, leaving three deep scratches across his cheek. He heard her screeching in anger as she sensed her prey escaping. Her cries, filled with so much anguish and pain, that he almost felt sorry for her.

"Don't stop Steve, just don't stop whatever you do don't stop." Beth had her legs drawn up in a fetal position, and Steve saw she was still clutching the doll to her chest like a protective charm.

He kept his foot on the accelerator as he ventured a glance in his rear view mirror and was so shocked that he almost went off the road. The thing was still right on his bumper, clawing and scratching, her ghastly face filled with hate and pain. He pressed down harder on the gas but how in the hell do you outrun a ghost?

Then, just like that, she was gone. One minute her whole face seemed to fill the rearview mirror and the next, she had simply vanished.

They hit Wagner Road at better than 70 miles an hour, and Steve didn't let up on the gas until he hit Foundry Road on the outskirts of Cambridge City. It was his plan to head to the police station and hope that Officer Channing was there catching a few z's instead of out rousting kids making out in the park. But he had no intention of going to the cops with his pants soaked in urine. If that got around everybody'd think he was a pansy. He pulled over next to a secluded copse of trees and shut off the car.

"WHY ARE WE STOPPING? STEVE, WHY ARE WE STOPPING?"

He shut off the car and looked at Beth. "It's okay. She's gone. I just got to do something first; then we'll go."

She looked at him with pleading eyes. "I want to go home Steve, *PUH-LEEZE, take me home.*"

"I'll take you home in a bit. Just settle down, I want to go to

Channing and report this..."

"Then let's go report it, but let's get out of here," she whined.

"Beth, I promise we'll leave in just a minute. I kind of wet myself back there, and I just need to slip on a pair of clean jeans and we'll go."

"I don't care. I peed myself a little too. I don't want to stop here."

Steve sighed and opened the car door. "Look, the Marcum's house is just across the street there. You can see their lights still on. Probably up watching Sammy Terry or something. Nothing is going to happen right here in town. I'll be right back."

"STEVE, COME BACK!" She yelled as he climbed out of the car. She rolled down her window and continued calling him as he walked behind the car and opened the trunk. He opened his gym bag and got out a clean pair of jeans he always kept for emergencies. He slammed the trunk and noticed four huge scratches going down the trunk. More evidence, he thought touching his face. His fingers came away smeared with blood. He'd have to get that cleaned as soon as he got home, no telling what kind of diseases that thing had been carrying.

"I'll be right back," he assured Beth as he headed for the privacy of some nearby bushes.

"Hurry!" Beth yelled out the window before rolling it up, as an afterthought she hurriedly locked all the doors.

She settled back in her seat, realized she was still clutching the Baby Tender doll, and tossed it in the backseat where it gave one last, weak cry before falling silent. Her heart was still thumping along like a steam locomotive as she glanced nervously from window to window, terrified that the next thing she'd see would be that grotesque, insane face staring back at her. She couldn't believe it had been real; it was just supposed to be a *story*, a scary little bedtime tale kids told each other for fun. Whatever that thing had been, it was much more than some mere spook or lost spirit, it had substance and mass.

What was keeping Steve? He should have been back by now; it doesn't take that long for a guy to change. Maybe he had to pee again? Her own bladder felt pretty full. She wondered if Steve would keep watch while she squatted behind the bushes. It would be embarrassing but not as humiliating as peeing all over his seat. She had dribbled a bit in her underwear when that hag had been attacking the car, but nothing that would show.

The back of the car settled for a moment and came back up.

About time, she thought.

She craned her neck to look out the back window, squinting

her eyes to penetrate the dark. She thought sure that had been Steve coming back, but she couldn't see any sign of him. He should have been back by now.

Not sure how much longer she could wait she used her left arm to unlock the door and pulled the handle with her right. The dome light came on, momentarily blinding her. She got out, surprised by how weak and shaky her legs were. She knew one thing for sure, she would never ever, not in a million years, go within a mile of Heacock Road. As quietly as she could, she closed the car door and turned to go find Steve.

The autumn air was crisp and chill, wet with the scent of coming rain. She shivered and clutched her sweater, rubbing her arms to warm them. Standing there exposed, she looked back in the direction of Heacock, uncomfortably aware of how close the bridge was as the crow flies. Really she could walk there in minutes if she crossed through the woods.

In the distance, she could hear the sound of a television coming from the Marcum's house. She could see the blue flicker of the screen through their picture window and considered crossing the street to see if she could borrow their phone. She had known the Marcum family all her life. She knew they wouldn't mind.

Still, she should have a quick look for Steve. She noticed he had left the trunk ajar and walked towards the rear of the car, suddenly feeling preternaturally aware of every sound around her; the Marcum's TV, the wind bustling the tree limbs, the crunch of her feet on the desiccated leaves beneath her shoes. She touched the trunk as a tiny whimper escaped her lips, and a rush of hot urine ran down her legs.

Steve's mangled body had been tossed in the trunk. At least she *thought* it was Steve. It was wearing the same blue Oxford and crisp jeans, but she couldn't be certain because above the neck...nothing.

As Beth backed away from the trunk, she felt the scream building in her throat. Somehow *she* had followed them, found them; sniffed them out like a hound following a coon's scent and just a few minutes before, Beth had become aware of how close the bridge was, how quickly one could walk to it. And a ghost? Who knew what was too far for a ghost?

From the darkness of the woods, The Crying Woman shuffled out; her ghastly, blood streaked face made even more hideous by the ecstatic, lunatic grin on her face.

"*I finally found my baby's head,*" she croaked in a watery, sepulchral voice that was almost tender as she held out Steve's severed head, its eyes and mouth opened wide in an eternal, silent scream.

Beth found that she couldn't scream after all, not when her head was being ripped from her neck.

Roger Cowin

The Servant of God

June 10, 1912

The Servant of God boarded the train outside Paola, Kansas, and took a window seat so he could watch the blighted landscape pass by. America - Sodom and Gomorrah, a country so infected with sin even the soil was diseased. It had to be cleansed one sin at a time or the whole thing purified by fire, but that would take the innocent as well as the evil. The Servant's way was better, though more difficult, slicing out the sin one cancerous piece at a time.

The train was always the same: cracked leather seats; dirty, nicotine-stained windows; and the ugly, faded carpet that ran between the aisles. The appearance didn't matter. It was the chariot God chose to convey him on his mission. God didn't promise luxury, only salvation.

The train didn't always feel right though. Sometimes it felt like he was the sole passenger, other times it seemed filled far beyond capacity; men and women, laughing and talking, itinerant travelers on their way from here to there. They didn't bother The Servant. They were just background noise. He didn't talk to them, and they didn't talk to him.

The demons were a different matter. They came when his mind was idle, not contemplating the Lord or his mission. Some were hideous caricatures of humans; black, reptilian monsters with horns and forked tongues that flickered in and out of their leering mouths. Others were quite fair and lovely, scantily clad women with luscious forms and angelic faces who came bargaining for his soul, tempting him with offers of the flesh, promises of pleasures. Lies fell as easily from their lips as dung from a horse's ass. But they were only a minor annoyance; The Word always sent them shrieking back to the Bottomless Pit.

The train rumbled to a stop right outside Villisca, Iowa, and The Servant heard The Voice telling him this was the place. Grabbing his battered, well-traveled Bible – his only luggage -- he disembarked, the joy of serving in his heart.

The jarring clang of church bells called the faithful to morning worship. He wished he could be in church with them, sharing the fellowship and mutual love for The Lord, but there was more important work to do this Sabbath morning. Someone would be chosen to meet the Lord this day. The Servant was envious. He wished his burden would be taken from him, and he would be allowed to rest.

Sighing, he listened to the Lord's instructions which were telling him to proceed through town to a neat, three-story farmhouse. Jesus had also prayed for his burden to be removed. If God didn't listen to his own son then why should he listen to the pleas of a humble, common servant?

He would do as the Lord commanded. That small, still voice speaking to him, leading him to a neat, three-story farmhouse. He walked around the back of the house and looked in the shed. An axe stood propped against the back wall; the Lord bade him take it and enter the house through the backdoor.

The door was unlocked, just as God had told him it would be. The house was empty; God had told him it would be.

Off to worship, no doubt, The Servant thought.

Diligently he began exploring the house, memorizing the layout, touching things, getting a feel for the kind of family that would live here. He would need to operate in the dark. He had to know every inch of the house.

The axe was reassuring in his hand. He was certain this was the family who would be delivered this night. When he was confident he would be able to navigate the house by only the light of the moon, he followed the voice of the Lord to an upstairs bedroom. Inside a closet, a short flight of stairs led The Servant to a tiny, cramped attic.

Making himself as comfortable as possible, he squatted on the floor to await the fall of night.

Hours passed. The heat of the room rose steadily as the day drew on toward noon, and

The Servant of God kept his mute vigil amid the clutter and dust, praying silently. Even when the family returned from morning service, he resisted the temptation to peek out the attic window.

The Lord demanded he remain patient and in return he would receive a very special reward. The children brought two friends home to spend the night. The Servant sighed in anticipation. He loved delivering children best.

He felt his member hardening between his legs, waves of disgust rippled through his gut. That was not a proper reaction to salvation. He intensified his prayer until his excitement was driven back, and the vile organ once again went limp.

As the afternoon dragged towards evening, The Servant dozed in a half dream state, his unconscious mind becoming attuned to the rhythms and sounds of the household as it went about its Sunday routine.

He heard the children playing outside; their high, infectious laughter and the cheerful, pleasant voices of the adults as they talked among themselves. Later, came the sounds of pots and pans rattling and the odor of meat cooking that announced the arrival of dinner.

Gradually the long shadows crept in, bringing the slightly cooler temps of evening and the anonymity of darkness. He felt his pulse increase as his excitement built but still he waited, caressing the axe with loving adoration.

As full darkness settled over the attic, he felt rather than heard the children as they prepared for bed. He joined them in saying their bedtime devotions, praying as silently and fervently as stealth would allow. It was not until well past midnight that The Servant received permission to act.

"Go now, commend their souls to Heaven," came the quiet voice.

His legs were stiff and numb, refusing to work after so much idle time. As they awoke from their slumber, needles jabbed into his flesh. He ignored the pain, stretching carefully to unkink the muscle. Finally, he grabbed his axe and descended the stairs.

The Father and Mother were the first to receive salvation.

Even when The Servant smashed the axe into the man's head, the woman never stirred.

God kept them deep in slumber. As promised, they felt nothing and, within moments, they were with the Lord.

Next, he sought out the children, feeling the righteous joy of serving The Lord as he dispatched each child to their heavenly maker. Each release brought him greater and greater joy. He was born for this and given enough time, he would deliver the world. Again and again, his axe descended, sending blood flying black in the moonlight, and never once was a scream uttered. The only sound was the thud of the axe on skull and The Servant's heavy breath.

Nearly dawn when he finally stumbles out of the house, his muscles ache from his exertion, but also feel oddly refreshed as they always did after a deliverance. His clothes were saturated in blood, but no one was awake to see him as he retraced his journey through the town.

Up ahead, that old Glory train awaited him. Waiting to take him to the next stop down the line, to another family, another deliverance.

As he climbed aboard the train, he was struck by how like the maw of a hungry dragon the open door looked. For a moment, he wondered if he might be insane, but the voice of the train, like that of God, was louder and more compelling and the thrill of his ministry too addictive to deny.

Aurora, he thought, *next stop Aurora, Illinois.*

John Stanton

Yard Work

Frank's next-door neighbor's toy spitz's given name was Pepper, but he usually called him Peter. Because it drove him bat-shit crazy. Frank had just to yell "Peter!" and the dog's lips would curl back, unsheathing those nicotine-stained needles. Then came the menacing growl and lift-off, usually followed by a resounding yelp when the leash nearly snapped his neck.

Frank caught the familiar waddle of Selma Pilchard as she strutted down her driveway and headed in his direction on her morning walk, no doubt to complain about the noise from his A.M. labors. Beak always pointing to the North Star, all she needed was a monocle to be the incarnation of the late 1920s *The New Yorker* caricature. As she stalked up to Frank, Peter bared his teeth, snarled and leapt from her arms. Frank took a step to his right. He felt a cold shiver of guilt as the mutt sailed past him and into the hopper of his Uncle Phil's woodchipper. Selma shrieked, then dropped to her knees.

Moments later, Frank was in his kitchen pouring a glass of ice water for her, thoughts racing on apologies and penance; especially to his wife Pammie, who actually liked the diminutive Pomeranian snotball. Peter would eat kibble right out of her hand.

Through the kitchen window, he could see Selma, now rocking side-to-side, keening, the sun glistening off her diamond earrings. As he opened the screen door, she stood tall for a moment then dove headlong into the wood chipper.

"Why didn't I turn the damned thing off?"

When he got back to the chipper, all that was left of Selma that wasn't mulch, was a single red shoe where she last stood. As Frank jammed his thumb into the "Off" button, electricity shot through him and everything went black. He didn't know how long it was before he could see again, but it seemed like hours before he could pull himself up enough to sit.

"Mister? You OK? Did you hurt yourself?" A teenage girl's voice cooed from behind tousled blond locks. Frank managed an unintelligible guttural.

"Dude, what the hell happened here?" echoed tinny from the male-thing hovering next to her. School must have let out.

"Two bits, four bits, six bits, a dollar . . ." they chorused. Christ, she's a fucking cheerleader. Man-boy laced his fingertips together, and the girl stepped in his hands, placing her palms on his shoulders. "All for Southwest, stand up and holler!" She arced gracefully above the horizon—the diesel whined while the chipper blades gnashed dense bones and gristle, then returned to its steady hum. The boy then threw a leg over the hopper, cheerfully doffed his cap and said, "G'day, mate!" in a fake Aussie accent before he slid in after her. Frank puked until there was nothing left to hock up.

"This isn't fucking happening," he could hear himself snort. "Maybe the mutt, maybe Mrs. Pilchard . . . but *nobody* is going to believe *this* shit."

When he could stand, Frank kicked the crap out of the chipper; he hopped around with a broken toe while it chugged menacingly behind him.

Leaning against a tree, Frank frantically punched the keypad of his cell until Uncle Phil's phone rang. Meanwhile, a fat squirrel scrambled up to the lip of the hopper, sniffed the air for a few seconds, then flopped in. Uncle Phil's phone went to voice mail.

Back in his house, Frank hobbled around the kitchen nursing a cold brew. "Who can I call? The cops? The fire department? The Bureau of Haunted Woodcchippers?" He heard the damned thing whine again and bolted back outside.

The letter carrier's mailbag, stuffed with bills and advertisements, sat on the sidewalk, but no sign of Balding Bob, the man that delivered his mail for the past six years. No point in looking at the growing pile of gore behind the chipper.

He backed the Mini Cooper out of the garage and used it to impede about half of the access to the chipper. A few minutes later, while rolling a wheelbarrow stuffed with bulky garage crap and yard gnomes out to block off the other side, he saw the Fatso's Pizza delivery guy scramble up the Cooper and do a cannonball into the chipper hopper. The more obstacles Frank placed in its way, the more determined folks became—it averaged four people and a critter or two an hour for the next three hours. He could have sold tickets.

Frank jammed his shovel into the spinning flails of the woodchipper, and all he got for his trouble was a dislocated shoulder, which he slammed against the garage door frame until bone popped back into socket.

Only when he had stopped screaming did he notice the shrapnel in his leg.

Frank used his belt as a makeshift tourniquet. He hobbled back to the chipper and watched with fascination as it gorged itself on an elderly man's leg. The old man sat on the lip of the hopper, weeping and wobbling, looking at Frank with pleading eyes. Frank obliged and gave the old fellow a helpful shove. Moments later, the crimson maw spat out a titanium knee. It clipped Frank on his left temple.

With the thud of metal to bone came searing pain–and epiphany. Prometheus. Odysseus. Kris Humphries. Frank realized he had joined the roster of those royally fucked by the gods.

He laughed until tears rolled down his cheeks. He pulled out his phone and flipped between numbers in the address book. Wilmer Gerhardt, his boss. Pammie's mother. Floyd Bishop, who had debagged him in high school. Clive Wilson, whom Pammie promised she'd never see again ....

"Eeny, meeny, miny, moe . . . which of you has got to go?"

Frank thought for a long moment, then dialed the number.

James Park

Zombi 6: Salvation

March 23, 2064

Dear Nobody,

I've struggled endlessly over the most appropriate way to address this letter. The truth is, I could have addressed it any number of ways—To Whom It May Concern; To Whom It Doesn't Concern; To Whom It Will Never Concern—and it wouldn't have made one severed-hand's worth of difference.

Given that our population has dwindled to meager proportions, Dear Nobody carries the charm—or better yet, *the genuineness*—that I'm after. I pity the imbecile that's chosen to carry on in this world of shit, just as I laugh at the nincompoop who truly believes that the world has reached its end. Our insignificance never occurred to us, *now did it?* We're nothing more than a supercilious species that refuses to acknowledge the fallibility of our instincts. We ignore our shortcomings, marching through life like a schizophrenic Third Reich, adamant that our demise will inevitably equate to the end of all existence. Well, I spit in the eye of those who refuse to acknowledge the footprints of those who've marched before us. Look at all the psychopaths we've lived with and ask yourself this, *how is it that the human species never managed to completely destroy the world?*

I credit our incompetence, for I know we tried. We bit the hand that feeds us many times, but we never managed to bite off any fingers. Sure, we left our share of scratches, some scars along the palm, but the damage wasn't anything that couldn't be ignored. We carried on, and we shouldn't forget that we're still carrying on. Our history hasn't completely ended. I'm still writing the written word, and that makes it true, that there's still a chance that we'll finally do ourselves in. Maybe we'll pull off the big one before the plague wipes the rest of us out. Maybe we'll bring back the bomb, and obliterate the ground that nourishes our tired feet.

Go ahead. Push the button. I dare you. It's the only thing left of value, so we might as well take it too. All other ideologies are lost. Nothing matters anymore, not one bloody torso, for my immortality is dying the same slow and agonizing death as the greater human species. I'm a published author, you have to understand, and I've lived the better part of my life under the misconception that my words will live forever. That's what we writers want, you know. We seek immortality. We want future generations to collect our works and preserve our thoughts. And even more so, we want coming of age geniuses to acknowledge the trail of inspiration that we leave behind. Let them read what we've written. Let them rise to fruition on the influence of our words. The path we're paving only matters so long as our followers continue to pave a path of their own.

My organs have always been destined to die, to slowly rot their way into the soil. *But the words I've written?* I used to fancy them living on in perpetuity. *And why not?* I've frightened thousands of people with my ghost stories, so much so that even the most devoted horror aficionado dare not read my work after dark. I'm brilliant, I tell you, I'm fucking brilliant. That's why it pains me to admit that the rate of conception is dwindling; they'll be no future generations to embrace my stories for the twisted rite of passage they are. I've dedicated my life and my blood to giving the world nightmares, and now that we're living in a nightmare there's no more interest in my work. We're a peculiar species, you have to understand, for we're easily captivated by stories that introduce the unfamiliar, yet we bore much too quickly with the perplexities of our own surroundings. The world used to embrace my nightmares, now we shun the horror of our survival.

Everyone says the end is upon us. I've seen it written across the countryside, painted on barns and rooftops, graffitied beneath the underbelly of metropolitan wastelands: *The End Is Here.* And when you come across a living, breathing human being (you know, the kind that has yet to die and then reanimate into a walking corpse), they'll tell you the same thing: "This is the end of the world."

I suppose we shouldn't blame them for thinking such simplistic thoughts. Without schools, education has become a burden of the past. Just ask the Jack Kerouac reincarnate, if you can find him. And if you can't then I encourage you to lament the fact that we no longer have the media to warp our thoughts. There's no more television, and radio broadcasts are the luxury of a long forgotten era. I can't even get a landline to work, let alone my cell phone. And the internet? It's dead and buried, just like Dan Quayle. We have no military, no coastguard, and no Interpol. They quit making cars in Detroit well over a decade ago. Smoke no longer gushes from factories into smog-infested skies. It's true, I tell you, it's true. You can walk down the street without a gas mask, though you'd be foolish to embark on such adventures without a samurai sword. I'll be the first to admit that I'm no Sonny Chiba, but I carry my weapon with pride, and I've slayed my share of reanimated dead.

Ugh. I quiver at the thought. It makes my stomach churn, like I've swallowed a strip of dirty blotter paper. The walking corpses are such a vile and disgusting continuation of our species. They carry no shame. *None.* It sickens me, but I'm not going to waste Nobody's time discussing the obvious, for when you've lost the ability to think, or even rationalize, *then what's the point in accepting shame?* All they know is hunger, but not a breed of hunger that shows in their eyes; all you see in their eyes is the blank nothingness of a drug addict. They crave our brains and our blood like a junkie craves a great big dose of nothingness simmering atop a burnt spoon. The similarities are countless, but there's one small difference, and this difference matters more than those reanimated slabs of death will ever understand. You see, the earth provides the junkie an endless supply of medicine; it's simply a matter of cultivation and distribution, which eventually works its way into a matter of preservation. The addict's stash may run low, and the occasional bout of junk sickness may take hold, but it's only a matter of time until the junkie finds warmth in a new supply. Zombies are different. Those piles of walking bones, wrapped in dead flesh that hangs from their shoulders and clings to their ribs, are not feeding on an endless supply of brains. It's a bitter truth, though they'll never understand the economics of their own demise. The sad thing is, the human species doesn't much get it either. We don't have television to inform us, just as we don't have journalists to mislead us. I can't even remember the last time I received a piece of mail, had one of my ghost stories published, or read any halfway intelligent commentary on the current development of our depravity.

Call it a big step backwards if you will, but this is not the end of the world; I don't care what anyone else has to say about it. Darwin figured out evolution on his own, and he didn't have the benefit of social media to help spread the word. It's true. But the man did have access to a printing press, and this seems to have made all the difference. I have no such luxury. When your resources include nothing more than a pen and a piece of paper, then you might as well stuff your letter in a bottle and hurl it out to sea. Or maybe tie the wretched thing to a birdie before he heads south for the winter. That's all the hope I have. Some of us will carry on, and my work might find its way into the hands of a survivor. But it will never be preserved in a library or garner the type of cult following that's previously been reserved for literature that rises from the catacombs of our bizarre sickness.

The human species is doomed, I tell you. But the truth is, I don't see the reanimated dead surviving this thing either. Sure, the fewer in number we become, the larger their population grows. I've watched them, and I understand their needs, but still, it's not what you think. This hunger that drives them, it can be satisfied only with human flesh. I've tried feeding them rabbits, even thrown a few rodents their way. They won't have it. I left the carcass of a freshly slaughtered boar on the roadside, and they hobbled right past it, arms outstretched as they wandered aimlessly in hopes of human flesh. You should see what happens when they go too long without. If you've ever taken the kind of drugs that you really shouldn't have taken, then you know what it's like to need. You've had every organ in your body working against you, collaborating in an effort to pump sickness through your blood, to the point that you want to crawl out of your skin. Watch what happens when the reanimated dead go without human flesh. They actually do it. The damn things crawl out of their own skin. Oh, it all starts with a little shaking, and you can see the agitation palpitate on the surface of their rotting bodies. Their fingers rattle, and if they've still got toes they curl them inwards while the rest of their body convulses. Some of them try to form fists, but they never quite succeed. What they do succeed at is ripping the skin from their skeletons. It's an intriguing yet disgusting spectacle. Their blood, for whatever reason, is black, almost tarlike. And their veins seep the depraved nectar of death. But even as their skin is separated from their frame, they're still undead, and they quiver on the ground, flapping like a fish that's been culled from the ocean and discarded along the shore. They gasp for air and clutch at the open wound of their dismembered torso, but the hunger is never quenched, and permanent death inevitably follows.

It's a most unnerving sight. And you, my non-existent reader, you might be wondering why I share such vulgar insight. Fact is, I shouldn't have to. The most rudimentary concept of economics is supply and demand. They're eating us faster than we can possibly reproduce. Much faster. We grow small in number as they grow dense in population. And now they're dying of starvation. That's why every survivor I encounter claims it's the end of the world. *This is the end, my friend, the end.* I've heard it everywhere I wander, and I laugh in the face of this ridiculousness.

I can breathe metropolitan air. I can walk down the street without the protection of a gas mask, though it's still not an enjoyable experience. *But do you know what has become an enjoyable experience?* Let me tell you. I've been living in the Maymont Mansion of Richmond for a spell longer than a year, and every week I catch some fish from a nearby pond. Mother Nature still holds employment, for seasons come and seasons go. It rains, and it pours. The sun rises and the sun sets. I've watched this happen, Dear Nobody, just as I've watched the Earth make an entire lap around the sun, and I swear the water in this pond looks cleaner than it did a year ago. It's simply astonishing.

Plants grow naturally the whole world over, yet it's been more than a decade since humans have smothered them with growth chemicals and pesticides. Things have changed. We don't drink from plastic bottles anymore, and we can't pilfer meat from the grocery stores. We kill what we need, and what we don't need keeps on living. *Quite amazing, wouldn't you agree?* Animals used to die needlessly, only to have their meat spoil on a shelf, all in the interest of providing the suburbanites with whatever variety might suit their whim on any given day.

They call the zombie apocalypse the end of the world, and I spit in the face of this absurdity. The humans will suffer their extinction, and the zombies will follow. But the world, if anything, needs this to survive. Our planet will continue to make laps around the sun, and the animal populations will grow larger and larger. All we're experiencing is the end of the human species. And I assure you of one thing, the other creatures have yet to express even the tiniest morsel of disappointment.

But let's not grow overzealous with the promise of a rejuvenated world for we're embracing the reality of our extinction. In a Henry David Thoreau sort of way, it's really not that bad. Oh, the bloody hypocrite hated humanity, but still he thrived on the notion that a literate population existed, for without one only Dear Nobody would have read his work. I have no such luxury, yet here I sit, pen in hand, leaving my thoughts behind. You have to trust me when I emphasize that it's not nearly as bad as you think. Ted Kaczynski survived just fine inside his little hut. Nature provided for him, and in return he did his part to control the population problem. Oh, the things society did to him. They certainly weren't kind. *But what more can we expect?* It's just like the masses to lock up a murderer, label him a madman, and then give the media free reign to exploit the innocence of his beliefs. Maybe the lies are true.

Maybe he deserved incarceration, for he was a tyrant to civilization, but to the world he was a bit of a savior.

We have a history of environmentalists being cast aside as crazies, and this history is a bloody one indeed. Charles Manson used to complain about factories built where his trees once grew. His water was so bad that the fish couldn't live. It's no lie. The polar icecaps have melted away, murdered by the hands of manmade machines. We never took the time to notice, and we're going to get what we deserve. But deep down inside, I know things could have been different.

When the holy wars moved upon the planet, Mr., Charlie Manson saw the blood splattered on the wall, and he warned us. He told the people to follow him, that they'd get free LSD and under-aged girls if they'd just quit cutting down trees and polluting the water. Call the man a lunatic all you want, but these days the offer doesn't sound half-bad, *now does it?* I'll take that deal. Really. Just give me a chance, and I'll ride dune buggies into the dessert. I'll wait there until the race wars are over. Hell, I'll even buy your music, Charlie Manson, and I'll listen carefully for your subliminal retort to the Beatles prophecy of that notion known as Helter Skelter. But in the end, no one cares to listen to the world's most outspoken malcontent, just as nobody places the good of the earth before their own need for survival.

Charlie took the world for what it was: just a great big prison. He understood that confinement doesn't begin and end at the gate, but that prison is in the mind, locked to one world that is dead and dying, and unlocked to another that's free and alive. It's all about atwa. Get it? It's about the air, the trees, and the water. Charlie grasped the true workings of the world. He's walking through forever, man. And look at us. We're clinging tenaciously to an immediate impulse called survival. It's because we refused to listen. We locked him up over a few measly murders, you know, just a couple of grocery store owners and a pack of celebrities that the world wouldn't have missed. And look at us now.

What's happened in the past is a shame, and what's happening right now is no small concern. Sometimes I don't even acknowledge the predecessors of my surroundings. I've seen cities overrun with the reanimated dead; it's like a great big fucking infestation of malformed vermin. But I've also seen cities that harbor nothing more than the stillness and finality of death. In the wake of our dwindling population, I've explored ghost town after ghost town, searching for answers from the dead. We have such a breadth of history to learn from, yet hardly a soul remains to inherit this knowledge. It's only a matter of time until we're down to none. But still I take refuge in the abandoned cities, even if the reanimated dead insist on scouring them for morsels of human brains.

No city has fascinated me more than Richmond, Virginia. The history here is so rich, yet so dated. I've been through the Museum of the Confederacy more times than I can count, and I never grow tired of the exhibits. When I wrote professionally, nothing tickled my interests more than a well-crafted ghost story. But sadly I no longer find solace in a world constructed of fiction; I'm left with no choice but to embrace the marvels of reality, and this museum satisfies my ravenous thirst. Brother used to fight brother, right here in our country. Now brother fights the reanimated death of his brother, right here in our country, and the whole world over. Man has killed man. Ape has killed ape. Though I've never seen a zombie kill another zombie. It's not a moral decision, I tell you. They have no understanding of shame, just as they have no use for cannibalism. It's human flesh and brains that keep them alive, and their supply keeps dwindling. Some might see this as a changing of the times, but my solitary school of thought argues that the times haven't changed much at all. It was about survival then, and it's about survival now. It's evident that we're losing, but I'll go against the grain and argue that we didn't have a foot in this thing to begin with.

I miss the old days when we lived under the guise that our actions were right, that they were just. We may not have been winning the war against our own stupidity, but our private sanctuaries were cozy, and we forced ourselves to justify only the wars we raged against others; only the crazies cared to acknowledge the war that we unleashed upon ourselves. Locking them up was much too easy. *Problem solved!*

Now we're left with nothing more than the records of our own insanity, and I'm still alive to read them. I'll take whatever leftovers I can get, for I've always been a sucker for nostalgia. That's why I slay the reanimated dead with my trusted samurai sword. It's also why I've helped myself to a selection of muskets from the museum. They're not for protection, I assure you. They take too long to load, and cleaning the wretched things is a chore I care not to endure. You see, I've selected one of these muskets for a far more important purpose. And because I'm a sucker for nostalgia, I've also helped myself to an assortment of lead marbles. It's quite marveling what the bullets of yesterday looked like. They got the job done then, and they'll get the job done now. It's true. I've tried out all the muskets, taken my target practice, and like anything else I've found some that work better than others. The musket that shoots best is named Charlene, and I know what you must be thinking. This is my rifle; there are many like it. Well, Dear Nobody, this is my musket and to my knowledge, there aren't any others like it. That's why it was in a museum. *And so what if I named her Charlene?* I speak to her daily. So go ahead, lock me up with the crazies. I expect nothing better from the masses. And I'll stand resolute, for talking to Charlene is a rather healthy practice. Given the bloodshed I've witnessed and the solitude I've worked so hard to protect, I have to speak to something. Charlene rarely talks back, but I have trust in her, and I know when the time is right she'll perform the task I've sequestered her to perform.

There are people out there, I'm certain, who wouldn't take the step I'm going to take. Those people will live the remainder of their lives behind an illusionary veil of self-inflicted deception. Like I said before, this is not the end of the world, but rather a much needed turn of events. This, Dear Nobody, is necessary to secure the continuation of the world. Mother Nature is seeing to it.

I've selected a lead musket ball that's certain to get the job done, and I've named the bullet Salvation. It will be sometime next week, I suppose, before I venture out into the historic heart of Richmond, but the journey will be well worth my trouble. I'm going to have myself a seat beneath the statue of Oderus Urungus. I'm going to load Salvation into Charlene, and then I'm going to blow my brains all over the graffiti-covered monument. That's all there is to it. I am in a world of shit, and I see no reason to continue.

Go ahead, call me names, ridicule my decision, for if you're the Dear Nobody who reads this, then you're living among the foolish. You're struggling to survive in a world that brought back the dead for no other purpose than to purge itself of human waste. The cleansing is almost over. When it's done, the seasons will come, and the seasons will go. Birds will migrate south for the winter, and flowers will blossom in the spring. The oceans will be blue again, same as the sky. And most importantly, we won't be here to ruin it. The death machine known as mankind is nearly extinct, and the world is already beginning to heal.

I wish you adieu, Dear Nobody, and I pity your struggle against the inevitable. You should follow my example while you still have the chance.

Regards,

Carlton Matthew Avery II

(aka, the William S. Burroughs reincarnate)

Charie D. La Marr

Candy

Every year on Halloween in a small town in Indiana, Maryanne Parsons went to school wearing a starched white blouse, pleated grey wool skirt, white ankle socks and saddle shoes with her hair neatly plaited into French braids. She sat in the middle of the classroom, surrounded by witches and goblins, princesses and cowboys, kittens and clowns. When the teacher passed out treats, Maryanne politely declined, sitting with her head down on folded arms. And every night, she sat on the couch in her darkened house, trying to sneak peeks at the kids trick or treating.

"Never you mind about them, missy," her mother Helen would say, pulling the shades down and the curtains closed. "That's devil's work they be doin'."

"Alice Watson came to school dressed as a princess, Mama. How can that be devil's work?"

"Acts like one, too, don't she? You know your seven deadly sins, girl. Vanity's a sin, sure as you put a gun to someone's head and kilt them. It puts you right in the same place—stokin' them flames in hell for the rest of eternity. No daughter of mine's gonna dress up like no princess."

"There's princesses in the Bible," she said.

"Sure there is," her mother replied. "And look how they turned out. Bathsheba, Salome, Tamar—raped and beaten by her own half-brother, Jezebel. Bernice—married three times afore she took up with her own brother all before she was twenty-three! Don't nothing good comes from bein' no princess."

Maryanne looked out the window and sighed. "Rachel Somers was a cat. What's wrong with being a cat? Ain't no cats in the Bible."

"Don't you say ain't to me, girl. And, don't you get fresh neither. There's no cats in the Bible because God wanted it that way! That must mean they's from Satan like that there serpent. Egyptians worshipped cats. What do the Bible say 'bout having no other Gods before the Lord? I bet she was a black cat, too. Dressed up in one of them leo-tard things they wear at that dancin' school with black tights and little whiskers painted on her face. And all day long, the men at that school had the lust for her, too, even though she's no more'en ten. That's what gets girls in trouble, Maryanne! They's just askin' for it!"

"Eddie Hoffman was a clown. He's funny. He can put a whole box of Milk Duds in his mouth at one time, chew them up and swallow 'em and then he burps real loud. Everybody laughs."

"Clowns is the worst of all, girl. Satan's most loyal soldiers they are. You know what they's always laughin' at? They's laughin' at those of us who live by the word of the Lord, that's what! Every time someone slides down that slippery slope into hell, the smiles get bigger! Clowns! You'll stay away from clowns if'n ya know what's good fer ya! Now walk away from that window, girl. Dishes aren't doin' themselves tonight just 'cos it's that witchin' day."

"Maybe they will," Maryanne said quietly.

"What? What's that you say, girl? The dishes gonna do themselves tonight? What are you thinking? Are you witched, Maryanne? Did they get to you? You know what witchcraft is? Nothin' but rebellion! You're not telling me you're rebellin' against your teachins, are ya? 'Cos if'n ya are, I got a right to cut me a fresh switch and beat that rebellion right out of you then drag you off to church to pray! You listenin' to me?"

Maryanne sighed. "Yes, Mama," she said, walking into the kitchen. She made quick work of the dishes and moved on to pots and pans. Last, she washed her mother's favorite blue mixing bowl. There was stuff stuck on it from the meatloaf her mother mixed earlier in the evening, so she filled it with soapy water and let it soak for a few minutes.

As she turned to put away the pots, the soapy water began to turn clear. Then the dried-on bits of raw meat began to release blood, which rose to the surface, spelling out, *"ANSWER THE DOOR!"*

The doorbell rang despite the darkness in the front room. Maryanne could hear kids laughing and calling out, "Trick or Treat!" She froze in place.

"No trick or treaters welcome here!" her mother called out. "Go away and leave us! Halloween's a lie of the devil! Read your Bible, you wicked children! "You belong to your father, the devil, and you want to carry out your father's desire. When he lies, he speaks his native language, for he is a liar and the father of lies. Yet because I tell the truth, you do not believe me!" The Bible say so! You're settin' a table for yourselves at Satan's table tonight and your parents for lettin' you!"

Eggs hit the door and there was the sound of more laughter. Then there was a knock at the back door. "Don't answer that!" her mother screamed. Then there was a knock at the cellar door. "Leave it!" she cried.

Tears streamed down Maryanne's face. She ran into the living room and fell to the floor praying. Her mother picked up a broom and ran to the front door. "Go away! You won't get no candy here, heathens! Hast thou found honey? Eat so much as is sufficient for thee, lest thou be filled therewith, and vomit it!"

"Screw you, lady!" someone called out and inside they heard the sound of a dozen eggs hitting the front door. Helen's face turned red with anger.

The three six-paned windows across the front of the house began to reverberate. Maryanne's mother held tight to her broom. "Cover yourself girl, they're going to blow!" Maryanne grabbed an afghan and pulled it over her head as the humming got louder. Suddenly, one by one the windows imploded— shattering the room with glass. "Six, six, six!" her mother called out. "The number of the beast! He's here, Maryanne! Pray! Pray hard! Pray for your immortal soul!"

The house began shaking. Pictures fell off the walls and glass figurines fell from shelves and shattered. In the kitchen, cabinets opened, spilling piles of dishes onto the floor with a loud crash. The chairs at the kitchen table rattled and the table lifted clear off the ground. Cracks appeared in the walls. The ceiling buckled and a white plaster cloud hung heavy in the room. Beneath the afghan, Marianne wept and begged for it to stop. The front door flung open, revealing a tall figure dressed in flowing black robes. He stared at Helen and his eyes glared blood red.

"Helen Parsons, you should have answered the door when the children knocked," its voice bellowed.

"Oh help me, Jesus!" Helen said, sinking to her knees, her fingers twisted and gnarled in prayer.

In the morning when Maryanne didn't show up at school and no one answered the phone, the police went to investigate. They found the child, her face smeared with clown makeup, sitting in a pile of Halloween candy, calmly stuffing it into her red painted, chocolate covered mouth.

"Mama taste good," she said.

Paul van Leeuwenkamp

The Clean Up

After he inspected the hall and put the remaining usable body parts aside, Thijs squirted a strong jet of water onto the floor and began to scrub, starting with the skirting boards and working his way out.

Spray, scrub, spray, scrub. The spilled beer and the accumulated filth had formed itself into a thick black goo, which he deposited, every meter or so, into a bucket. In addition, of course, he used his scrubbing brush and dustpan, because even though he had his gloves on, you never could be too safe. He wouldn't be the first to pick up a broken syringe needle infected with AIDS.

Before he threw the goo into the bucket, he wiped it a few times with the brush and carefully pulled out a few stray coins. There was money strewn around everywhere and was one of the reasons he kept on working here, since the salary itself wasn't much. The second reason was the body parts, which could make good money on the black market. Every little bit helped and as a student he had to pay for everything himself, his tuition fees, his rent, the food that he ate... He could probably borrow some money at the going rate, but that wouldn't be enough. He had to earn some extra money. Therefore, he performed the monotonous spraying, scrubbing, dumping goo into the bucket, spraying, scrubbing, dumping goo...

It took Thijs a couple of hours before the main hall was clean enough for the performance of some rapper tomorrow evening. Beneath the radiators he found some eyes and fingers and in the corner, behind the chairs, a whole foot and even a forearm. He put the body parts into a plastic bin bag and added the arms and head he had found earlier. These were wild nights and many of the participants wouldn't have been able to stand up or even see clearly by the end. This was all part of the fun.

Finally, Thijs took out a stepladder and removed the last of the already shredded posters from the walls.

The posters for the 60's were all taken down and for the next few months he would only have to deal with vomit, syringe needles and plastic cups. Then the over 60's dance would happen once more and the oldies would go mental yet again. Thijs grabbed the bin bag and walked out of the hall, whistling merrily to himself as he made his way to the Commercial Management exam he needed to take.

(Translated by Ernst van Leeuwenkamp & Graeme Phillips)

Lori R. Lopez

Deadman Tales

Bones can tell a story if you listen
To their pithy piteous clink and clatter
Seemingly devoid of substance
Yet voicing no false notes of chatter
Of wasted breath and hollow chords
They speak of death in a guttural rasp
And reek with the stench of solemn despair
Hark the scarce audible hint of a final gasp
That bleeds through lips no longer whole
Revealing a grin to hide their silent grief
Each bone will sing its shard of history
Once shed to earth like an autumnal leaf

I doubt any of them died without regret
At the loss of open-eyed chances never known
There's no telling how uncomfortable it is
To lie eternal, in one position, prone
And I wonder too if it pains them to be jarred
Each time the earth gives itself a quake
We tend to worry about the living in disasters
Nobody asks the dead if they withstood a shake
Yet since I was a child I felt a kindred spirit
Between myself and those interred below
I prowled their resting places curiously
In a reverent quest to spy a wisp or glow

The thing about skeletons is underneath
We look the same, regardless of skin or health
Of color and scars, age lines or weight
The differences of class and wealth
Everyone's closet holds a suit of bones within
For it is what a ghost will wear to sleep
Like a pair of pajamas for lying in their tomb
Do not disturb the dead or they will creep
Through the fog and dark with clanking bones
And you may suffer an excruciating fright
That chills your whim, curdles blood to slush
Then tears you limb from limb by jacklight

Pay heed to the dreadful deadman tales
As they wail with a clash of fury spent
In frustrated ruts and rites long gone
Beyond the grave's guts where Time is bent
And the deceased are never in a hurry
Everything takes forever and a day
Pick them clean like a flock of buzzards
Glean what you will, they have much to say
In the death-rattling groans of polished pieces
Like a poltersnake that is coiled to strike
There is wisdom in a pile of bones
And yet none of them sound alike.

Lori R. Lopez

A Hard Rain

It rained bones
The world was pliant
Springy or fluid
Without edges and boundaries
There was no anger
No cuts to make them bleed
They had no pain or trauma
And the bones landed
Gently in a soft society
Without harming anyone
Dissolved by the soup
Of a crackerless ocean
Or bouncing upon
Some gooey plain
Falling through the substance
That once was life
Or down the gaping chasms
Of its bottomless wells
Where lay the cast-off emotions
Like clothes that didn't fit
Or were inconvenient
Filling cisterns with tears
And the anguish of old stones

Invisible, insubstantial
Ignored and disbelieved
As if they did not exist
Rolling like ghosts through
The fields of melting Time
A surrealist's landscape
But the bones were genuine
Perhaps the only thing
Accepted yet often rued
For spoiling the clarity of day
Though sorely needed
For they replenished this swampland
Fed its wobbles and waves
Quenched a mad desire to be dry
And firm, to step on solid ground
Not flow or ripple or quiver
Watching the sky
With fervent anticipation
A sense of joy at the tapping
The storm's rhythmic patter
When at last bonedrops showered
Breaking a drought of sogginess
The lengthy wet spells between
Their flood, their exuberant clamor
Bumping together in the air
A cascade of windchimes
Tuned and melodic with hope
Their knocks echoed, a solid drizzle
In a deathly quiet world
Of mushy quagmire sentiments
The supple bend of wills
And squishing of resolve
A wishy-washy bubble
Of mist and vapors
In a spiritless heaven
Waiting for the bones
Of petrified ways
To burst its balloon
With a hard rain.

Photography by John Stanton

Mike Jansen

Caligo

The ice and snow on roads and sidewalks lasted well into March that year. Talk of global warming was again rife, the yeays and nays fought openly in the mainstream media. Peter Adema could not care less about them. He was a born skeptic and he only needed to know if he could take his bicycle to work or if he would have to take public transportation. He preferred the bike, although riding it over icy patches had caused him to fall several times.

The road to Hadlin & Sons pharmaceuticals led him across the bridge over the Spaarne river in Haarlem, in the Netherlands. He lived in one of the worker neighborhoods in the north of the city, neat rows of small nineteen-thirty homes, quite different from the larger house that his ex-wife Marie still lived in with their daughter, Elana.

He looked around his small living room with its drab walls and the small open plan kitchen. Boxes filled with books and comics were stacked in one of its corners, and the furniture was hand-me-downs. His gaming rig had a prominent place in the other corner. He was yet to unpack when he moved in, two years ago. Somewhere in the back of his mind, he had come to realize, he still figured Marie would take him back.

His Facebook pinged. One of the reasons Marie gave for their separation, his obsession with social media. To it, she added the endless gaming sessions on World of Warcraft, his frequenting of many X-rated sites and perhaps the occasional liaison with likeminded women he met online.

He typed a quick reply. *Yeah, I hope spring will finally start tomorrow. The forecasts seem nice, sunshine for a change.*

He checked Marie's Facebook account. She had not dropped him and he found that looking at her photos brought back memories, most of them good, and he had to admit he missed her. And Elana of course, although he saw her nearly every other week. Still his mood turned sour.

The evening went by in a flash, doing a raid with his guild online.

When he stepped out the door the next morning, he walked into a world of dimmed light and sound. A thick fog had developed during the night and he could see only a few yards ahead. Although it wasn't freezing, the cold went right through his layers of clothing.

Peter shook his head a few times, zipped his coat closed a little more and unlocked his bicycle. It was wet and cold from the fog

A car drove by, his neighbor's silver Honda, its headlights penetrating the thick white clouds only partially. Its engine sounded muffled and, within seconds, car, light and sound were swallowed by the dense mist.

He rode the bike through the wet streets. After a few hundred yards, he encountered people exchanging insurance information. There seemed to be hardly any damage to their cars, but the fog made it difficult to assess.

Near the bridge, he drove past a heavier accident, several cars that crashed into each other. Firefighters were trying to pry open one of the cars to get at one of the victims. He overheard a police officer say that the city was a madhouse with smaller and larger accidents.

He checked in at work and dealt with the various matters that his job required. Several people called in sick and two of those were in the hospital because of car-accidents. The paperwork kept him busy all day.

At the end of the day, he rode back. Cars that passed him on the road he heard more than saw, even their headlights were but momentary white globes in a sea of dark, roiling fog. They drove extremely slowly, a few miles per hour tops. He could just see the road beneath the wheels of his bike and he followed the intermittent white stripes in the center. At regular intervals, he passed streetlights that cast a faint, yellow glow that marked but not so much illuminated the area.

He passed another recent accident. People were extra careful in this weather but the fog seemed to do strange things to drivers' eyesight, causing people to scrape past other cars or hitting the brakes just too late to avoid a fender bender. He was glad he rode his bike.

At home, he took a pizza marguerita from the freezer and put it in the oven. He ate it behind his computer and washed it down with a bottle of soda.

Have you seen the accidents today? he typed at Joanie, one of his online friends.

Nah, was cuddled up on the couch, tea, biscuits and TV, she wrote back.

How is the weather forecast?

The anchor said they were taken by surprise, mentioned some

old peasant sayings about March's fickleness. But tomorrow should be good.

He switched on the TV, just in time for the end of the weather. They showed satellite pictures of Western Europe covered in fog and attributed the unexpected weather to a combination of cold sea temperatures and weird atmospheric fluctuations. In other words, they didn't know.

He zapped through some channels and noticed news reports about fog in Japan, Australia and several of the coastal cities of North- and South America.

Perhaps those climate people are on to something after all, he wrote.

Joanie wrote, *Maybe, ttyl*.

He sighed. It had been a while since he had seen Joanie or any of the other women he was in contact with and sometimes visited. He needed to feel a woman again. He looked up Marcia and Stephanie who were often in for a good time, but they did not respond to his messages. *Trust me to pick the night they're not behind their Facebook.*

The forecast for the following morning was sunshine and reasonable temperatures. He hoped it would be so. He could use it after months of grey skies and dark clouds.

Falling asleep took some time. His dreams were dark and filled with unseen, unremembered things that slithered through his mind.

When his alarm woke him up, he didn't feel rested. Instead, there were half perceived shadows of memories, in the back of his mind, whispering about horrors he witnessed in his dreams.

From his bedroom window, his small garden was near invisible, only a few close-by branches of the apple tree with rows of ponderous water drops.

After a shower and a triple shot espresso he felt a little more awake. The weather anchor explained that the fog was unexpectedly stubborn and that this day would again be drab, grey and cold. In fact, she said, this type of fog could hang around for days. She showed images of New York where just a few skyscrapers rose above the dense white fog covering the city. Pictures taken from one of those showed the blanket of low clouds that stretched as far as the eye could see.

Peter shook his head. He had a hard time believing that the images he saw did not serve a purpose. Sure enough just after the thought entered his mind, the anchor started an impassioned plea to reduce air pollution and global warming. For now, he just longed for warmer weather. "Tell me something new," he said and switched off the TV.

His Facebook feed wasn't very busy and several of his contacts were offline, probably on their way to work. He would catch them later.

In the hall, he noticed a wisp of fog just inside the door. He wondered about that. Still, outside it was cold and wet, so he could understand fog forming near the doorsill. He raised the thermostat to twenty degrees Celsius. That should keep his house warm and the fog at bay.

Outside felt even colder than yesterday. His bicycle was ice cold and frost covered most of the metal parts. The lock seemed frozen and he had to hit it a few times to get it to open.

Much fewer people were on the road than yesterday. That allowed him to make good time to the office and he came in fifteen minutes early, for which he was thankful. The fog had an eerie quality today, almost as if he was under scrutiny. The slow undulating movements made it seem a living entity dedicated to sucking the life or, at the very least the warmth, from those who dared venture through its domain.

A few of his colleagues were around, but not as many as usual. He assumed most would remain at home, especially those who came from outside the city.

The phone on his desk flashed a signal that a dozen voicemails were present. He pushed the button and started listening. A dozen people were ill, with symptoms ranging from fever and vomiting to headaches and nausea. He made notes and his list grew steadily. Nothing to worry about yet, an average flu season saw more absentees.

More worrying was the number of people that hadn't called in sick, but also had not appeared at work. He called several of them at home, but no one answered the phone. When he made his final notes he looked up. The office was awfully quiet and the fluorescent light was incapable of conveying warmth. The windows were disturbingly white, as if the fog formed a fluffy cold blanket that shrouded everything.

The corners of his eyes worked overtime and each time he checked his computer screen for Facebook and Twitter updates or new, work related emails, he thought he observed movement in the fog.

This isn't working. Three on the clock and two more hours to go before he could leave. He switched off the screen. The silence was overwhelming. He only heard the soft, intermittent drip of water somewhere far off. He gathered his coat and bag.

"I'll do the rest from home," he said aloud, glad to hear the sound of his own voice, although there was no one to hear him. His co-workers hadn't shown up in the office and he knew the factory was running at only half production, but there wasn't much to do about that.

Friday would be his regular afternoon with his daughter, after school, and he was looking forward to spending time with her. His divorce had been painful, bitter and costly, especially since his feelings for Marie still existed. But in Elana he saw Marie like he first met her, pure, fresh and positively complicated. Being with her brought back good memories.

On the way home he stopped at the supermarket to get some groceries for the next days, but also to get out of the cold for a brief time and to be with other humans again. The stillness of the outside world was getting to him. Beyond the sliding doors he walked into a sea of fog with aisles of groceries like weird, rectangular islands sticking out.

There were a few shoppers out, but not nearly as many as usual. This supermarket was always busy, day and night. The people he did see were dressed warm, their faces pale because of the long winter. He picked up some milk, bread, apples and flour to bake apple pie with his little girl. He decided on a TV dinner for that evening, a large piece of fresh lasagna from the delicatessen section, still slightly warm.

While he walked to the cashier, he thought he saw movement underneath the cover of fog, near the meat section, as if something large wallowed and turned, causing the white fluff to roil and ripple. His logical mind told him he was seeing things, but almost involuntarily he steered his cart along a different aisle, forgoing the ham and bacon he wanted for breakfast the next morning.

The cashier had a pale, haunted look. It was obvious she wore multiple layers of clothing, but she still seemed cold. He paid in cash and as he handed her the euro bills he touched her hand. It was clammy and far colder than he expected. For a moment he looked into her eyes, dark brown, and he recognized fear in them, somewhat obscured by the onset of tears. He wanted to say something, but didn't know what, so he packed up his groceries and took his change.

"Have a good shift," he said when he left. Lame, he knew. At least it broke the silence. Leaving the store he looked back at the cashier. Not a hint of a smile.

His hallway was filled with fog that reached to his knees. He sighed. *So much for increasing the temperature of the house.* His home was cold and damp and when he checked the thermostat, he saw that it was just fifteen degrees, although he had set it to twenty. He put his groceries in the fridge, then placed towels in front of the door and the windows to keep out the cold and the fog. It was after all an old house; there were gaps and chinks between walls and windows and beneath doors.

He checked Facebook and Twitter. Apart from some messages about the fog and some nonsensical status updates there was no real news.

The TV showed static on several channels. He zapped until he found one that talked about the weather, although it soon degraded into a discussion about the Rapture and the end of times. With a sigh, he looked further until he found a panel of scientists on CNN International.

"We think the fog is a rare occurrence that happens only once every ten thousand years, usually near or during a time of climatic upheaval. We've dubbed it 'Caligo', after the Latin for fog," said one of them. The presenter showed satellite pictures that displayed overcast skies on most of the continents. The discussion became too technical for him after that although he thought he heard a tie in with global warming proponents.

A local TV station mentioned that most cell phones had problems picking up signals due to the extreme level of water in the air. In combination with spotty GPS coverage, many people got lost in the dense fog. This caused a lot of missing person reports. Finally something that made sense to Peter.

He took his own cell phone. It showed five bars of reception, the maximum. On a whim he decided to call Marie. She usually didn't pick up the phone, but he hoped she would feel lonely and perhaps just a little afraid. Like him, he had to admit. It was a busy neighborhood and he was used to the sounds of people moving about, doing stuff, driving cars, yelling at each other. Not now. There was an unnatural silence, like the world had somehow emptied of humans and left a few stragglers behind to fend for themselves.

"Peter?" Marie's voice was shaky.

Peter choked up. "Hey," he croaked. "I'm glad to hear your voice."

Marie waited before answering. "Me too." To which she immediately added: "But you're not sleeping over. That was once and I still regret it."

"No, no, that's not why I called," Peter said. "Are you and Elana ok? Are we still on for this weekend?"

"Yes, no... I don't know," Marie said. "There's fog in the living, Peter. Everything is cold and damp."

"I know. My hallway has the same. These old houses have gaps and chinks everywhere. I wouldn't be surprised if it gets in through the floor. Will you be alright?"

"We're going to bed early, maybe watch a movie if the electricity keeps working. It's been off a couple times today."

Peter thought about his heater. It needed electricity to function. Now he understood the low temperature of his house. "I haven't heard anything on the news," he said.

"It was probably just local," Marie said. "We'll see you Friday, Peter."

"Can I say goodnight to my daughter?"

"Elana is upstairs, getting ready for bed. By the way, I'm keeping her with me tonight. She's got trouble sleeping. Bad dreams."

"That's ok, you take care and I'll see you Friday."

"Goodnight, Peter."

After she hung up he tried to surf the Internet, but everything was dog slow. Not much was going on anyway. Most of his Facebook friends were offline and the topics he followed were completely dead. He turned in early, hoping for a better tomorrow.

His dreams were filled with despair. Unseen, dark things followed him through shadowy labyrinths, mazes in dank forests, always close on his feet. He heard their slavering breath and dripping bile from venomous jaws. Once, he saw a pair of glowing red eyes in the distance, the owner obscured by the ever present fog, quickly closing in. He ran until he could run no more, then he woke up.

He had a quick shower in, at best, lukewarm water, then some breakfast. During the night the fog had infiltrated his living room, forming a thin, cold, damp layer around his feet.

His mood was darker even than the days before when he left his home to go to work. He didn't see a point in going, yet he gave in to his sense of loyalty, even if that was only to the regular paycheck.

On the corner of the street his neighbor suddenly appeared from the fog. He was breathing heavily.

Any company was good at this point. Peter tried to strike up a conversation. "Hey Joe, how've you been?"

Joe grabbed his steer and gasped for breath. "They're everywhere. We have to run!"

"What do you mean? From what?" Peter looked around, anxious. When he looked back, Joe had already left, vanished into the thick fog. He shook his head and sighed. He had almost forgotten what it was like, actually talking to someone, face to face.

He rode his bicycle along frosted streets. The soft sloshing of the river sounded far away as he crossed the bridge. There were no other people in sight and even the street lanterns were switched off, adding to the eerie quality of his surroundings.

At the company, the lights were all off and the doors were locked. He looked into the hall, but apart from a thick layer of fog, illuminated by the sickly green light of the 'Emergency Exit' sign, there was no one at the reception desk. He noticed the total absence of noise coming from the factory itself. He realized no one was there at all.

He waited for at least fifteen minutes before he too decided to go home. By then the cold had gone right through the layers of clothes he wore. Right now his mood told him to lie in bed with thick blankets to regain some warmth. He could watch a movie; maybe play some games, if the Internet worked. Even that thought hardly appealed.

He rode his bicycle along the shortest route he knew. A feeling of urgency drove him on and he moved as fast as he dared, barely missing obstacles in his path that would appear fractions of a second before he registered them.

Halfway he halted, breathing heavily. Somehow he felt watched, although his logical mind told him that no one could see him any more than he could see others. He blinked his eyes and just for a fleeting moment he stared into a pair of red, glowing eyes, three dozen yards away, several yards above him and belonging to something that cast a huge shadow on the surrounding, billowing fog. Blink. The fog was back, covering up whatever it was he had just seen.

He stood very still for what seemed like minutes, not sure what to do. When he finally dared move, he stepped on the pedals like never before, rushing back to the safety of his home.

With all the locks in place, he made coffee and switched on the TV, his mind already at work rationalizing what he had just witnessed, yet failing at every turn. His core remained cold, detached and in denial yet emotion, mostly fear, swamped his brain and kept his adrenaline pumping.

First, he pondered getting in touch with Marcia or Stephanie, but he just wanted –sexual- oblivion, no complicated games of seduction, so finally he switched on his computer and watched

X–rated movies all day in an attempt to divert his mind.

He went to bed early, raw and sore, but with all his nervous energy spent. Tomorrow was Friday, when he would pick up his little girl at the end of the day. He hoped against all hopes that the weather would improve. And of course he really needed to go to work. He had a responsibility to get the workers back to the factory to man the production lines.

The slow dripping sounded close to his head, volume increasing to thunderous splashes on wet flesh, accompanied by a deep, threatening growl with an occasional low, rasping breath from a non-human throat. He stumbled about blindly in the dark, knowing that light would just show him the fog whose icy fingers touched and stroked and sucked all warmth from him, chilling him to the core of his being.

Somewhere he knew he was dreaming again, his logical mind telling him that he was merely reliving events of the day. However, his usual control over waking up or continuing the dream was absent and doubt set in. *What if all this was real?* Ahead of him the dark seemed to lift. Cold grey fog swirled around him, agitated by unseen and unexplained air currents. Light or dark, he might as well be blind. He saw nothing of his surroundings or people or things in it.

A shadow appeared, approached and he felt relief at not being alone. He thought he recognized the shape of a woman, but when of a sudden she was before him her pale face had white in white eyes and small icicles hung from her limp dark hair like softly clinking beads. Her breath held the stench of a thousand graves when she opened her mouth, revealing bloody, razor like teeth. He attempted to step back, but her hands with claw like fingers caught his head and with inhuman strength she pulled him toward her, as if to kiss.

Sweat coursed down his body and he heard a scream, his own voice, as he switched on the light. For once he was grateful to whatever God that the electricity worked. Seeing the patch of fog below his bedroom window did not surprise him, yet he worried. How long before his whole house was inundated in the stuff? The time on his cell phone said five fifteen, still quite early. He knew sleep was out of the question now; his heart was still racing from the nightmare.

The shower started out nice and hot, but halfway through it turned ice cold and wouldn't get warm anymore. He cursed. He skipped his razor and just brushed his teeth. Instead of a neat shirt he put on a warm, brown cable sweater to work. He didn't really care about anything but keeping the cold out.

His hallway had a yard of fog in it, his living room half a yard. Fortunately the coffee was hot. More channels on the TV now displayed static. Intermittently the power seemed to drop, causing the image to falter and then come back again. An obscure German station rattled on about a flood of missing people and companies struggling to keep up production as more and more people never showed up for work.

Outside the weather hadn't changed. His bicycle was still frozen and the world was a quiet, desolate place. The roads were slick with patches of ice, worse than before so he moved with great care. At one point he halted to continue on foot. As he stepped off his bike the fog swirled and just for a moment he could see further than a dozen yards and looked right at his ex, Marie. Her wet, dark hair hung in limp strands around her face and she stared at him with empty, white eyes. The fog closed in again.

Peter almost choked. His heart hammered in his throat. 'M- M- Marie?' he whispered at the fog, but there was no answer, just the steady dripping of droplets falling off nearby branches. He pulled out his cell phone and speed dialed his ex-wife. After a few seconds there was a 'no connection' signal.

He got on his bicycle and with near reckless speed sought his way toward his former house where his ex lived, with their daughter. When he thought about Elana he felt a deep fear. Would she be alright?

Six streets further he found the loose stones in the pavement and he knew he had reached the house. He dropped his bike and half walked half ran toward the front door. He wanted to ring the bell, but in a momentary lapse in the fog covering everything, he saw them through the front window, Marie and Elana. Both dressed in their night gowns, dark, wet hair around pale faces, both staring at him with wide eyes, white in white, dead eyes. Elana jerked her hand up against the window, a fraction of a second, before the fog closed in again. It was enough to show him elongated, bony fingers ending in knife point nails.

Fear and desperation shot through him. "No, noooooo!" He shook his head, felt tears run down his cheeks in hot rivulets. He stumbled back to the street, finding his way half-blind through the obscured neighborhood where silence now reigned.

He reached his home, fumbled the key a couple of times, got in and closed and locked the door behind him. The lights were off and the heating seemed cold. The fog had inundated the ground floor.

He ran up the stairs to his bedroom where the fog roiled around his bed, closed the curtains and his door, then threw himself on the bed and pulled the warm covers around him.

Only then did he calm down.

"Marie, Elana," he whispered. "What the hell is going on?" He knew they were gone, felt it in his heart. In the silence that answered him the only thing he heard was the soft dripping of droplets that reminded him of his nightmares.

A text message notification broke the silence. He checked his phone. It was from Marie! He shook his head, then noticed the time stamp on the message. It had taken nearly sixteen hours to arrive.

With trembling fingers he opened the message. It read: *P if u rd this, help us. Smn in house. On strs, cming up. Hurry!* It had only just arrived. He pushed his fist in his eyes and felt tears burning and sobs welled up from his throat.

He buried his head in the blankets, trying to pretend none of this happened, that when he would sleep and wake up, the world would be back to normal.

Then he heard the bottom step of the stairs creak, followed by slow, heavy footsteps.

Please let me wake up, please let me wake up, please, please, please!

Nienke Pool

Cenotaph

Baltimore, October 2 1875

"Coachman, take me to Bond Street. Number 80."
"Number 80, sir. Are you certain?"
I nod and get in while studiously ignoring his gaze.

Am I certain? It is odd I feel nervous thinking of this re-acquaintance. He receives no living soul, rumor has it, or, more likely, no living soul will see him. Staring Death in the face is all in a day's work, so that is not the issue; holding onto this life at all costs is what would scare me; and holding on is what he does.

I take the note from my jacket pocket. As I smooth it, some coagulated blood sticks to my fingers. My eyes scan the characters, but again the content eludes me. I must see him. The words repeat in my mind during the rest of the trip:

Fate that once thought him too light
Hate that once was his plight
Evil that bound him in lies
Now glorifies his cenotaph

A cenotaph, that much is clear. Why her dead fingers clutched it, is a mystery to me. One of many.

The coachman halts. As soon as he receives my payment, he turns and disappears into the dark of night. The whinny of the horse echoes in the deserted lane for a long time. It seems to me he is running away. I pull my fur collar tight around my neck, and observe the mansion before me. Not a candle lit, and I know why: no fires.

I fear meeting him, but if I want to solve this case, I will have to confront him.

The cold night forces me to move, but the endless approach does not strengthen my resolve such that I can use the knocker resembling the Goddess Athena. Just when I decide to turn away, Charles opens the door.

"Good evening, Mister Reynaard. Please come in. Mister Bernhard is expecting you."

Why am I not surprised? Charles does not even offer to take my coat. He places my hat on a table beside the door. Only then, I notice that he wears a winter coat. He points upstairs, but does not lead the way, signifying Bernhard's difficult visage. Reluctantly I mount the stairs and count the steps.

"Enter." Bernhard's voice is hoarser than I remember.

When my eyes adjust to the darkness, I see my old friend in the middle of the room. His back toward me, he pores over stacks of newspaper clippings and dossiers. There is no need to count them; there are eighty stacks. I observe the photos on the wall. I shudder when I notice her. Sarah was the first. Her braided hair lacks the usual care that I witness tonight, as the braid that hangs from a tree marks her grave. I will carry the image with me all my life. One does not grow accustomed, ever. Tonight is no exception. Every time the almost loving care of the murderer touches me.

Julia. Number eight. I have so many questions, although all answers so far have led nowhere.

He is behind me. I can feel it. How do you greet an old friend after so long?

I look past him at the fireplace that holds no flames. I can see the small clouds of my breath float through the high ceilinged room. He speaks, but his words only register slowly.

"Jenny?" I ask in surprise. "She is splendid. Yes, of course, I'll give her your regards."

"No need," he answers, "She's here every Wednesday. Has she not told you that?"

No, I have no clue, I think, but I am also not surprised. It has been a while since I knew, or even cared, how or where Jenny spent her time.

I stare at Sarah's photo again. He moves his chair past me and stops beneath her murdered image. Only now with his wheelchair before me, dare I see his face . . . or what is left of it.

"The pain can be unbearable," he says. A tear wells up in his good eye.

I give him the note. He reads it, moves toward the dossiers and starts rummaging through the stacks, babbling feverishly as he searches for God know what. Do these words mean anything to him, where sixteen detectives fail to comprehend? I take a chair and sit next to him to study the various documents. I am surprised to see he has all our information. Handwritten copies of secret files, photos of all the crime scenes, neatly placed throughout the room.

"He's developing," he murmurs. "To him it's a work of art."

"He makes them Vestal Virgins. They're all adulte..."

"A Vestal Virgin defended Rome's holy fire," he interrupts, "and should she display lewd conduct, she would be buried alive. Some food, some water and an oil lamp would accompany her in the grave, to make certain she would die a slow death."

"So why leave the cut braid in the tree, the wedding gown, both ancient symbols of virginity and part of an inauguration, not of an inglorious death? What is the murderer telling us? Why the ambivalence?"

He does not answer my questions, but reads the verse aloud. Suddenly he seems to remember something and he rides to the bureau before the window. The light from a lantern outside illuminates his face. My breath halts. His face is unrecognizable from scar tissue, his nose is just a fleshy ridge and his right eye is gone—yanked out, I know. I read the files, at least eighty times. His halting breath returns me to the present.

He offers me today's newspaper.

"Poe was reburied today. This cenotaph is in his honor. How fitting—the master of the macabre rules beyond his grave."

I pull the paper from his hands and read the article about the sober reburial. We have thoroughly investigated the suggestion that the Vestal murders, as christened by the press, were inspired by his nauseating literature. I support, in part, the conclusion that such intricately described horrors cause more violence and should be forbidden, but must admit there is no solid proof.

The murderer obviously admires a past much further removed than the writing of this poet.

I sigh.

"Next you're going to tell me the cenotaph contains a cryptic message. Or do we have to open Poe's grave to search for the next corpse?"

He turns to me, allowing me a full look at him. His body is halved. His legs were burnt to such an extent the doctors needed to amputate. His mouth hangs open. Shortage of breath is his biggest adversary. It still is. His good eye stares at me. I look away; his gaze is too intense. We sit in silence.

Finally, he says, "Today's grave is a cenotaph." His voice sounds pedantic in a way I remember well from our glory days. "Poe himself still lies in his decrepit grave."

I know my friend's obsession.

"Grave number 80," I say. "No one should die so inglorious."

"There's no glory in dying. No honorary columns will change that," he says and rides past me to file the article with the poem.

This is his life, I think, and now that I see his room, I understand why. Or did I already know?

"What symbolizes the Tarpeian rock this time?" he asks, looking at her photo.

His use of words touches me. This is *his* case as well as mine.

"A man was pushed from the second balcony during a performance of Shakespeare's *Julius Caesar*. Exactly as the stabbing occurred, the man fell down. He held a pig's genitals in his hand, just like the others."

"Was he the lover of this night's victim?" he asks.

"I never said we found another victim last night."

"You're here, that tells me enough. So that makes it eight in all."

"Eight adulteresses and their lovers," I say. "Except Sarah: she was alone." I feel nauseous.

He rides further. The darkness does not bother or hinder him. People whisper he only lives at night. In the middle of the room is a wheeled blackboard. I follow him and listen attentively to his lecture.

"The similarities are clear: an adulterous relationship is punished by interring the woman while alive, like a Vestal Virgin, and letting her rot in the ground, while the man is pushed from a symbolic rock. The murderer evolves: he gets surer of himself, although, unfortunately, for us, no less the careful perfectionist. In fact, he seems to become more careful. He is toying with us; every murder has discrepancies. Focus on the differences. Therein lays his message."

"Message," I repeat. Every time I think I comprehend this killer, really understand him, he eludes me. Nevertheless, I persevere: I have read all the gothic works by crime authors, I have studied the ancients during many sleepless nights and I have visited the sites where the dead bodies lay countless times. Yet, nothing brings me closer to a solution. I only find more questions.

Baltimore's populace is getting restless. Fifteen deaths in a year and a half negatively affect the sleep of innocent souls. Fifteen! Moreover, in my opinion it should have been sixteen.

He looks at me, stares. I can no longer avoid his gaze. My legs tremble. My uncertain voice scares me. "There are discrepancies; the men, especially. All of them somehow thrown to their death from a great height. All of them held a pig's scrotum in their right hand. Sometimes it seems there is hatefulness in a murder. The one last night looked more like a cold-blooded killing. The lawyer, on the other hand..."

Fierce gasping startles me. My friend seems to suffocate. Quickly I ride him to the window and open it to allow the freezing air to enter. It is cold inside anyway, so it will not make much difference. Is he dying? God, he reeks of urine. I observe this once virile man. The anxious rattle continues.

"Is there anything I can do?" I ask, while I search for a glass of water.

He shakes his head and clutches his chest with his hand, making me realize all of a sudden that he is laughing. What can be so funny?

He points at the photo prints of the dead lawyer. I follow his gaze. The scene shows the lawyer, dumped in a room, belly up, surrounded by pig's intestines and bloody slabs of fat. Unlike the other male victims, this man was already dead when thrown down upon the smelly offal. His hands and head were already missing. Those severed limbs stood in the center of the room, impaled on long spikes, like a salute to the police upon entrance. The reference to that ancient lawyer still grips my stomach and most certainly does not amuse me.

"Cicero, the lawyer who once successfully defended a Vestal Virgin—in the end he paid for his wiles and deceptions," Bernhard says with a bitter smile. "The citizens of Rome knew how to deal with a treacherous snake like he."

"The Vestal Virgin was his sister in law, like with our lawyer. The man had an affair with his brother's wife," I say. I remember the deceived brother well. He was a highly respected judge. We shadowed him for weeks, but his alibi for the other murders was impeccable. We could not touch him. He was another dead end street, like so many before.

"Which in your opinion was the most heinous of all these murders?" he asks.

Of course, Sarah is my first thought but what is the use in saying it? Why rub salt in open wounds not yet allowed proper time to heal?

"The death of Julia, this night, has touched me deep," I therefore answer.

Bernhard seems surprised.

"You just said the man's death was straightforward. What was it about her?"

I remember the events earlier this night, the abandoned ship in the harbor anticipating the thaw, where a long blonde braid hangs from the mast. Beautifully woven red ribbon fluttered in the cold winter night. I knew what to expect once we found her, still the sight of her nearly overwhelmed me.

"She was quite young," I begin, "beautiful too. Her mouth was tied with a silk scarf, her hair was cut; she tried to resist. There were deep knife cuts in her neck and it must have hurt. She wore the bridal gown that she got married in only a year ago. Her head was on a pillow. Oddly enough, with her hands tied, the water and food were pointless. The silk muffled her last cries. The oil lamp burned for some time, so she must have seen the rats arrive."

"Rats?"

"Place was crawling with them."

"My friend is silent. He closes the window and looks outside . . . With longing? How long has it been since he ventured outside?

"He's a monster," he contemplates. "What astounds me is that he seems to evolve. I cannot help you, inasmuch as I would like to."

Bond Street is a mere ten-minute walk from the police headquarters. The cold invigorates my brain. There is no use in going to sleep at this time of night. Perhaps the coroner can tell me more; I think and hasten my steps. My thoughts wander and I think of Bernhard. Such terrible suffering, inhuman almost.

Tick, tick, I hear in the deserted road.

I look back, looking for source of the sound. Nothing. A dog crosses the street. Automatically I check my pistol in its holster, while holding on to the small weapon in my pocket. There it is again. Tick, tick, followed by the sound of wheels. I stand still again and inspect the alleys between the town houses. Nothing. The murders are playing tricks with my mind, I think and I shake my head.

There is a solid blow against the back of my skull. Dazed and powerless I notice a cloth bag thrown over my body. I only vaguely recollect the rattle of the wheels of the carriage on the cobbles of Bond Street. Then all is black.

I awake. When I try to grab my head I find my hands tied behind my back. I am still inside the cloth bag. As I try to discern my surroundings, I focus on breathing steadily. There is a room with a warm fire. I hear voices of at least six men, maybe more. They mumble, but I recognize the educated accents and realize this is not just riffraff.

I gasp for breath when the bag is removed,. A torch is held close to my face. Silhouettes resembling my own I see, gentlemen wearing high hats.

"What the hell is this?" I ask in my sternest voice. My head hurts and I can smell my own fear.

"We want to make you an offer," a voice says.

I know that voice, I am certain I do.

"An offer. That sounds interesting," I say.

"You're the detective charged with the investigation of the Vestal Murders and you are out of clues." The certainty is such that I do not attempt to deny it.

"We can solve this for you."

"Solve? I think only the killer knows exactly what is on his mind."

"Of course."

The truth of these simple words hits me hard. My head hurts even more than moments ago. "What is it that you want?"

"We spared your life, with Sarah," the voice says. "We all know you should have died, for you were the Tarpeian rock that night."

I know who he is now. It's judge Williams who so tragically lost his wife last year. She was number four. I followed him for weeks after his wife and brother were killed. I was so sure he was somehow involved, but the evidence proved otherwise. Now he tells me they spared me?

"Spared? How so?"

"Sarah,' he answers. "Bernhard's wife, the one you had an affair with."

I dig through my memories. "Bernhard was... is my friend. That night he outsmarted you. He discovered the whereabouts of Sarah, where you buried her."

There is a snigger behind me. What are they laughing about?

"She was underneath the catacombs of an abandoned monastery. How do you think he found her? Why was she the only one who burned? Fire destroys all traces, you should know this."

I do not understand. They are laughing again.

"What is your offer?" I finally ask.

"Join us. We are men, like you. Married, and, in the end, deceived."

"Deceived? You mean by Jenny? The fire of our love had subsided. I had Sarah. Jenny knew that."

"Meanwhile she cheated on you with your friend Bernhard. Even now, she is faithful to him. You have seen him. She chooses that husk of a man over you. That must hurt. People are laughing behind your back."

My heart skips a painful beat. How long was I going to deny it to myself?

I see Sarah's burned body before me, thinking of the oil lamp that fell on her while Bernhard tried to save her. Or did he? What if Bernhard had lied to him? Was he aware of their affair? Did he really try to save her that night?

The silhouettes shake their heads and wait for my response. "Are you beginning to understand?"

David Slater

The Devil Moves in Mysterious Ways

(please don't shoot the messenger)

In the disquiet of your loneliness
The silence is not as it seems
For echoes harbour spirits
And not all shadows are vacant of substance
Amid the dreaming nights warmth
Beyond the deepest sleep befalls
Tremolos of subconscious fear
To seize hold of of the souls disquiet
And quiver any a stalwart heart.

Shall I play softly with your hair
Glide my retched fingers between tumbling tresses
Quicken thy blood in porous beads of tenderness
Your eyes deceive, for I wear no shadow
Desires flatter in tongues of twisting lies
To enchant and entice, these poisonous whispers of mine
As your body exhales
My kiss upon your soul you happily greet.

Anticipation races throughout every sinew of this languid flesh
As your closed eyes dance
I sit weightless upon your rhythmic pulse
Starring wildly unto your heaving bosom
Tranquility escapes in a rush, carried upon your exhaled sigh
As my twilight spell weaves its insidious magic
This beckoning sings your sweet surrender
Possession is not by 'rules' my game
Simplified, demonic irritant!

Sanity's fall is what sustains this carcass
As you break, releasing energies I breathe you in
The fullness of your essence, as I drink of you within
surrendering
Hell works in mysterious ways; "please don't shoot the
messenger"
So do not stir, do not waken
Feel free to resist my dark intrusion

For there is no joy in easy persuasions
Fragility of your sleeping labours, limbs set in frozen numbness.

Please, lay still
If you wake things could turn serious
Stopped of illusions of my mystery, I would not hesitate
To snap you like a twig, for you could let slip my secrecy
Then again, such a waste of suffering
For they'd say that you have gone mad
And I shall enjoy your torture all the sweeter
Sullen evenings filled with teasing insanity, how delicious
To watch ecstatically as you slide ever deeper unto my realm
That taste of your womanhood flowering
In the scent of culminating fear as your predicament peaks.

Self-disgust in your melodic moans as I ply
Caressing between soft thighs within your reflective pupils
I sip with delight of your inevitable peril
Your wanton lust shall taint this room
With the eagerness of your tentative release
Thus the games all too soon fade with the approaching dawn
Never the less, I shall bide my time, here
Nestled deep within your unsuspecting skull
Praying on your shattered sensibilities as I devour your strength
From the inside out.

Until twilight returns with my conjurations
Bubbling with such insidiousness, and your wasted flesh
I will feed to lesser demons
Set free from their shackles with a silent glyph
Then they and I will feast and dine to our evils content
And I shall return to the nether regions, with a fulfilled quota
And release my burden upon his eminence's command
And His torture shall be unfathomable
Upon an eternity of sweet black sufferings.

David Slater

Beyond the Last Day

The passage of the tempest left calamity in its wake
A chill in the coolness of the night's breeze
A lucid malady spewed from the very bowls of the earth
A malodorous so bitter sweet
All minds and hearts shall fetter and bleed
Upon a vortex of madness so complete
Shall flood the flesh in total grief
And show to all the very pits of hell
A lifetimes despair such vacant faces bare witness
From which there will be no such relief
A cocktail of generic decay of cognitive cranial cohesion
As the hourglass of time beckons inexorable minutes
As the flesh tears within minds cold, a contagion so final, so complete
From earthy soiled mounds now unfold
With eyes that have no soul, stomachs, dead to its hunger
Yet the mind shall be wandering mire, forever reaching
Clawing to set free its carnage, to set free a ravenous rage
Within a lumbering rotting carcass

In the eerie silence there is respite
As towns and vast cities unfurl into a grey lifeless canvass
This plague that swept upon ravaged winds and dusts of red
Caught, between that rock and its hard place
Safety was now in the hands of solitude
For there is no love lost here, amongst the debris of civilisations
Key to survival is watchfulness
Least you get caught up in someone else's mistakes
As the evening chill sets the scene to this unfolding nightmare
Never restful are those dead walking
Within this crazed madness the insanity of self fractures
With each passing day and it's equally careful footsteps
Caution becomes a steadfast friend, as every shadow begs attention
And the new days sullen sun shall bring forth little comfort
Each wakeful moment brings its own tests
In this new world, where hell has breached its gates

Saturating the very core of society's fragility
Upon this singular stroke
There shall be no warmth within its chaos
No solace amongst once friends and neighbours
Just unhinged civility
But the dead walking are not the true enemy
For those whom survive this insanity of hell on earth
Upon the desperations that cling to our every breath
Shall now show itself in deeds of true evil !!

Photography by John Stanton

David Slater

The Devil moves in mysterious ways II

What is this !

Gapping fissures of flesh
Crimson pools glistening as they slowly lose their lustre
Black globules congealing around splintered bone

Why ?

Is my breath so uneasy
Of fear, exhilaration and excitement
This isn't me ...... I am ......
'Praying deep within my subconsciousness' ...... Normal !
Yet, this is far removed from normality
Has insanity finally exhumed this utter barbarity
Of flesh, bone, blood and madness

Time,
Has vacated all sense of moments
Minutes, hours, all have melted into a deranged red haze
The dank smell
Wrenched my stomach into somersaults
Bittersweetness of macabre decaying corpses
Each carrying with it vivid disturbing memorial visions
It's heat nearby was too eagerly rank with festering scents

Oh,
Oh to dream of glorious blooms wafting upon the breeze
Twilight creatures entertain
With their scurrying routines
And oh, to feel the breath of the chilled cold winds upon this
flesh
How nearer to desire was this, bountiful fantasy
Once perhaps, eons ago
Cobwebs of thought had wafted through this cranial cesspit
The cesspit that you folks call features, portrait of face

Alas,
There are no mirrors here in eternal darkness

Save for the red pools of the Damned
I am but a servant of a higher order
The minions of Hell's pyres
Yet am I any less of a creature than any other !
Am I not allowed to dream !

And yes ... The devil does indeed move in mysterious ways...

T.S. Woolard

Why In Hell

Joe was a serial killer, had been his whole life on Earth. He took his first life when he was fourteen, his sister. His last was at the age of forty-four. The police apprehended him at forty-five, and he was put to death at forty-six. He lay on the lethal injection table and went to sleep. He awoke in Hell's Hospital, the gateway to the underworld.

With thirty years and thirty-seven murders to his credit, Joe was a consummate professional when it came to killing. Serial killers have reasons for the things they do, passions and desires, but he had nothing of the sort. He didn't care how they died. He didn't keep trophies. The only thing that mattered to him was taking life from another person.

He had always loved the last exhalation. The sweet smell of death blowing from the lungs of the victim fueled him. It was like they blew their soul into the air he breathed. For a man with no heart, feelings, or soul, it was his life force.

Before Joe took his sister's life, he always felt like something was missing. He couldn't put a finger on what it was, but he knew he lacked it. It was the reason he attempted suicide when he was twelve, and twice at thirteen. Then he learned why the attempts failed—to kill *others* was his sole purpose.

He felt as though he did the Lord's work. It was like he was put on Earth to cleanse the world. He believed this was the serial killer's job, their purpose. It was the reason for their particular tastes in targets and the strict M.O.'s they followed. They help God thin out certain kinds of people.

Hell, however, was much different than Joe had expected. It was nothing like the eternal suffering and everlasting fire lapping at his soul he heard about in Sunday school as a child. There were streets, apartments, and people milling about the sidewalks. Everyone ate breakfast, lunch, and dinner, and folks even slept at night.

One major difference was the landscape. Where grass and shrubbery should've been there was ash and piles of burning coal. Flames shot as high as trees in the barren areas. When storms brewed, they blew in with clouds of gray powder and orange-red lightning bolts.

Two people slept in each apartment. The buildings were six

stories high, six rooms deep, and six rooms wide. There were six-hundred sixty-six buildings on each street.

The rooms were as nondescript as possible. They had white walls, blue commercial carpet, a small kitchen, a smaller bathroom, and two single beds in the common living area. They smelled like ashtrays bursting with old sweat. Living conditions were horrible, but they were in Hell. Joe didn't expect The Marriott.

Every day the citizens of Hell had appointments in which they went to the big building in the middle of Hell, known as The Epicenter. The tenants of each apartment building loaded onto huge, matte black buses with thick, red stripes down their sides. Two buses were always at the curb of The Epicenter. One loaded a group to take home; the other let its passengers off.

All of Hell's inhabitants reported to The Epicenter every day. On Earth, most people observed Sunday as a day of rest, because God took Sunday off after creating the universe. However, this was Hell. They didn't celebrate Sundays as God's day. They also didn't celebrate Good Friday or Christmas. Every day was a day for The Burning.

The Burning was the punishment everyone in Hell had to endure. There were certain punishments for each individual, but The Burning was for everybody. They checked in at the desk in the lobby of The Epicenter, and then went to the rooms matching their apartment numbers. Inside the room were cylinders that looked like stand-up tanning beds. Each person did thirty minutes of The Burning.

The idea behind The Burning was to burn off the evil. Evil seeps out through the pores and onto the skin. When evil is allowed to grow and fester, the host must get it off in some way. Usually, it's what got them sent to Hell.

Joe missed his burning for four days. His own evil caked on his skin like dandruff. He felt it becoming a more prevalent part of who he was. He was turning more evil than man was. Thus, his serial killer ways returned.

A woman by the name of Salem Hawks caught his eye one day on his way to The Epicenter. She was boarding the bus, leaving from her burning.

Joe couldn't comprehend how she had made it this long without him noticing her. She was just what he liked to hunt when he lived: an alcoholic, abusive, single foster mother who moonlighted as a prostitute when times got hard. She ended up in Hell by murdering foster kids and collecting the Social Security money for their care. The ones she did let live she treated worse than swine, a speed bump on the way to a smooth blacktop that took her to easy money. As soon as the watchful eye of the social workers relaxed, she tossed them screaming, sometimes with relief, into the old stone well under her house, like all the other paychecks. Moreover, Salem was a redhead, his favorite kind.

He followed her for days. Everywhere she went Joe was behind her, if only steps. Sometimes he got so close the smell of fermented strawberries tickled his nose. She seemed to sweat wine and a quiet disregard for the living. She walked lightly, barely making a noise on the pavement under her heels. Her red hair hung to her nipples, and always appeared disheveled. She also made sure to be indoors every day by dusk.

Salem lived one building over from Joe, in Apartment 137. Thirteen and seven were his lucky numbers on earth. The symmetry intoxicated him.

Joe hadn't killed in Hell. He hadn't killed in over a year before his execution. He was jonesing bad, especially since he had skipped The Burning for so long. The catalyst for his serial killer behavior was Salem. She sent him into a tailspin. Killing was his addiction.

Since it had been so long, Joe decided he would beat her to death, or maybe strangle her, something with his hands. It made the murder more intimate. Besides, he always enjoyed a good strangulation. He usually did it with a rope or something that wouldn't leave evidence, but this was Hell, so he wasn't too worried about getting caught. There was no death penalty here. He had already done that, but didn't get the t-shirt.

Salem stepped onto the sidewalk with the bottle of wine she had just bought at the grocery store. The coal moon set alight her pale face, making the sweat on her cheeks sparkle. At high noon, the coal moon burned like a charcoal briquette. At this time of day, it winked out to an ashy, gray orb. Joe followed her, taking a deep breath of the noxious air polluting Hell's atmosphere. He was beginning to loathe that smell, the stench of familiarity. Lit

His target made it into her building at the same time the coal moon went dark, like every other day. He followed her without her noticing him at all. He was like a shadow moving in unison with Salem, attracting no more attention than a blade of grass shaking in a light breeze. He was close now.

She went into her apartment. Her roommate wasn't home, never was except when she came down from massive highs. Her roommate would stumble into sleep it off. When she woke up, she'd pull another five-day meth binge, and the meth in Hell was a bitch.

Joe pressed his ear to the door. On the other side he could hear Salem walking around the room, opening and closing drawers— getting clothes out, most likely. Then he heard the *click-click* of the lid screwing off the wine bottle. It was unmistakable, the sound of a false savior, the sound of a wasted life.

It was exactly what he wanted, Salem to drink herself unaware. He did it himself several times, between kills. Every time he got the urge, he tried to swallow it like a chalky, over-sized pill, but it never went down. Therefore, he drowned it in bourbon.

He jimmied a pocketknife inside the lock and pried the blade until he heard the lock release then turned the knob. He took extra soft steps on the dingy, stained carpet of the living room. He heard water running, hitting and splashing on the floor of the tub.

Steam billowed into the hall. The soft yellow light on the ceiling illuminated the dense cloud collecting around it, a glowing cloud of vapor. Joe's lungs filled with the moist humidity. He missed his home and the warm muggy summers in North Carolina. The dry, desert heat of Hell wasn't nearly as pleasant.

He poked his head around the corner and looked into the bathroom. Salem lay on her back as the water filled the tub, rising up to the bottom of her small breasts. A dripping arm hung on the outside, gripping the neck of the wine bottle. She didn't bother with a glass. Her eyes closed, and her chest rose with deep, relaxing breaths.

His heel was silent on the tiled floor. He took another short step and was before her, towering above her as he stared at her lying in the tub.

He reared back and slammed his fist down onto her face. Her orbital bone broke from the blow. Her eye squirted out of its socket, squishing between his knuckles and her cheek. He pulled back and struck her again in the same spot. Through experience, he knew attacking the wounded area again intensified the pain and pretty much crippled the victim. Afterwards, he owned them.

Salem's head dipped below the surface of the water. Bubbles rippled and popped as she tried to breathe beneath, her throat filling with warm bath water.

Joe grabbed clumped handfuls of her red hair and jerked her from the tub. She sprawled out on the cold tile. Joe snatched the shower curtain rod from the wall and began beating her with it. Blood splattered and flung around the room. Little drops and large arcs of crimson decorated the walls, ceiling, and floor. He was painting his masterpiece.

Salem went into shock when her skull fractured on the left side. Pudgy round chunks of brain wiggled out and tangled in her hair. Joe felt a raging hard-on coming, but kept beating her until the curtain rod broke.

He tossed the rod in the tub and tried to pick her up by the hair again, but plates of skull—still attached to red ropes of soaked hair—come away in his hands. He threw those in the tub, too.

In frustration, he began stomping her. His heart pumped wildly and sweat dripped from his nose. Salem continued to shake until her rib cage cracked and pierced her lung. She just gargled, trying not to die, but she did when he stomped one of her broken ribs through her heart. He felt it, that miraculous moment when he took her life.

He sat on the edge of the tub savoring her last breath; that release, that high. A tear gathered in the corner of his eye and threatened to spill onto his cheek. But before it could, Salem sat up like the undead, a stiff ninety-degree angle made of flesh, bone, and rigor mortis.

Joe reached for the wine bottle and raised it above his head. He couldn't imagine how she was still alive with her face and head caved in. Pieces of bone were missing; exposing brains that looked like graying scrambled eggs with blood drizzled over them. Her eye was gone, her teeth knocked on the left side of her mouth. Still, she made to get up. He began beating her again.

Wine, blood, glass, and brain matter flew all over the bathroom. The bottom of the bottle shattered on Salem's face, leaving deep gouges in the meat. She made no noise while the cheese grater of a bottle stripped away at her.

Joe licked the strawberry-copper flavor of the wine/blood combo from his lips. The wine fragranced the air with a sweet, rotten fruit aroma. He was at peace in the presence of chaos, violence, and death.

Finally, Salem lay still, and Joe rested in the disgusting puddle his labor produced. The warm liquid soaked into the seat of his pants. He exhaled a satisfied breath.

Again, to his horror, Salem sat up in the same rigid manner she had before. Joe jumped to his feet and backed away so haphazardly he fell into the tub. Water overflowed onto the floor, washing away the death spray of blood and wine. He flailed and flapped his arms, trying to grab something to pull himself from the water. With a slick hand, he gained hold of a handicap rail on the shower wall.

He stood and chased her down the hall, half of her head missing from her shoulders. He caught her as they came out into the kitchen and punched her in the base of the neck. She fell facedown and hit the floor.

In a drawer beside the refrigerator, Joe found a steel chef's knife. He turned Salem over and dragged the knife across her throat with a long, dramatic stroke. No blood oozed from her arteries. Nothing happened aside from a gash, like another mouth, opening under her chin.

She clamped her hands over the wound and crawled away. Joe couldn't believe his eyes as she opened the door and set off into the night.

He breathlessly followed behind her. He jerked the door open, but on the other side stood a man. Pale with a diminutive, pointed chin and curly black hair, the Devil looked down upon him. Thick horns, curled like a mountain goats, grew from his head above his ears.

"Joe Thomas," said the Devil. He buttoned his black suit jacket over his red vest. "I'm sure you know me, but you can call me Lou."

Joe nodded. Lou stepped inside and closed the door.

"This is your punishment," said Lou, "for your crimes on Earth. You will hunt and try to kill your prey for the rest of eternity without the sweet release of the death of your victim. At the end of each attempt, you will begin again, none the wiser."

Joe said, "What?" and clearly distraught.

"Welcome to Hell, Mr. Thomas!" The Devil laughed.

A woman by the name of Salem Hawks caught his eye one day on his way to The Epicenter. She was boarding the bus, leaving from her burning.

Joe couldn't comprehend how she had made it this long without him noticing her. She was just what he liked to hunt when he lived: an alcoholic, abusive, single foster mother who moonlighted as a prostitute when times got hard. She ended up in Hell by murdering foster kids and collecting the Social Security money for their care. The ones she did let live suffered worse than swine, a speed bump on the way to a smooth blacktop that took her to easy money. As soon as the watchful eye of the social workers were relaxed, she tossed them into the old stone well under her house, like all the other paychecks. Moreover, Salem was a redhead, his favorite kind.

He followed her for days. Everywhere she went Joe was behind her, if only steps. Sometimes he got so close the smell of fermented strawberries tickled his nose. She seemed to sweat wine and a quiet disregard for the living.

Dona Fox

Satan's Heart

(*Editor's Choice Award Winner*)

The snake stretched in the brittle sun of Hell. "Am I beautiful?"

"Surely." The woman ran her fingertips down its glistening scales.

"Pick me up; let me curl around your hand. Feel my warmth; lay me against your breasts."

The woman did everything she was asked.

"Do you feel a stirring between your thighs?"

"I do," the woman said.

"Lay down with me." The snake coiled around her and, again, she did as he asked.

The man came and joined them. The snake blew vapor into the air, intoxicating the man and woman. Their bodies vibrated. They cried out with pleasure until they were sated.

"Will you worship me now?"

"What is worship?"

The snake sighed. "Will you love me?"

"What is love?"

The snake sighed again. "When you want always to be with the other; when you want to be one; when you want only to please the other. Do you love me?"

"We love each other." They pressed their naked bodies together.

The snake grew. His head became massive; his body split--he stood on mammoth golden legs. His voice thundered as the man and woman cowered in his shadow: "Each other! You are but clay!"

And he smashed them.

Lilith approached, wiping the red mud from her face. "What have you done, now? Another failure, my son?"

"No, I don't fail. I'm just playing." Slowly his face morphed from the giant Gila it had become in his anger back into the perfect planes of his father's dreams. His muscles rippling beneath near crimson skin, he smiled as he reached for her. Whether in anger or love, she stayed his grasp. As a sobbing boy approached through the vapors, Lilith slipped away.

"What is your story, boy?" He drew the young man onto his

lap.

"I know I was my father's favorite—the smartest, strongest, and most handsome. Yet he took my brother to his bed instead of me—not that I wanted that. Oh, no, never, yet why take him and not me? But then, perhaps it's not even true, I have only the word of my brother."

"Yet you believe it. Why do you believe him?"

"I have a doubt because I remember the way my brother flirted with my father as we ate, in front of the other men, and how angry my father became. But that's not proof."

"I will allow you to return. Go back and plunge a knife into your brother's heart. Watch his blood soak into the earth and the life breath leave his body. Kill your brother as you would kill a lamb."

"That's it. That's what I shall do. Thank you." The boy kissed Satan's feet. "I love you."

"Go. Go, before I change my mind." Satan smiled then he whispered to himself, "And I shall call it Murder."

Rebecca choked, sputtered and gagged.

"No, no. Not on me." However, before Satan could move her, she threw up a mass of green water that flowed down his chest and into his lap. Satan cried out. "In Beelzebub's name! What is this great waterlogged mass that has landed in my lap?"

Satan pushed Rebecca's long, black hair aside and drank water off her face. Her huge, frightened blue eyes glared at him. Cords binding her hands and feet held her in place.

"Devil's Cat got your tongue?" He laughed.

She opened her mouth. Red water poured out as she forced the bloody stub of a tongue between her lips.

"Let me see if I can guess." He looked her over. A rock tied to the cord bound her legs. He pushed up her skirts. Shapely legs.

He examined her body further. Tiny waist, ample breasts. Dress cut to entice yet that purpose was not obvious. Black dress. Extremely long straight black hair. Lips tinted with berries. He smelled her neck and between her breasts—herbs, not flowers—not a prostitute. This was, well—had been, a witch.

"Witch, huh? They treated you especially cruel—did you kill someone?"

She shut her eyes. A tear ran out.

He nodded. "I've seen it before. The young mother lied to you about how far along she was. You loosened her up so her blood would run, then much to your surprise you had a body to dispose of. They caught you burying her."

She had turned her head away.

"Well, now you're here. If it's any comfort, they'll all be here too when their time comes —they'll be here for killing you." Satan hugged her and rocked her, even though she was a sodden mess—he had a soft spot for witches, even when they weren't young and beautiful as this one. He understood how it felt to be misunderstood, persecuted.

Nonetheless, he took this one to his chambers and explored how loud she could scream without a tongue.

Then he made the biggest mistake of his career—he decided to let her cycle through again.

Satan smelled the burnt powder in the air, but he hadn't heard the gunshot that woke him. Likely, the shot hadn't happened in Hell; usually, they didn't.

Then he saw the young woman. A girl, maybe nineteen, perhaps twenty-something, but thin—excruciatingly so—barely able to lift the gun she still held with both hands, pointing out— out in the same direction on which her stunned gaze was fixed.

He followed her line of sight to her target, another tag end Millennial, the dregs of Gen Y—her mirror image—except this skeletal figure was a young man. He also held a gun in both hands, pointed at his sister. Shock froze upon on his narrow face.

Satan saw that a bullet had just entered the girl's heart from the gun the boy held, and another bullet had entered the boy's brain from the gun the girl held. Amazing. Their deaths must have been instantaneous—and simultaneous, or at least almost so. It had been a long time since he'd had one of these—and rarely twins.

Satan was shocked to see them here. The girl ran at the boy and began hitting him with the gun she held. "I hate you, I hate you, I hate you!"

The boy grabbed her and started biting her, "Damn you, bitch!" He screamed between mouthfuls of her flesh. Then he spit the fresh meat from his mouth and straightened his back—becoming another person, as if possessed.

"Money. Money. Bills. Bills. Bills. You can't stop spending. Someday, I'm gonna get a gun, and I'm gonna blow your brains out. While you're asleep. Put a hole in the side of your head. Blow all my problems away. Bam. Bam. Pow! Pow! Pow!" His voice got louder and louder as white foamy spit flew from his mouth.

"Shut up. The kids will hear you. Shut up. The kids will hear you." The girl dropped her gun and put her hands over her ears. "Shut up. Shut up. The kids. The kids."

"I'll blow them away too. Who wanted kids? I'll kill the fucking kids too." Now the boy was screaming, tears ran down his beet red face.

"Shut up. Shut up. The kids will hear. Shut up. The kids. The fucking kids." The girl was spinning with her hands still over her ears.

"Money. Money. Money." The boy jumped up and down.

"Shut up. Blow them away. The fucking kids." The girl ran over and beat on the young man's chest with her fists.

He pushed her away then pointed his index finger at her where she'd fallen, even though he still held the gun in his other hand. "Pow! Pow! Pow! Bam."

Both of the twins were screaming at the same time. Screaming and crying. Louder and louder.

Satan stepped back just as their parents popped into his chambers—careful bullet holes in the sides of their heads. Satan laughed and clapped his hands. They had written the script to their own murders. This was a good day in Hell.

The sparkle and crack of electricity warned him of incoming. This didn't happen nearly as often as it used to, or as often as Satan would like but it was a real high when it did. And, boom. The man landed in his lap, still convulsing and still giving off a faint charge. Satan could have done without the damp of the urine and the horrible smell of the shit, but they did insist on giving them that damn last meal.

"Hey, hey, its okay, you're here now. It's all over. It's not as bad as you thought it would be." Satan shook the man.

"Wha? What?" The man looked up. His eyeballs rolled back down to where they belonged in his sockets. "What the fuck? Where the Hell am I? Who...who the Hell are you?" He pushed himself out of Satan's lap. "Get your fucking hands off me, you pervert!"

Satan threw back his head and laughed.

"That's just it. You are in Hell. And it's not half as bad as they told you it would be. It was harder getting in—that little electric chair bit was worse than anything I've got down here. So, what's your story? Who'd you kill?"

"I was innocent." The man rubbed his hands across his bald pate as if he were used to having hair that needed pushing back. "Innocent. I didn't do it."

"Nah. See, you wouldn't be here if you were innocent. This is sure-fire, not like some jury bought or misled by a clever attorney. You're guilty. What's your story? Who'd you kill?"

"Myself." He hung his head.

"Nah. Try again. You don't get the death penalty for killing yourself. That's almost like an oxymoron. You guys get more interesting all the time. Who did you kill?"

"I told you. I killed myself. Just let it go, okay."

"No, no, no. I get to hear the story. This is my joint. You get it? I run the place. You will tell me your story. I have all the time in the world...I'm waiting."

The man sighed.

"Okay." He swallowed. "I'm not the guy that was supposed to be executed. I was the guard that was supposed to bring the prisoner to the chair. I was getting ready to come to work last night and my gun was gone. Actually, both of my guns were gone. I don't wear the guns to work, I was just checking them before I left—I was going to lock them up. But they were gone."

"I searched the house. Nowhere. I tried to call my brother. They'd been over the night before. He didn't answer. He always answered. I finished getting ready thinking I'd stop by his house on the way to work, just to check—probably he was messing with me."

"Their cars were in the drive but they didn't answer the door, or the phone. I went around back and used my key."

"Oh, God." He buried his face in his hands. "My brother and his wife were in bed. Blood was all over the sides of their heads. Apparently, the kids had shot each other across the bed. Lucky shots, unlucky shots. I don't know how they did it. They were so young. But they used my guns." He sobbed.

Then he straightened up.

"I walked right out of there, got in my car and went to work. We had this execution planned for that night. Luck was on my side, lots of flu—staff was short. Lack of planning was probably on my side, too, couldn't have gone smoother for me if I'd planned it—probably wouldn't have.

"The piece of crap's probably waking up about now wondering how in hell he's still alive and in a guard's uniform. The shit is really going to hit the fan." He chuckled softly, sadly.

"So see. I killed myself. I had to do it. Damn. I'm a sad son of a bitch, lousy fucking excuse for a man. If I could kill myself again, I would."

Satan watched as the woman faded in and out on his lap. Suicide—it was pretty trippy, almost hallucinogenic as she bled out somewhere else. He could see her story as she mumbled to herself. She didn't know if she had committed murder or not.

Good one.

Shannon had been depressed as hell—she couldn't sleep, she was exhausted. The baby cried all the time. There was nobody else to take a turn and get up and feed the little one or see why he was crying.

She was a single mother on food stamps with a big dog dumped on her by the absent father. And then the baby was crawling, getting into everything. Shannon was bone tired, and she couldn't keep up with the damn screaming, crawling baby—always putting stuff in its mouth.

Did she see it take the big chunk of dog food? Alternatively, did she actually give it the dog food from somewhere in the thick, dark fog she had been living in?

Did she just stand there and watch? Or did she pick the baby up and shake it to dislodge the food? But, wait, you're not supposed to shake babies, right? So maybe she didn't do anything. Maybe she couldn't do anything. But watch.

She doesn't know what she did or didn't do, or why she did or didn't do it. But she was confused, depressed, and guilty enough that she was now on the floor of her kitchen bleeding out—in and out of Satan's lap.

Maybe Satan would tell her what happened, and maybe he wouldn't.

The baby's father, Nate, had a new girlfriend. The new girlfriend was jealous and worried Nate would have to give Shannon money someday—or maybe he would even go back to Shannon, because they shared a son. The new girlfriend snuck in and gave a piece of dog food to Shannon's baby. The bitch stayed and watched until she thought it was too late, then she slipped back out the door. By the time Shannon found the baby she also thought there was nothing anyone could do, and she panicked.

Nate had good intentions, just like his new girlfriend feared. When he got himself fried in the electric chair, he had no idea that Shannon was also dying. He thought he'd done a good thing when he left his dog to protect Shannon and the baby—and he had.

His dog nuzzled the baby. Its instincts took over, and it saved that baby's life. Dogs are like that.

Shannon's best friend, Thea, was a witch, and she was mad as hell.

Thea was ready to do battle against Satan. If Satan hadn't invented murder, then her friend Shannon wouldn't be dying.

Lilith came to Thea. Lilith told Thea she had lain with and been in love with the original man and woman that were created before Adam—the couple that Satan had smashed. She told Thea that she had been in love with the brother Satan had murdered—the first murder. After that, Lilith dared love no mortal again. She hated Satan.

Lilith showed Thea the past. Thea had been named Rebecca—she had been murdered for being a witch, and then Satan had used her cruelly in his chambers before he let her cycle through again.

In her passion Lilith told Thea the Secret—if a mortal could eat Satan's heart, his whole warm, beating heart, at one time, Satan would be overcome forever.

Thea tried to still her mind so he would not sense her approach.

With no thought for herself, she jumped from a cliff and rushed into Hell, plunged her dagger up beneath Satan's ribs, reached in—grasped his beating heart—and yanked it from his chest.

As she brought the foul mass into the light, it appeared as a giant black toad, too enormous to plunge whole into her mouth. She sank her teeth in for the largest bite she could take into her mouth. She gagged on the odor as she swallowed. Cruel bile bit back at her tongue and poured down the sides of her mouth.

She sank her face into the putrid mass for another bite even as it seemed to grow. The foul heart glowed and growled at her through sudden yellowed teeth.

Satan's arms reached for her as his body rose to its feet. She stepped back, sliding in his black blood. She regained her footing, then stepped farther and farther away. She sank her face into the mass in her hands for yet another mouthful even as her stomach convulsed.

She tried to think of pleasant smells, pleasant tastes—cool, clear water. Fresh air. Even cigarette smoke would be more pleasing than the charnel house stench of his heart. It was dark and horrid. Rancid and rotting.

She tried to keep it down. There was one bite left, and she was losing. Tears poured out of her eyes as her body convulsed, and she realized she had lost, the cruel bile was rising—it was over, Satan had won again.

Just as she was about to vomit, slender arms encircled her and Lilith pressed her mouth over Thea's as she muttered, "We will not let that bastard win again."

A handsome young man landed right in The Devils' lap.

"Tell me your story." Thea smiled, parting his hair with her long, pointed nails. "Tell it quickly, we want to take you to our chambers and punish you for your heinous sins." Lilith smiled also, as she ran her hand slowly down his chest.

Author Bios

Charie La Marr: Author of Circuspunk book "Bumping Noses and Cherry Pie" and NYzarro book "Squid Whores of the Fulton Fish Market" Available at Amazon

Mike Jansen has published flash fiction, short stories and longer work in various anthologies and magazines in the Netherlands and Belgium, including Cerberus, Manifesto Bravado, Wonderwaan, Ator Mondis and Babel-SF and Verschijnsel anthologies such as Ragnarok and Zwarte Zielen (Black Souls). He lives in the Netherlands, in Hilversum, near Amsterdam. He has won awards for best new author and best author in the King Kong Award in 1991 and 1992 respectively as well as an honorable mention for a submission to the Australian Altair Magazine launch competition in 1998. In 2012 Mike won awards in the SaBi Thor story contest, the Literary Prize for the Baarn Cultural Festival and the prestigious Fantastels award for best short story. More recent publications in various English language ezines and anthologies, among which several publications with JWKfiction.com, Encounters Magazine and others. For a full list please refer to Mike's site: http://www.meznir.com

Dona Fox
Dona Fox's short stories and poetry have appeared in Eldritch Tales, Haunts, Thin Ice, Cemetery Dance (Issue #1), Beyond, and New Blood. Recently, her work has appeared in a number of James Ward Kirk Publishing's Anthologies including Bones I and II, Ugly Babies Volume I and II, Cellar Door Volume II, Indiana Horror Review 2013, Memento Mori, Serial Killers Quattuor, We are Dust and Shadows, and Demonic Possession. Her short story "Grace at the End" is one of the two Editor's choice awards in JWK's Memento Mori. Dona will have several poems in The Best of James Ward Kirk 2013. Dona also has a short story and a poem in JWK's Terror Train anthology; she will be part of a special segment of the online radio program "Whispers in the Dark" where she will discuss her writing and how great it was to work with the rest of the Terror Train team.

Essel Pratt

Essel Pratt pens horrific tales of terror and fright. He is currently published in over twenty books. He also writes fantasy adventures, as is evident in his debut novel, Final Reverie. From animals to zombies, nothing is off limits.

Murphy Edwards

Murphy Edwards is the award winning author of Snapped, Dead Lake, Serious Money, Bumper Music, Heavy Weather, Noodlers, Ace of Spades and The Last Days of Maxwell Sweet. His supernatural crime novella, Stone Cold is featured in Four Ghosts. Edwards' dark and deadly fiction has appeared in Morpheus Tales, Trail of Indiscretion, Hardboiled Magazine, Barbaric Yawp, Samsara: The Magazine of Suffering, Nocturnal Lyric, Night Chills, Big Pulp, Criminal Class Review and in the anthologies The Terror Train, Dead Bait, Dead Bait II, Dead Bait III, Assassin's Canon, Abaculus II & III, Morpheus Tales: The Horror Fields, Night Terrors, Splatterpunk Saints 2013, Unspeakable: A New Breed of Terror, Bloody Carnival, Indiana Horror 2011, Indiana Horror 2012, Grave Robbers, Serial Killers Iterum, Hell and Indiana Science Fiction 2012. Edwards is the 2011 recipient of The Midwest Writers Workshop Writers Retreat Fellowship Award for Fiction and his short story, "Mister Checkers", was chosen to be among the best in science fiction, fantasy and horror of 2009 for the Leucrota Press Anthology, Abaculus III. He is the Co-Editor of Indiana Crime 2012 and Indiana Crime Review 2013. In addition to the United States, Edwards has been published in Ireland, Australia, South Africa, and the U.K. His third novel, Kingfish, is currently due for release in late fall of 2014. He likes his music loud, his knives sharp and his turtle fried. Visit him on the web: http://murphyedwards.wordpress.com

www.facebook.com/murphy.edwards.96

Edwards loves to hear from his readers. Drop him a line at:

murphyedwards@etczone.com

D.S. Scott

When D. S. Scott was fourteen, a friend suggested he write a short story. He began writing and immediately took an interest in it. A couple weeks later he finished and was surprised to find how much he enjoyed writing it. In the years since, Scott has written in several genres but has found a particular interest in horror and suspense. He enjoys writing poetry, short stories and has started on a novel. Finding writing to be a creative outlet, he kept with it and followed his goal to publish.
He currently lives in North Carolina with his dog, Bandit.

Lemmy Rushmore

Lemmy Rushmore is a mechanic by trade and father of three who occasionally dares dabble in the world of words.Until recently unpublished,his pieces touch on many topics,but tend to lean toward the darker side of those things encountered daily.Ranging from emotionally dark to horror,some of his work can be seen in the anthologies We are Dust and Shadow, Demonic Possession,and No Sight for the Saved,which features the superbly dark art of Niall Parkinson.All have been released by James Ward Kirk Publishing and are now available.His newest work can be viewed on the Facebook page,the P.R.S. Project as he is currently involved in a unique collaboration with the extraordinarily talented artist, Niall Parkinson.

S.L. Dixon

Former print-journalist, S.L. Dixon is a Canadian author residing in the northern portion of British Columbia, Canada with his wife and cat. He has written four novels and five collections of stories, as well, has contributed several stories to magazine publications. The bulk of his work falls into the horror field, but occasionally steps outside the genre to write science-fiction and humor.

Gary Murphy

Born 29th January, 1969, G K Murphy (or Gary), lives in Egremont, West Cumbria, UK, where he writes full-time and as well as having over 70 short stories published in varied horror and sci-fi anthologies is the author of horror collections 'Nerds Unite', 'Scared Shitless', 'Pulp Horror', 'Zombie Tax – Paying What Is Due' and the 'Wick'd North' anthologies (volumes 1 – 2) and 'Infernal Highway' as well as superhero collection 'Smalltown Superheroes', radio-plays 'Controversy' and 'Cobweb Chance' – as well as pirate/horror novella 'Hellish Redcap' published by James Ward Kirk Publishing and the sequel/prequel 'Beginnings'.

He is currently studying for a BA Honorary degree in History, tries his hand at electric-guitar and produces electro-transient beats with the help of a rickety old MicroKorg synth. Gary fantasizes one day one of his books, or short stories, will make the transition and get adapted for television or film, often penning screenplays with this in mind. In the meantime, he maintains he'll just write more and more horror until the day comes he can't publish any more. Lots of his stories can be found within the folds of many Horrified Press publications, as well as other publications, books, magazines, and webzines such as Schlock and Death Throes, who have featured him a lot online. Gary can be located on Facebook by simply 'Gary Murphy', or emailed at gazvespa69@hotmail.com. He is currently working on novellas 'Kooky' and 'Savage Lunatics.' He welcomes fans new and old and is always willing to chat. Feel free to get in touch.

Tony Bowman

Tony Bowman writes Horror, Science Fiction, and Thriller novels from his home in Raleigh, North Carolina. He is a native of the Appalachian Mountains of Virginia, and grew up in Butcher Knife Holler (or, "down on Butcher Knife" as the locals would say). It was a magical place where witches, bigfoot, and UFO's were considered fact and no street lights blocked out the view of the milky way at night. Tony learned to read through comic books like Creepy, Turok: Son of Stone, and Superman. Later, he devoured the works of Heinlein, King, Bradbury, and Koontz.His beautiful wife Laurie is his biggest fan, and his beautiful daughter Sara is his inspiration. Tony's other works are available through http://thattonybowman.blogspot.com

Timothy Frasier

Timothy Frasier is a novelist, short story writer, and poet. His work appears in over twenty-five horror anthologies from James Ward Kirk, Thirteen O'clock Press, Static Movement, KnightWatch Press, and various other anthologies. A collection of his short stories is now available titled Dark Frequencies. He is co-author along with Elizabeth Loraine of the zombie series Pathogen. Frasier lives in rural Kentucky with his wife, Lisa, and German shepherd, Chief. He is an active member of the Hanson Writers Workshop in Hanson, Ky.

CS Nelson

CS Nelson holds a BA of English and has appeared in US and Canadian ezines and anthologies. When not writing, he spends time with family, plays metal guitar with his invisible friends who are all orcs, and serves as a US Army Cav Scout out of Fort Irwin in the Mojave Desert. He raises Asian forest scorpions as part of his Tiny Tickles Scorpion Rescue project. His website is at www.nelsoncs.com.

Mathias Jansson

Mathias Jansson is a Swedish art critic and horror poet. He has been published in magazines as The Horror Zine, Dark Eclipse, Schlock and The Sirens Call. He has also contributed to over 60 different horror anthologies from publishers as Horrified Press, James Ward Kirk Fiction, Source Point Press, Thirteen Press etc.

Homepage: http://mathiasjansson72.blogspot.se/

Amazon author page: http://www.amazon.co.uk/Mathias-Jansson/e/B00BTDBYBQ/ref=sr_ntt_srch_lnk_4?qid=136680 6658&sr=8-4

Jon Wesick

Host of the Gelato Poetry Series, instigator of the San Diego Poetry Un-Slam, and an editor of the *San Diego Poetry Annual*, Jon Wesick has published over seventy short stories in journals such as *The Berkeley Fiction Review, Space and Time, Zahir, Tales of the Talisman, Blazing Adventures,* and *Metal Scratches.* He has also published over three hundred poems. Jon has a Ph.D. in physics and is a longtime student of Buddhism and the martial arts. One of his poems won second place in the 2007 African American Writers and Artists contest.

Judith Skillman

Judith Skillman is the author of fourteen collections of poetry. She holds an MA in English Literature from the University of Maryland. Her poems and collaborative translations have appeared in Poetry, FIELD, Seneca Review, The Iowa Review, Southern Review, BEACONS, Ezra, and other journals and anthologies. Skillman is the recipient of an Eric Mathieu King Fund Award from the Academy of American Poets for Storm, Blue Begonia Press. She has taught at City University, University of Phoenix, Richard Hugo House, and elsewhere. Angles of Separation, her new book, is available from Glass Lyre Press: www.glasslyrepress.com or visit www.judithskillman.com

John Ledger

John Ledger lives in central Pennsylvania with his angel Erica and their four children; Carson, Kaila, Logan and Layla. John has published several short stories in anthologies such as Bones II, Memento Mori, We are Dust and Shadow, Demonic Possession, No Sight for the Saved and Deathmongers. He has more stories awaiting release in anthologies such as Dynatox a Go Go, Axes of Evil 2.666, Cherry Nose Nightmares and Bones III. John enjoys punk rock, serial killers, dogs and Chinese food. You can find him talking a bunch of nonsense on Facebook.

Stuart Keane

Stuart Keane published his first novella, The Customer Is Always... in April. It has slowly garnered critical acclaim, including a CWA Dagger in the Library nomination, and is slowly rising through the Amazon ranks. His debut novel, All or Nothing, will be published by J Ellington Ashton Press in 2014. His second novel, Boys, will be published in 2015. Wet was a story born out of slipping in the bath. The rest came from his horrific mind.Ever the busy author, Stuart will see several of his short stories appear in anthologies before 2014 draws to a close. Dead Harvest - A Collection of Dark Tales, Axes of Evil II, Journals of Horror: Found Fiction, and Floppy Shoes Apocalypse are just a few of the books that contain short stories from Stuart Keane. He is also working on Carnage: Extreme Horror with three extremely talented authors. When he isn't writing, he can be found on Facebook or Twitter. He regularly chats the night away as he constructs stories and destroys worlds in the process. Stop by for a chat sometime, he isn't shy. He currently resides in Ipswich, UK with his wife and an unhealthy caffeine addiction.

Roger Cowin

Roger Cowin currently resides in Centerville, IN with his wife Barbara. His poems have been appearing in journals and anthologies for the past 3 decades. He is the author of the poetry collections, "Passing Through Darkness & Other Poems" and "Succulent Flesh," published by JWK Fiction. His first short story will be published in "Axes of Evil II: Rise of the Metal Gods."

John Stanton

John Stanton's stories, novellas, essays, poems, and articles have appeared in *Mount Zion Speculative Fiction Review, The Indianapolis Star, CompuServe Magazine, MIND, Static Movement, Theatre of Decay, Yellow Mama, Tales of Bigfoot,* and other print and on-line magazines and anthologies, as well as technical articles and documentation. His photographic art has been used as covers and internal illustrations for *Not One of Us, Black Petals, Twisted Dreams Magazine, RAZAR I* and *II, True Police, Literally,* and the anthologies *Indiana Horror Review 2012* and *2013, Indiana Crime 2013, Bones, Cellar Door: Words of Beauty, Tales of Terror, Of Shadow and Substance, Requiem for the Damned, Studies in Scarlet,* and House of Horrors' *Tales of a Woman Scorned,* among others.

Stanton was a field investigator for APRO, the Aerial Phenomenon Research Organization and maintains a blog on all things Fortean and synchronicity at http://johndstanton.blogspot.com/. He explores graveyards, abandoned and haunted sites with his wife Flo for inspiration. They live next door to a house haunted by a murder-suicide that happened as they slept just a few yards away. Find out more about John at www.3amblue.com.

Lori R. Lopez wears many hats, literally and otherwise. She is an artist who designs her book covers and illustrates some of her tomes. As an author she writes poems, short stories, novels, children's books and songs, as well as a humorous-slash-serious column called "Poetic Reflections" at Fairy Fly Entertainment. She is a musician, actress, filmmaker, tree-hugger and animal-lover. A vegetarian, her work often contains themes of conservation, animal rights, and the rights of children. Lori unapologetically takes pride in creatively bending and reshaping the rules of writing when it suits her style. A horror fan since small, she roamed graveyards as a kid and conducted funerals for dead birds, squirrels, insects and spiders. Lori has received various honors for her novels THE FAIRY FLY and AN ILL WIND BLOWS. She was named on an Examiner.com list of "92 HORROR AUTHORS YOU NEED TO READ RIGHT NOW" for WOMEN IN HORROR MONTH 2014. Her books also include CHOCOLATE-COVERED EYES, THE MACABRE MIND OF LORI R. LOPEZ, OUT-OF-MIND EXPERIENCES, DANCE OF THE CHUPACABRAS, POETIC REFLECTIONS I and II: KEEP THE HEART OF A CHILD and THE QUEEN OF HATS; THE MUDPUPPY and THE FOX TROT (based on childhood experiences). Her stories and verse, featured in THE SIRENS CALL E-ZINE, on HELLNOTES.COM, and at SERVANTE OF DARKNESS, have been published in anthologies such as TERROR TRAIN, JOURNALS OF HORROR: FOUND FICTION, CURSED CURIOSITIES, WE ARE DUST AND SHADOW, BONES II, MIRAGES: TALES FROM AUTHORS OF THE MACABRE, MASTERS OF HORROR: DAMNED IF YOU DON'T, DARLINGS OF DECAY, I BELIEVE IN WEREWOLVES, THE EPOCALYPSE: EMAILS AT THE END, THIRSTY ARE THE DAMNED, and SCARE PACKAGE: 14 TALES OF TERROR. Fifteen of Lori's poems were published for an anthology titled IN DARKNESS WE PLAY.

Paul van Leeuwenkamp Stems from April 1st, 1955, no joke. He works in IT and has been doing so for the longest time. Apart from IT design and information analysis, he writes and publishes stories and poems. So far his work has appeared mostly in Holland and Belgium in such magazines as Holland-SF, Ballustrada, De Leeswolf and various anthologies such as Black Stars, various Ganymede short story collections and Ragnarok yearbooks. His poetry won several prizes and Paul has published several poetry collections.

Nienke Pool publishes shorter and longer stories in numerous magazines and anthologies in Belgium and the Netherlands. With her historical background she loves to write about ancient times and heroes of the past. She has won awards in writing contests and is named 'the promise of the year 2015' by CapslocSpeak, a Dutch spoken word platform. She has published in the Fantasy Yearbooks of Ganymedes and Fantastisch Strijdtoneel, but also appears in literary magazines. Her story about Ancient Egypt has won a "Vlaamse Filmpjes" publication and is distributed to all primary schools in Belgium. Only writing for one year her short stories have already appeared in three countries and she is proud of her first English publication with JWKfiction.com. A full list is on Nienke's Linkedin: Nienke Pool and on her Facebook page Stympahtica,
https://www.facebook.com/pages/Stymphatica/1381276285451294?fref=ts

Charie La Marr

Author of Circuspunk book "Bumping Noses and Cherry Pie" and NYzarro book "Squid Whores of the Fulton Fish Market" Available at Amazon